Luna, the Lone Wolf

Luna, the Lone Wolf

Forest Wells

Luna, the Lone Wolf

Written and published by: Forest Wells (ForestWells.com)

Artwork by "chickenbusiness" (DeviantArt.com/ChickenBusiness)

Cover design by Sophia Feddersen (FrostCovers.com)

Edited by:
- Edge Of the World Editing
- Hollie Hausenfluck (WriteYourWayEditing.wordpress.com)
- Trisha Tobias (TrishaTobiasEditorial.wordpress.com)

Interior layout: Charlie Pabst (CharfishDesign.com)

Praise for Luna, the Lone Wolf

"I love how well and accurately the author portrays the wolves. He's obviously very knowledgeable on them. Each character is so unique it makes the story riveting. Overall it's very well rounded and engaging. I'd recommend it to everyone. (And I have.)"

— Jensen Reed

"Wolves have been at the core of American culture and lore for centuries, and (Forest) Wells takes all the charm and characteristics that have so fascinated us about the species, and lends to them a new depth and meaning."

— Sammie B

"Luna the Lone Wolf is more than just a thrilling tale featuring wolves, humans and the problems that arise between them. It's a journey. Forest leads the reader on an emotional journey with Luna. The reader will laugh, cry, and sometimes even shout as they travel with Luna. An imaginative tale told from a whole new perspective, you won't be disappointed. Luna the Lone Wolf is a novel everyone can enjoy, from a YA reader, to a classic fiction reader; everyone will find something to enjoy."

— Hollie Hausenfluck

Author Foreword

THIS NOVEL HAS BEEN many years in the making, and I would need another novel to properly thank all of those that made it happen. The best I can do is simply state here how amazingly grateful I am for everyone that endured the many days working with me on this, even when I was driving them crazy. Some of which include:

The late Mary Rosemblum, who never stopped answering my questions, no matter how stupid. I'm sorry you never got to see the fruit of that patience. Laurel, my first fan, who kept asking me when it was coming out. My mother, who God bless her, even at her most tired, remains my sounding board. My brother and family, who are always ready and willing to give advice and help where they can. Samantha Leigh, who put me on a path that would lead to everything coming together in just over a year. Jane Lindskold, my good friend and mentor, who would have never let me hear the end of it if I gave up. Barbra Savage, God rest her soul, who would have slapped me a dozen times for the same reason. Cheryl Pensis, who saw my potential through the scars and the anger, and helped me learn how to live with Dysgraphia. The many artists and professionals, who stayed patient with me as their client, and deserve more pages than I can give them. My beta readers, Jensen, Samantha, Karina, Julissa, and Jaimie, who came in when I needed that final, critical eye upon my work.

Even this list is incomplete. People who helped in ways I'll never know. Those I've forgotten through the fog of Dysgraphia and time. Still others simply because I didn't want to fill an entire page with every single name on the list. People may talk about how I overcame my learning disability to write this novel, but I couldn't have done it without all of you who stood with me over the years on my journey.

And finally, I must say something about my dedication. On September 11th, 2001, 2,996 people lost their lives. Families across the nation lost someone. Meanwhile, in the little town of Thermal in the Coachella Valley, one life was saved.

I was one bad day away from suicide when I woke up to those towers burning on the TV. The full impact didn't hit me until a full list of the dead was printed in the newspaper the next year, but its effect began on that morning. I'd always written stories when we had journal time in school. Yet it wasn't until a classmate read of poem about the attacks that the muse woke up. I wrote my own poem that afternoon. I wrote horrendous first drafts months later. I believe this novel was actually born somewhere in the following October, or November, I'm not sure which. But most of all, it woke me up.

I saw how fragile life was. I saw how important it was to try things, to do things, to take advantage of the days I have, for I may not have many. I took life by the horns and made it work for me for a change. I still had bad days, but because of those events, and that poem, suicide was no longer an option. I found my passion, my reason to fight on, and for the first time, I found a pack to run with that, three years later, would rise to defend me.

In the famous "Last Lecture", Randy Pausch said that walls are there to test how bad we want something. Because of 9/11, no wall could keep me from writing, and because I had my writing, I was able to keep on going. I wish it hadn't happened. My life isn't worth that many, but I can't change the past. I can only use the future they gave me.

On September 11th, 2001, 2,996 people died. On September 12th, 2001. Forest Wells, the author, was born.

Nothing I do or say can make up for that loss, but at least because of it, I have the opportunity to try. Because of them, this lone wolf found his pack, his purpose, and overcame his pain, to become the person so many thought I could be.

To them, and to everyone that helped me get here, "thank you" is not enough.

"It doesn't matter how long it takes to get there.
It only matters that you keep plugging along."
– Forest Wells

Dedication

To my mom,
go ahead, embarrass me.

To Mary Rosenblum, Barbra Savage, and Jane Lindskold,
here is the fruit of your patience, advice, and and friendship.

And to the victims of 9/11,
without whom this book, and this author, would not exist.

Chapter 1

I AM FEARED.

The feeling coursed through my veins as I followed a scent through the forest. The trail led me toward something that would soon be my next meal. A rabbit based on the soft, earthy smell on the wind. I only had to find it, and catch it.

It was about time too. Three moons old, and growing fast, my siblings and I saw no reason to be treated like pups. Wolfor's fang, we didn't even look like pups anymore. Much of my puppy fur had turned gray and silver, darkening on my back. The "silver sheen," as Mother called it, on my neck and hackles had only gotten brighter, though a slight touch of black seemed to outline it.

Father and other adults followed nearby, but this hunt was ours, and ours alone. I followed the trail through brush and leaves, sniffing so fast I might as well have been breathing through my nose. My only pauses came when the trail seemed to thin, or even vanish.

It was during one of these pauses that my brother, Rajor, tried to push past me to find the trail. Much like the rest of us, his puppy fur had taken on adult coloring. In his case, his fur was turning solid black, aside from a hint of a gray tint. He also needed reminding of his place. Pushing past me like that was an act of dominance he had not earned. As such, I snarled and nipped at him, threatening to do more if he didn't submit. Rajor froze, while his ears and tail fell in submission. They didn't stay down long, but I accepted it even so. He kept an ear turned my way as he hunted for the same trail.

About time that happened too. Seems he'd finally begun to respect my position as alpha male of the litter, if only a little. *I hope it stays that way.* The fight it took to claim that spot from him hadn't been easy. I did not welcome the thought of having to do it again.

I snorted and pressed on with the hunt. The scent was so strong and clear, I wondered why I couldn't see my prey. I trotted along its path, with Rajor and my sister, Jinta, beside me. The rest of the litter were caught among themselves, trying to find the very trail we now followed.

I wanted to run full sprint after our prey, but we only had the scent to follow, and sprinting would make it impossible to find. So the three of us walked on, sniffing at every turn to make sure we didn't lose it. We were getting closer, and my heart pounded with every step. At last, *my* hunt, *my* kill, all I had to do was... dig it out of the ground?

The trail had gone into a hole much like one Rajor had found before, except this one lay under roots as big as Father's legs. I'd never fit in the hole, and I wasn't about to stick my muzzle into it and carry the same scratches on my nose as Rajor. That was one mistake I did not intend to repeat. *Of course, if he did, that'd be okay.* When Jinta and Rajor followed the scent to the same end, they slumped with a frustrated growl.

Then Jinta looked at me. "Now what do we do, big brother?"

I turned my ears back to say I didn't know, then looked to my father. His fur was a dark gray on his back and hackles that quickly faded around the edges to a more medium shade on his head. His legs and underside were cream and white, as was his face and muzzle.

"Father," I said, "how do we get to it without getting our noses scratched like Rajor did?"

Rajor gave a short growl, while Father's ears flashed back in a cringe. "Luna, you're old enough," Father said. "It's time you used my name. They are part of our identity, and we must not allow it to be lost. As for the rabbit, you have to scare it out. This one chose its den well, but it's not perfect. For one thing, the den seems rather new, which means it hasn't had the chance to dig other exits yet. Here."

Fath... Toltan gently nudged Jinta and Rajor into positions around the hole. "Jinta, Rajor, you two stand at the entrance. Leave enough space between you so you won't bite each other. Luna, when I tell you to, dig on the other side of the roots. The rabbit will think you're digging toward him. When he tries to run, he'll run right into Rajor or Jinta."

I thought about insisting I be part of the kill, but being the reason it happened was enough. Besides, maybe the gesture would earn me some respect from Rajor that didn't require my fangs. While Rajor and Jinta found their distance, I chose my point of attack from the other side. The rest of the litter caught up to us, and Father told them to watch and learn. When he did, a rush went through my body that made it feel like I could tear the tree right out of the ground if I had to.

This kill would belong to the three of us, no one else. Our first of many, and I would lead it. It didn't matter that Rajor glared at me the entire time, or that he might get the kill. It was *my* hunt. I tried to avoid breathing too hard as I waited for Toltan to give me the word.

Toltan glanced at Jinta and Rajor, flicked an ear, then turned both ears toward me. "Okay, Luna. Dig!"

I tore into the dirt with all my energy. Earth moved in paw-filled piles, slowed only by roots quickly torn through by my claws. An excited growl vibrated through me with every paw of dirt I flung out behind me. As I got deeper, I could hear something. A rustling, skittering sound, like twigs bouncing off each other. I could only guess it was my prey. It seemed to be moving back and forth, as if unsure which way to run. As my paws got closer to the sound, for a moment, I wondered: *will I get the kill myself?* My paws didn't have much farther to go. I only had to dig a little more, break into the den, and I'd be able to land the killing bite myself. I could prove myself a skilled hunter in one act.

As the dirt softened, a streak of fur flashed out of the corner of my eye. When I looked up after it, I found Rajor and Jinta staring after a rustle in the brush nearby.

Toltan sighed while rubbing Rajor's cheek. "Try harder next time."

"Yeah, like at all," Calon, another of my brothers, said.

While Toltan snapped a reprimand at him, I growled at my sinking heart. My hunt, my kill, denied by a brother who hates me. I had to wonder if he missed on purpose. After three moons of bullying, I wouldn't put it past him.

"We'll find him later," Toltan said. "Right now, I want you to practice the basics. There's a field near here full of mice. There, you'll learn the simple techniques you need to—"

All ears perked toward an odd sound from deep within the forest. At first, it sounded like thunder, but it didn't rumble, nor did it linger. Just one sharp *craack*, then an almost whistling repeat of the same sound as it faded. Toltan stepped on stiff legs toward the sound, his ears up and alert. The rest of the pack watched and waited, though some drifted closer to the pups.

Craack!-cshoo-shoo

Everyone flinched, with more than a few pups dropping their ears. The adults scanned the forest with straight ears and darting eyes. Noses and eyes searched for threats, though some tails were close to tucking as they did.

I moved closer to Toltan, trying to deny my own fear. "What is that?"

Toltan's voice, for the first time I could remember, wavered. "I'm not sure. I've only heard it once before. We never found the source then either."

"It sounds like thunder," Rajor said.

"Yes, it does. Just like the thunder I heard before—"

Craack!-cshoo-shoo

I hugged the ground, again startled, though my ears stayed up in search of the source of this new sound. Part of me wanted to find it so I could know what it was, and then maybe learn it wasn't worthy of my fear. The rest of me decided going the other direction made more sense. More so as new smells floated on the wind. One was dirty, almost stifling, while others were sweeter, and still more were somehow tart and bitter at the same time. I think I smelled fur too, but it was unfamiliar, as was a kind of sour I'd never smelled before, and something close to... smooth rock? It was the only description that came to mind when I found a scent of something sharp and tangy. *What is out there?*

"Back to the dens," Toltan said. "Things are not safe here. Keep your ears open and your nose alert. If something seems wrong, voice it."

Rajor looked after our prey. "I'm not leaving. We came out here for hunting lessons, and you can't make me..."

Toltan went stone stiff. His ears were forward, his hackles started to rise, and his eyes narrowed as they locked onto Rajor better than any bite. There his gaze stayed, ready to bore a hole straight through Rajor if he didn't back down. We pups, and much of the pack, called it the "death stance." When Toltan entered it, you only challenged him if you wanted to die. The rare times someone did, they were always pinned before they knew what happened.

When Rajor's ears and tail fell, Toltan only moved enough to speak.

"Your lessons can wait. Now move!"

The pack moved in a tight group back to the meeting area. The pups were kept between the adults, never allowed to roam past for any reason. Every adult continued to check the winds and the forest in search of danger, some with still low tails. I looked back the way we'd come, longing for the kill that got away, but also keeping my ears up in case that weird sound happened again. I heard only the steps of the pack, and my sigh at excitement unrewarded. *Next time, I get the kill.*

The group didn't spread out until we had arrived back home. Mother... Martol greeted Toltan with a rub and a soft whine. She had a pelt of thick silver fur that looked smooth and flat, as if it only knew how to be soft.

"Everything all right?" she said.

"No," Toltan said. "Did you hear the thunder?"

"Yes. Gave us quite a start. I was worried—"

"Luna!" Lonate, our primary pup-sitter, interrupted my perked attention of my parents. "I said follow me. I want you pups where I can watch you."

I couldn't resist. "Watch us, or just Rajor?"

Lonate growled and snapped at me. I fell onto my side with a whine of submission, more so because his fur made his glare that much worse. It was mostly white below, but black covered his back, neck, shoulders, and top of his head. His face and throat were white, forcing my eyes to focus on his. Worse than angry, they were heavy with his own brand of disappointment. One that somehow made you hurt as if he'd bitten you.

"I thought better of you," he said. "An alpha should have more respect for his members. Especially his own brother."

Did you bother to tell him that? "Yes, Lonate. I'm sorry."

"Good. Now come."

Despite the scolding, Lonate gave me a soft nuzzle on our way toward a hillside on the edge of the meeting area. The pack's dens had been dug into the base of that hillside, which only had one tree at its top. The hill itself went straight up about as high as two adults or so, yet it tapered down the sides enough to be easily walked on.

As we walked, I took Lonate's nuzzle as a sign of respect, though it didn't make me feel much better about myself, or the day.

Much as I hated to admit it, he was right. Rajor's lack of respect for me did not mean I had the right to disrespect him. The thought festered in my stomach, tightening even more as I noticed the adults had made a border around me and my siblings. It made it quite clear how little freedom we had at the moment. More so when I looked at the wolves near the dens and saw them give any pup who came near a straight-eared glare.

Sure, we had an open area among the trees to play in, but we didn't dare play near the dens, because one of them held a new litter from Solas and Carfen. Toltan had made it clear: no one plays near them, which meant our limited area was even smaller. I tried to listen in on Toltan and Martol, but my head slumped onto my paws when I found I couldn't hear them. *What a fine end to a fine day. A failed hunt, lessons stopped by a strange thunder in the forest, Martol and Toltan appear worried, and now Lonate's mad at me. At least there's nothing else I have to deal with.*

"You're scared of it, aren't you?" Rajor asked in his usual mocking tone while also giving fake whines. "An odd noise in the woods. Like thunder, yet not like thunder. It just fills you with fear, doesn't it?"

I should have drowned him at the river. "Go away, Rajor. Leave me alone before I pin you again."

Rajor growled with a glare to match. I sighed while preparing for yet another fight with my brother.

CRAACK!-cshoo-shoo

All ears shot up toward the forest, save for Rajor's, whose went flat against his head just as fast. *Who's afraid now?*

Squawking soon followed, coming like a strong wind from the forest. I stood with perked ears as I tried to understand what it meant. I knew it was birds, but far more of the same kind, at the same time, than I'd ever heard before. They were flying in a single flock that blew overhead like a cloud rushing by. Most of it was just noise, but I was able to catch something from the mockingbirds.

"Beware the two-leggeds, bearers of thunder. Beware the two-leggeds, bearers of thunder."

Over and over, they cawed as they flew. The pack watched the flock pass, with Lonate in particular transfixed on them. His ears were up, but there was an odd darkness to him. Something I'd seen on my parents not long ago when they came back without a kill. Toltan seemed particularly worried, while Martol mentioned something about "not having a Mesin problem," whatever that meant. After seeing this darkness again on Toltan just a moment ago, I realized it was fear, but a kind different than the one that still had Rajor's ears flat against his head. *Wolfor's fang, what is going on out there?*

I hadn't noticed Martol approach until she barked to call the attention of the pack. Once we were all gathered, she addressed us. "Everyone, listen up! I want a hunting party to gather some meat for the pack. The pups will remain here for now." She glared at Rajor. "*No* exceptions! When the pack is fed, we will meet, older pups included, to discuss what we've heard today. That's all."

Toltan gathered a hunting party without many words to anyone. Rajor tried to join them despite Martol's warning, but Lonate's fangs, sharp enough to draw blood this time, put an end to it. Rajor found a spot to be alone and sulk, too hurt in one form or another to bother anyone. *Thank you, Wolfor*, I thought. The last thing I needed was another fight.

Not that I could relax either. I could sense tension from every adult, particularly Lonate and Solas, like some kind of black cloud coating their fur. Their scents felt thicker, harder, like I was breathing dirt or water instead of a smell. It turned parts of my insides in a way I had never felt before. The only feeling that came close was when Toltan, Martol, or Lonate were angry, and I wasn't sure if they were mad at me or not. Much like those times, I found myself watching them for some sign of what to do. Solas spent the day talking with the other high-ranking wolves, while Lonate sat on top of the hillside, watching the forest as if something might jump out and bite him.

That more than anything kept me from joining the other pups as they filled their time with playful roughhousing. Lonate had always been so controlled, almost an alpha himself in his own way. Now he seemed more like an omega, utterly subordinate to something only he could see. As much as I wanted to understand it, I didn't bother trying to ask him, or anyone else for that matter. After all, I was still a pup to them. Until that changed, I wasn't going to get answers or freedom. That left me with nothing to do except enjoy the soft glow of a half-moon as it rose in the sky. While not as calming as the glow of a full moon, right now, even a tiny bit was welcome.

It proved to be more calming than expected, as I found the tension falling away. The silver of my hackles caught just enough light to reflect, making them appear to glow. I never could tell if they really were glowing, or if it was just the reflection. I only knew that when they did, I was able to relax in a way different than any other. My nerves and frustrations hadn't left, I was just too far away for them to reach me.

It had been that way since the first time we were allowed to leave the den. While my siblings had gotten lost in the scents on the wind and the vast open space we had only heard about, the full moon had called to me. My hackles, with the same "silver sheen" then as now, began to glow, and somehow, it relaxed me. More than that, at the time, I felt safe, protected, though I still didn't understand how.

My name came from the same source. Lonate had seen my fixation, and mentioned "Luna," the eternal forest where wolves go after death, and the only territory we had a name for. It is said this forest resides on the moon and is watched over by Wolfor, the great alpha wolf that created us. We call ourselves "wolf" to honor him, and according to Toltan, though Wolfor lives in this "Luna," he still watches over us, at times guiding and even helping us when we need it most. Martol and Toltan thought Wolfor's dwelling called to me, so they gave me the same name in honor of it, and him.

I sometimes wondered if any of it were true, but there was no doubt that something about the glow of the moon seemed to put me at ease. Martol said it was proof of Wolfor's blessing, Rajor mocked me for it every chance he got, while Jinta playfully teased that I had been born with a dash of Wolfor's home in my fur. Whatever the reason, I only cared that right now, it meant a moment of peace was not hard to find.

That peace ended when I heard the hunting party return with a kill. The meat was distributed among the pack, with some going into the den for Carfen. The hunting party gave us older pups a share as well, some of it nice and fresh, instead of regurgitated like we usually got. At least something had changed with our age.

I ate my share quickly, not wanting to miss anything that might happen in the meantime. My reward was catching Rajor heading to steal Calon's share. Calon's fur was an almost solid pelt of smooth silver, except for his back, where it became a darker gray, and a lighter underside. Every strand was soft and relaxed. He was unaware of the brother moving to steal part of his meal.

Before Rajor could get there, I snuck up behind him and snarled right at his tail. While hardly menacing like the adults, it still accomplished my goal. Rajor snapped around to face me, ears and fur on end like he might leap out of his skin. Calon jerked too, but when he looked back to see me, he gave a growl of his own. When he did, Rajor turned to him, then back to me, then at last, Rajor's ears fell.

"Better," I said. "Now go back to your own share."

"And what if I don't, Mister Silver Sheen?" Rajor said in a mocking tone. "Are you going to pin me again?"

I bared my teeth. "I just might."

"Careful. Remember what Father—"

"Toltan! We are to use his name now, remember?"

Rajor's ears fell further, then they raised with what little pride he had left. His tucked tail betrayed the truth. "He told us that wolves don't kill their own young before they see their first winter. It's a law passed down from Wolfor himself. So I don't have to be afraid of you."

Don't be so sure. "Who said I would kill you? I've pinned you before. What's to stop me from doing it again?"

Rajor tried to find an insult. I could see his lips searching for the right words. I deepened my growl, at least as much as a pup can, and he finally lowered his ears.

"Someday, I'll be alpha," Rajor said. "You'll see. I'll lead this pack, then I'll put you in your place."

"You'll have to beat me first," I said, still growling.

"I will. By Wolfor, I swear, I will be alpha."

I huffed as he left. *That'll be the day.*

I turned to reassure Calon that I would defend him, only to find that instead of his growl fading, if anything, it had grown louder. His glare was locked on me, as if he could bite me with his eyes.

"What?" I said.

"I could have handled him!" he said. "I didn't need you."

You're welcome. "It doesn't matter if you did or not. I'm not going to let him—"

"I can fight my own battles! I'm the big brother. I don't need you to defend me."

I think that stick up his tail went deeper. It first appeared when Martol mentioned that he was the first to be born. Ever since, Calon had touted himself as our "big brother" despite being smaller than all of us. Even Rajor was talking about pinning him for his own good, and I now wondered if I should let him. Maybe he could knock Calon back where he belongs, or create a situation where Rajor's focus would shift to him instead of me. I'd be happy with either outcome.

I left Calon to his meal, perking my ears when I saw Toltan taking meat up to Lonate. With most of the adults talking, or transfixed by some rough play that might be too rough, I was able to sneak close enough to the hillside to hear their conversation. With any luck, I could avoid being run off before I got some idea of what had the adults so nervous.

"Come on, Lonate," Toltan said. "You have to eat."

"I can't," Lonate said.

"Why? You feel sick? Were you bitten by something?"

"It's the past. Something I thought I'd left behind."

"What are you talking about? What does the past have to do with—"

"Toltan, Lonate," Martol called. "Come down here. It's time we talked to the pack."

Toltan growled annoyance, and so did I. *So much for getting answers.* If anything, I'd only gained more questions. What could Lonate have "left behind" that would have him so nervous? Somewhere in the back of my mind, there was the question of how worried *I* needed to be, but mostly, I was just confused. And the lack of answers was starting to prick at my nerves, because I didn't know what was going on or how I needed to react to it.

Lonate turned down the hill without his meal, which seemed to draw another growl from Toltan. He carried Lonate's share down, stopped in front of him, and dropped it at his paws. Toltan's fur rose, until Lonate looked at the meat like he might throw up.

Once Toltan noticed it, he continued glaring, but somehow softer, and without his fur rising. "You will eat that, or I will stand here and watch you rot."

Lonate's ears and head fell, but Toltan didn't flinch or change. He continued to stare at Lonate as if he could will him to eat. Eventually, Lonate sighed and dug into his share. I had to join the other pups before I saw him finish it, though he soon rejoined the pack, licking his lips. I still had my ears bouncing between him and Toltan. Lonate for whatever "past" he was talking about, Toltan as he talked with the higher ranked adults a short distance away. *All this because of some thunder?*

I didn't get to think about it before Toltan and the others returned to the pack. Everyone perked their ears forward as Martol stepped out to speak.

"By now, you have all heard the odd sounds in the forest," she said. "I'm sure many of you remember hearing it before. We believe it is not thunder. Old legends told of great creatures that could kill from long distances. It was said, when they killed, a sound like thunder could be heard far away. The birds' call has confirmed that there *is* something to fear out there. Therefore, new rules are being imposed."

Toltan's ears kept shifting as he stood beside his mate. "No hunting group shall be smaller than five wolves. Pups shall be guarded by two wolves per litter. If a smell of smoke is found, the pack must be informed without fail. If anything besides a bird is seen with two legs, you will give a howl of warning. Thunder sounds shall be treated with great caution. Any questions?"

One adult said, "What do we do if we find one of these things?"

"Avoid them. They may or may not be as dangerous as legend tells."

Another adult asked, "Is it the same legend Mouler talked about? Is it real and out there, hunting in our forest?"

Toltan hesitated and cringed in pain, much like Lonate did some time ago. Unlike Lonate, his lasted only a moment. "I don't know. I pray to Wolfor it isn't."

I couldn't stop the question. "Will hunting lessons be affected?"

Toltan's ears and voice turned hard. "Still showing initiative, I see."

Might as well keep going. "It's a valid question, isn't it?"

"You're right, it is. The answer is no. We'll just be more careful. Anything else?" The pack replied with silence and backward-ticking ears. "Very well. It's been a long day for many of us. I suggest we remain here for now, try to get some rest. Conditions permitting, we'll take the older pups out for some hunting lessons when daylight returns. That is all."

The pack scattered, many talking about the new rules. Lonate made a point to walk beside me. "You continue to impress me, Luna. Not many pups would follow up on such a question. I can't wait to see what kind of adult you'll become."

My ears fell in blush. I couldn't even manage a thank you because I didn't see anything special about what I did. It seemed like a valid question, especially if it meant it would take even longer for us to prove ourselves. With the adults all worrying about this strange thunder, I didn't want us pups to be lost in it, so I spoke up. That didn't mean I deserved any credit for it, though I must admit, receiving it did feel pretty good.

I tried to find words, but by the time they came, my ear turned toward Calon as he started muttering.

"'So impressive, Luna. You're amazing, Luna. Can't wait to see what you do, Luna.' Might as well be Wolfor's son or something."

What's wrong with him? Being mad at me for "not letting him fight his battles" was one thing. This was sending a chill down my back. It was as if some part of me knew something the rest didn't. Part of me wanted to ignore it, while another said to watch and listen, just in case something came of it. One Rajor was bad enough. Having a second would make my life unbearable.

～～～

Chapter 2

MY PAWS MOVED CAREFULLY, not making a sound as I emerged from the brush. Eyes watched me, but not the ones I had to worry about. Those eyes were focused on whatever Jinta was chewing on in the middle of the meeting area. I couldn't quite see it because Lonate lying between us obscured much of Jinta. I could see enough of her to admire her changing pelt. She was becoming a white-gray mix, with most of the gray on her head, neck, and back, as if someone had sprinkled it there. Her tail had also developed a black tip larger than even the adults.

I had a feeling she would become an impressive adult someday, but for now, all that mattered was that neither fur nor ear suggested she knew I was there. Her focus on her chewing gave me the freedom to slink forward, unheard and unseen, wondering just how close I could get. My only concern was how Lonate would react. I would have to go past him for the pounce, and even if Lonate didn't react at first, once I attacked, my little game could turn unpleasant very quickly. Even so, I pressed forward, enjoying the hunt, even if I'd never get to make the "kill."

As I got closer, one of Lonate's ears turned my way, followed by his eyes. I went stone still, except for my ears, which perked forward. They waited to receive whatever reprimand or warning Lonate gave. Except, instead of either one, Lonate ticked his ears forward at me. I didn't understand what it meant until Lonate turned his head back around without a word. *He's giving me permission!*

Energized by this, I flowed fast and fluid, paws moving without thought. I risked using Lonate for cover, which the den guard ignored, suggesting he didn't mind. I peeked around my cover to check on my prey, seeing now that it was a small bone she was still chewing on. *Must have come from the last kill.* I didn't think we'd come away with such a piece, but now that I saw that we had, I decided the bone would be my prize, at least at first. I'd tease her with it a little while, have some fun, then give it back.

I tucked close against Lonate's rump to maintain as much cover as possible before my pounce. Jinta was still chewing on her bone, and she had turned so she was now facing away from me. *She'll never see me coming.* I crouched, sinking bit by bit as I prepared for my strike.

Once ready, the tension was unleashed all at once. I sprinted straight toward her, almost running over another pup tucked against Lonate. By the time she heard me, it was too late. I latched onto her scruff and pulled her onto her side before she knew what hit her. Jinta rolled onto her back, giving a full puppy growl as she tried to paw me away. I growled as well as I fought off every paw to get through. When I went for her neck, Jinta tried to block with her muzzle, but I pushed around and past it to plant my jaws on her throat. Though her growl was as loud as us pups could manage, she only tugged a little. I gave a soft compression of my jaws, then lifted my head and tail in triumph.

"Killed you!" I said. I stepped off of her, going for the bone. "I guess that makes this mine."

Jinta rolled onto her paws with a renewed glare. "Hey, that's mine! Filinsit gave that to me from our kill."

"And I killed you. That means it's mine."

I snatched the bone up in my jaws and walked away with my tail in the air, signaling my place as alpha. I waited for a playful growl or more protests of the same from my sister. What I got was a very real whimper, which stopped me cold. Such games usually went on past the "kill," but this time, Jinta sounded disappointed for real. It caused an ache in my heart that drew a sigh through the bone in my mouth. *So much for the fun.*

I turned around and dropped the bone in front of her head, which had sunk onto her paws.

"I wasn't going to keep it," I said. "Besides, I killed you anyway. I don't need a bone."

Jinta lifted her head, but her ears weren't all the way forward. I had seen the posture before, when Toltan was disciplining an adult. She was seeking permission to stand. While I liked the respect, I didn't like the fear. Not from her.

"Go on, little sister," I said. "I'll get my own later."

I left without waiting to see her reaction, half to hopefully reinforce my words, the other half because I didn't want to see her fear any more.

"Nicely done," Lonate said. "A good 'kill' and a kind heart. You know you had every right to that bone."

"I didn't need it," I said. "I never really wanted it. I just wanted to tease her with it for a while."

"So why give it back?"

"I didn't like hearing her cry."

Lonate ruffed amusement, then added a thoughtful shift in his ears I didn't quite understand. "Luna, you remind me of my younger siblings. One of them was just like you. He..." Lonate suddenly cringed, as if something had bitten him from the inside. "He was the best of my former pack."

My head tilted, confused and curious. "Former pack? You didn't come with Toltan and Martol from theirs?"

He cringed again, and I looked for something chewing on him. "No. I joined the day you were born. I was... I was orphaned. The last of my pack. I found Toltan's pack and begged to join. He agreed."

A mocking tone from someone else broke in. "And then you saved us all from a mountain lion, and now you've been given the task of watching us. How wonderful."

My ears turned to find Calon as the pup I'd almost run over a moment ago. He was curled next to Lonate, the last of his share still on his muzzle. *You don't want me fighting your battles for you, but you seek protection from Lonate?* There had to be something I was missing, but it didn't matter. While Lonate had appeared to ignore his comments, I refused to let them go.

"Shut up, Calon," I said. "We're not talking to you."

Before I could think about what I wanted to do next, Calon leapt from his spot, baring his teeth. While they weren't fully formed yet, they caused pain as Calon's first bite landed on my shoulder. We traded growls and then I sunk my teeth into Calon's neck just above the shoulder. We pulled away from each other, both preparing our next strike.

Before we could make a move, Lonate's head appeared between us, as did his adult growl.

"That's quite enough. I suggest you drop it before you two get left behind on the next hunt."

I lowered my ears, tail, and body in surrender. Calon held his ground until Lonate growled at him again. Then he too submitted to Lonate's authority. When Lonate's growl faded, Calon slunk away to play with the rest of the litter.

Lonate watched him for a while, until another adult stepped closer to watch.

"Thank you, Luna," Lonate said.

For what? "He shouldn't talk to you like that. Besides, like I said, we weren't talking to him."

At first, he cringed, then Lonate gave me an oddly affectionate rub against my muzzle. "Don't lose that, Luna. Not ever."

I only accepted the rub because I didn't understand what I was sensing from Lonate. It felt like pain, but of a kind I couldn't understand or describe. My ears shifted up, down, and sideways, trying to understand the feeling, and how I should be reacting. Even after Lonate stopped to watch Jinta return to her chewing, I had no idea what I should do or feel. Eventually, I shook it off, too confused to try and sort it out.

My eyes instead swept over my siblings, most of whom were playing in the meeting area. Calon had joined them for a moment, but it wasn't long before he was off to the side, finding a bone of his own to chew on. I turned my ears back, still trying to figure out what was wrong with him. He seemed to have as much attitude as Rajor, but his was different, and there seemed to be more to it than him just hating me.

As for Rajor himself, he was prancing toward Martol with a hunk of meat in his mouth like he'd made the kill. *That wolf puts more effort into himself than a family of beavers could put into their dam. If he'd put his energy somewhere else, with a little more attention to common sense as well, he might become a good hunter someday.*

As welcome as the thought was, I didn't expect either to happen anytime soon.

Of course, I had to wonder when he *would* carry a kill of our own. Despite us being over half the size of the adults, Toltan still wasn't letting us prove ourselves. For a moment, it had looked like he might. During the hunt earlier, I'd gone searching for the trail, I'd found the doe, and he'd praised me for my efforts. Except he also said my initiative would get me killed one day, and then told us pups to watch and learn. Never mind the fact the doe was badly wounded, or that it had an equally weak foal. All he saw was a mother with her young, and that was that. I'd have been happy to go after either, to show him what we'd learned, but he refused to allow it.

So I had to watch him go for the doe while the foal slipped away. Another kill denied.

As I tried to find sleep, my mind ran through how we could have done it. I imagined me and my siblings waiting for the adults to attack. When the foal bolted, we'd have been there, to conduct our own hunt. Young prey versus young hunters. I don't know if Rajor would have followed my orders, but the others would have. It would have been enough. We'd work around it, pick our chance, then when the time was right...

I nearly jumped out of my fur when something landed on my back. I yipped in surprise and whirled around, tossing whatever it was onto the ground. I expected to find some crazy eagle looking for a meal it had little chance of carrying. Instead, I found one of the younger pups panting laughter.

"You should see the look on your face," she said between laughs. I growled at her, to which she pretended to swoon. "Oh, come on now. I was only playing."

Does the law about killing pups apply to stupid two-moon-olds? "I don't like surprises."

The pup rose with a sigh. "Well, you're no fun at all."

"Estrella!" Solas, her father, called from the den. "Get your tail over here."

Estrella's ears fell while she slinked back to her father. Lonate arrived with an amused ruff while I watched her go.

"I'd keep an eye on that one," Lonate said. "I hear she asserted her dominance before she left the den. Since then, it's been no contest among her litter. Kind of reminds me of... never mind."

"Of what?" I said.

"Nothing. Just the past."

You're not getting off that easy. "Which is what? Lonate, why are you so obsessed with 'the past'? Why does it keep you stuck on that hillside every day?"

Lonate's ears fell while his eyes went to Estrella. "It's not something I intend to share, Luna. Not even with you."

"Why not? I don't understand..."

A scuffle among the older pups drew our attention. Rajor was at it again, this time trying to steal Calon's bone. Unlike my game with Jinta, Rajor wasn't going for a play kill, he was biting and snarling to get Calon to submit to him. As usual, Rajor was doing so with far more aggression than he needed. If he didn't stop soon, he might draw blood, puppy teeth or not.

Lonate turned with rising fur, but I barked after him.

"Let me," I said. "I'm going to stop him for good this time."

"Don't do anything stupid," Lonate said.

"Please, I'm not my brother. Only thing I have in mind is his pain."

I sprinted at Rajor in full snarl before Lonate could reply. Rajor had gotten Calon on his side and was going for the pin. Rajor was so busy gloating over his coming victory, he never saw me coming. I hit Rajor with all my speed, my jaws landing on his neck. Rajor tried to pull away, but all he did was send us rolling. While the tumble shook me loose, he took a moment to shake himself. I didn't need to slow at all. I charged back in the moment all four paws were on the ground. Rajor's eyes went wide just before I laid him flat on his back. He bit and pawed at me, but I had every advantage. I bit on a paw, a shoulder, a few misses, then I got a hold of Rajor's neck. As I squeezed to make my point, a part of me wanted to end it once and for all. I could have. I even thought I should. I'd be doing the pack a favor.

It wasn't the first time either. When we were learning to swim, another fight saw him pinned under the water. I had thought about killing him then too. Like now, for a moment, I had wanted to. There was no law then to stop me either. For my sake, and for the sake of my siblings, it seemed best to remove him from the pack for good. Yet, in spite of all that, I couldn't bring myself to make the kill.

I couldn't do it now either. Perhaps it was the law, or maybe Wolfor wouldn't let me, I don't know. Whatever the reason, my bite was only strong enough to cause pain. Though I made sure to cause as much as I could.

15

Rajor kept fighting until another strong bite tucked his tail and brought on the whines. I bit down once more, to be sure he got the message, then held him still with my growl still shaking us both.

When I finally released him, I stood over him and glared straight into his eyes. "No more. I don't want to see you harassing anyone, ever again. Fail to listen, and I'll see you live your days as the omega." I ruffed in his face before stepping off. Rajor again promised to punish me, but I ignored it as I went to check on Calon. "You all right?"

"Fine," Calon spat. "Just fine."

More than his tone, Calon's glare had my ears straight in surprise. *Some gratitude.* I'd just helped him with Rajor, yet he seemed to be angrier with me. I could only guess he was mad at me for once again not "letting him fight his own battles." Considering I'd yet to hear a "thank you," I was starting to wonder if maybe I should do just that. He didn't seem to like it when I helped, so what was the point of continuing to try?

Lonate trotted up to me. His ears were up and forward, beaming pride through his usual stern expression. "You continue to amaze me, Luna. A fine eye for hunting, a kind heart, and a firm muzzle with your pack. The next few moons will be very interesting."

My ears lowered, blushing my embarrassment. *Not sure I'm that good.*

As Lonate nuzzled me and left, my ears turned up again at Calon's mutterings.

"'You amaze me, Luna. You're so perfect, Luna. You're gonna be the best alpha ever, Luna.' What a bunch of—"

I stopped listening to him at that point. I didn't want my mind cluttered with that kind of language. However, the more he fumed, the more uncomfortable I felt around him. There was something there. Something my instincts were trying to tell me, but I didn't understand the message. I only knew he worried me in a way I couldn't understand or describe.

Lonate's "next few moons" started with more hunts where Toltan told us pups to "watch and learn." Though we were granted a little more freedom at times. On one hunt, Rajor and I, by some act of Wolfor, were allowed and able to take down a lone foal more or less on our own. Okay, as usual, he tried to take most of the credit, but it was a start. We had worked together to make the kill, giving birth to the hope that maybe someday, he might respect me.

However, a start was all it was. The adults still wouldn't let us hunt with them as equals. We were getting closer to their size and our puppy fur was gone, it was time we took our place in the pack. But Toltan was adamant, and I knew better than to fight him on it.

Thus, we followed him, flanked by adults, of course, into a part of the forest we'd never been to before. It was the same as the rest, but Toltan had yet to claim it despite how long we'd been there. It made sense to look though, as other wolves were starting to arrive in the forest. Only one or two packs so far, but Martol made it clear that more would follow soon enough. That meant more competition for prey in the forest, so the more territory we could claim now, the better we could provide for our pack. At least, that's what the adults kept saying.

As far as I was concerned, they could have this part of the forest. The sun moved steadily across the sky, and we found precious little. A couple of rats for the pups, three rabbits we stashed for the time being, otherwise, there was nothing. Just trails that were weeks old and others that quickly went cold. When we found one trail that was fresh, I didn't care that it was another wolf's. Or that it was mixed with more of those strange sweet and tangy scents from the day we first heard the odd thunder. I was happy to have something to track for a change. That is until I saw Toltan's ears were straight up, and his tail was level. Something about the scent had him nervous.

I sighed a growl as I exchanged looks with Rajor. In a rare case of mutual understanding, he ticked his ears forward in agreement. With Toltan nervous, we both knew what was coming next. The hunt was over. Just as well given the lack of prey, but that didn't keep me from wanting to be treated like a member of the pack. I turned back the way we'd come, about to lead the other pups "to safety" with me.

"Where are you going?" Toltan said without moving.

My ears perked in surprise. *I can't be that lucky.* "Don't you want us to go back where it's safe?"

"The safety of one wolf is the power of his pack. We have enough here, and there isn't a territory marker, so the risk is minimal. Stay close, control your initiative, and you'll be fine. Now follow."

He started forward carefully, the other adults following almost step for step, with me and my siblings in the middle. Rajor stopped near me long enough to roll his eyes at me.

I turned my ears forward in agreement. "It's a start."

Rajor flicked an ear, then half-pranced to catch up with Toltan. I growled annoyance, but let him be. It wasn't worth the effort.

Toltan led the group forward, following the trail deeper into the silent forest. His ears were perked the entire way, while his tail remained level, ready to react to whatever we found. I tested the air while also searching for any sounds. I found only the same wolf mixed with other scents, and dead quiet beyond. It was as if the entire forest were hiding from us.

We eventually came to an area where a small pond had formed from the rainstorm we had a few days ago. It sat in the middle of the forest, with several small creatures scattering the moment they saw us.

Toltan was more interested in what lay between us and the pond. His eyes were focused on the body of a wolf that had only recently been found by scavengers. The skin was broken in several places, but they had taken little meat thus far. Toltan told the group to hold while he went forward to investigate the corpse.

"That'll be you someday," Rajor whispered. "Yes. I can just see it. You'll show just how bad you are, then I'll get to be alpha. It wouldn't take much. All you need is—"

"One breath to pin you if you don't shut up," I said. My hackles and tail rose to remind him of my position, which Rajor, thankfully, responded to by lowering his ears and tail. His glare hadn't cooled, but with the other signs of submission, I let it go. Now was not the time for another scuffle.

Toltan was sniffing at the dead wolf, searching for something. I asked Lonate what he was looking for, but he too was unsure. The only clue we got was when Toltan tried pulling on one of the wolf's forelegs.

When he did, we saw that something was attached right above the dead wolf's paw. At my distance, it appeared to be hard as stone, but thin and curved like a bent piece of bark. The bark... stone... whatever it was, formed a half-circle, and I thought I saw a line that went along the middle of it that looked like teeth, with the wolf's paw trapped in this line. As Toltan pulled, the paw itself flopped around wildly, no doubt broken when it had been caught. The wolf's blood dripped from his claws as it hung in the air, further suggesting a recent death. The stone itself seemed attached to a series of more, smaller stones, that were looped around and through each other. This line of collected stones ran a short distance to where they appeared to be rooted deep in the ground. Each time Toltan tugged, these stones chinked against each other, yet never seemed to chip.

"What is that?" I asked.

Toltan dropped the leg and came back to the group." I don't know. I've never seen or heard of anything like it before. Smells strange. It's acrid, tangy, almost like rock, but not like any I've ever seen before. I wonder what happened after he got trapped."

"What do you mean?" Lonate asked. "Didn't that stone thing kill him?"

"No. It wounded him, but he wasn't here long. A day at most. Much longer, and he would have gnawed his paw off to get loose."

My stomach churned at the idea. *How desperate does one have to be to literally chew their own leg off? And what good would it do? Once you're missing a paw, you won't be able to hunt as well, so you're dead either way. Assuming your self-inflicted wound doesn't kill you first.*

As I tried to get my insides settled, Rolin, one of my brothers, stepped out to sniff at another part of the ground.

"Hey look," he said. "A dead rat. There are quite a few here. At least we can feed ourselves."

"Careful, Rolin," Toltan said. "It might be too long dead."

"Smells pretty fresh. I think it's safe."

Rolin reached down to eat the rat, and the pack jumped as another of the strange stones, this one bigger than the other, snapped up onto his neck. Rolin slumped to the ground without so much as a yip.

The pack stood frozen, many, myself among them, trying to find their breath. The rest were merely silent, save for Toltan, who gave a single, soft whine of pain. When it became even harder for me to breath, I looked down at my leg to refocus my mind on something else. I couldn't bear to see my brother with his neck caught in one of those things, so I trapped myself in thinking about what it would be like to chew my leg off. In an odd way, I found it an easier thought than the broken neck of my brother. It turned even more sour when I looked at my paw and realized just how close I was to finding out.

Toltan turned my way when my breathing came close to panting. When he spoke, his voice was still heavy. "Luna? Luna, what is it?"

I could only stare at my left forepaw, or rather, the dead rat right beside it. My insides wanted to shake, but the rest of my body didn't dare let them. Another claw to the right, and I would have stepped right on it. I tried very, *very* hard not to think about what came next.

Toltan followed my stare, then gasped. "Don't touch it. Pick your paw straight up, then take a step back, nice and slow."

No argument.

I moved as slow as the sun, while my heart raced enough for three sprints. The image of the stone popping up to catch me had my insides rolling around like a pebble in the river. I tried to focus on not trembling, hoping it might push everything else out of my mind. When that didn't work, all I could do was concentrate on moving back, nice and slow, placing my other paws where they'd been a moment ago. I put my forepaw down away from the rat, then retreated the rest of the way at the same pace.

I breathed great relief when nothing jumped to bite me after a couple of steps. My breath disturbed some of the leaves, nearly stopping my heart again. There, in the ground, sat more stone teeth sitting upward, ready to bite. Somehow certain of safety, my fear weakened in the face of curiosity. *I wonder if that would work again.* I stood stone still and blew. More leaves moved, showing the teeth made a circle around the rat. The line of connected stones lay under it, no doubt rooted like the others.

Relief was compounded by a sense of pride. Just by accident—*thank you, Wolfor*—I had discovered the secret of the stone teeth. The dead rats somehow caused them to jump up and latch onto their prey. While I couldn't understand why they never did more, the fact that I'd found out that much had me almost giddy. That, or it was the fact that I'd been that close to being caught myself.

"At least we know how it works," I said almost laughing.

"At too high a cost," Toltan said. He stared at Rolin's body a long time before giving a sigh of his own. "Everyone, back to the den."

My joy faded when I too looked after my brother. *If only I'd found the secret first.* "But what about Rolin?"

"We can do nothing for him. We'll mourn when we are safe. Come on."

We grabbed the few kills from before and left, never to travel in that part of the forest again.

～～～

Chapter 3

"**I** SWEAR, MY HEART STOPPED FOR A MOMENT."

All of the pups, younger and older, were gathered around me. Though all were listening, some ears were more perked than others. All four of the younger pups sat still, transfixed by every word, while most of the older ones did little more than pay attention. Lonate stood over us, at times ruffing in amusement for some reason. I certainly didn't find any of my tale funny. Rajor, of course, glared and rolled his eyes every sentence or two. For once, though, he was outdone. Calon had a glare worthy of Toltan's death stance.

"So the grand Luna escapes death by a claw's width," Calon said. "I can't believe you're listening to this."

"Shhhh, quiet!" Estrella said. "Luna is talking, not you."

Calon pretended to cower as if submitting, but sarcasm laced every word. "Oh, I'm sorry. I didn't mean to offend you. Please forgive me."

Estrella growled at him, though it sounded closer to a raspy whimper than a growl. *Did we really sound like that at her age?* I looked at Lonate, who ticked his ears forward to answer my silent question. I panted a short laugh, rather embarrassed at the idea of ever sounding so... harmless.

I flicked an ear as if I could toss the feeling away, then returned to my tale.

"Wolfor was watching over me, I'm sure of it. He kept me safe, and he showed me the secret. I blew away the leaves by accident, and I saw the stone teeth all around the dead rat. That's when I understood it. If you touch the dead rat, the stone teeth will jump up and bite you. If they catch you, they won't let go, ever."

"Ooooooo," the younger litter said.

"Runts," Calon said. He trotted off, continuing to grumble.

Lonate ruffed at him before turning his attention on the younger ones. "All right, that's enough for one day. Your parents want you back near the den, now."

"But Lonate," Estrella said. "I want to——"

"Now."

Her ears fell with a small growl more pitiful than the last. I turned my ears back at her as Lonate led Estrella and her siblings to their den. *Tell me we weren't like that.*

Rajor, for once, didn't say a word. That left me with Calon, who had somehow gotten to the edge of the meeting area without anyone stopping hm. Even at a distance, I could see he was still muttering. No doubt the same rantings I'd heard before. With Lonate preoccupied, and Toltan in deep conversation with Martol and others, I felt I had to deal with Calon myself.

Calon kept going, and I followed him. The only adults nearby were too busy listening to Toltan to notice either of us. Calon ignored them, while I slipped past, staying a few steps behind him. I only hesitated when a strange sensation tried to overwhelm me. It was as if a wave of panic swept over me, forcing my ears back. Yet at the same time, I didn't feel any real fear. It almost felt like there was a voice inside me, trying to tell me something.

Without any more than the sensation to go on, I pressed forward. I knew I could handle this alone. If I could pin Rajor over and over again, dealing with Calon shouldn't be an issue. Besides, I wasn't about to have another Rajor in my pack. One was more than enough. I saw Calon approach the river, and I had to push down another wave of that strange feeling before moving forward. I needed to keep my head clear if I was going to handle this the right way.

As Calon leaned down for a drink, I stepped forward, calm and steady. I didn't want a fight, I wanted answers. I kept my tail level to avoid any air of dominance. I hoped it would be enough.

It wasn't.

"What do you want?" Calon said.

For a moment, I couldn't tell which was rushing faster: the river, or the blood in my ears. The latter I didn't understand and thus ignored.

"What's wrong with you?" I asked.

Calon's eyes widened. "What's wrong with me? Do you really want an answer?"

"I asked, didn't I?"

"You are." My head tilted in confusion. Calon went on. "For moons, all Toltan and Martol and Lonate talk about is *you*. 'Luna did this. Luna did that. Luna will be a great alpha someday. You could learn a lot from Luna. Luna is your example; match him.' They talk like you're Wolfor's chosen leader or something. You and your 'silver sheen.'"

"And you blame me for that." It was more a statement than a question.

"Why not? You won't keep helping when we don't need it. You won't let us fight our own battles. You won't let us get the preferred teachings. You won't let us be the top wolves we should be."

"Calon, I'm in charge. It's my pack, or at least the litter is. It's my job to enforce order."

"Says who?! Who decided you get to lead when everyone knows I was firstborn? I'm bigger, stronger, and faster. I'm better than you in every way, but you won't let me prove it!"

I huffed and turned my ears back. *So much for no argument.* Once I realized he wasn't going to listen, I let my tail rise to show dominance. If talking wouldn't work, then I had to make sure I ended Calon's challenge before it got anywhere.

"Now you're sounding like Rajor. I suggest you remember what I've done to him before you talk about taking over my pack."

Of all the things Calon said, he was right about one thing.

He was faster.

Calon clamped his teeth on my shoulder before I even realized he was moving. Instinct alone had my jaws snapping at him to retaliate. I missed, but my quick twisting and the near misses shook Calon free without a pant. Speed seemed to be his only advantage, though it was more than enough to be a threat. Calon snarled and continued to lunge at me, landing only glancing blows, sometimes not even drawing blood. I countered as much as possible, too off-balance to retreat or call for help. The best I could do was keep him from getting to my neck or underbelly. What few bites I landed did more surface damage than true injury, effecting a stalemate.

That is, until Calon charged. I blocked his jaws, but not the rest of him. Both of us rolled, legs entangled, into the river. I pushed off to get away from him, only to regret the success of my choice. The current took hold, drawing me away from my pack and the shore. I whimpered in panic, more so when I saw Calon still fighting and kicking to catch up with me. The look in his eyes was the worst. This wasn't just anger. I could see my blood in those eyes. Even above the rush of the river, I could hear a true, fierce growl in his throat. *And I thought Rajor was bad.*

I swam as hard as I could toward the shore. My paws kicked with all they had while my head twisted around in search of something, anything, that could save me. The best chance appeared to be some rocks near the edge of the river that might be low enough to climb onto. I fought with every kick to get there, even wagging my tail in the hopes it too might offer some help.

I managed to fight the current just enough to get my paws on the rocks. My claws dug in, finding enough hold to keep me in place. My hind paws found traction soon after. I heaved myself out of the water, panting in terror and exhaustion.

"No!" Calon said. "Get back here. I'm not done with you."

Calon still hadn't given up. He was fighting hard to get to me. He wasn't able to achieve as much movement as I had. I could tell the river would take him past the rocks, but too far out to get as much traction as I did.

The panic returned, but this time, it rushed up from my heart. The rush gave me a burst of energy, which I used to plant my paws at the edge of the rocks, take aim, and reach for Calon. I tried to get my fangs on the scruff of Calon's neck, or onto a paw if I could. Either would have been enough to pull him to safety.

Instead, I jerked back when Calon bit at me. He had come so close, I could feel his nose brush the fur on my throat. But once again, it was his eyes that haunted me. I saw it there, in those eyes, in Calon's raised hackles despite being soaked. A cold hatred. One that had only one goal on its mind: my death. I watched him pass by, horrified that my own brother would hate me so much... would... I couldn't even think it.

Calon kept fighting, but because he was trying to get to me instead of the shore, the river continued to take him downstream. Despite Calon's hatred, the panic remained. *No. No, I can't lose another brother.*

I turned for the bank, careful not to slip and fall back into the river. Once I was on dirt, I followed the shore, trying to find Calon. I let out short howls, or rather long, loud whimpers, as I ran. All the while, I was praying. I begged Wolfor to help me. I asked him to keep Calon alive until Lonate could save him.

My legs burned from running, swimming, and minor wounds. My tongue flapped in the air with each bound. My chest demanded I stop, but I ignored them all. I couldn't stop. Not yet. I had to find him. I had to...

Near a fallen tree in the water, I saw a figure. A shadow I didn't want to believe. I sprinted to the edge, climbed on the trunk, and found Calon stuck under the surface. Ignoring the burn and throb in my limbs, I reached in with my jaws in the hopes of helping him get out of the river. I got a firm hold on Calon's scruff and pulled as hard as I could. Calon never moved.

At least he's not biting at me anymore. It was a lie I barely registered. Not only had he not budged, he hadn't moved at all. Even his eyes were closed. *Must be really stuck. Come on, Calon. Budge!* I tossed my head side to side, at last feeling Calon's body move. Another hard pull to the side, and I almost fell in again when Calon came free all at once.

I dragged him all the way to shore, then shook myself dry, nearly fainting from exhaustion. Calon still hadn't moved or opened his eyes, and nothing I did would stir him. I nudged him, pawed at him, even bit his muzzle and ears. None of it worked. Try as I might, I could not change what my nose was already telling me.

"No," I said. "No, Calon. Calon, come on. Come on, wake up. By Wolfor, wake up!"

My ears fell. I couldn't lie to myself anymore. Calon was dead. Killed when he hit the tree, drowned when he couldn't get free... it didn't matter. I'd lost another brother.

I heard the pack arrive, but I barely processed it. My heart was too heavy.

Martol was at the head of the pack.

"Luna? Luna, what... no. No, not another one."

As much pain as I felt, I could only imagine how much she was hurting. It felt like the howls for Rolin were still in my ears, and now here was Calon, also dead. I watched her try everything I had tried to wake him up. She got the same reply, but she kept trying. She tried so hard she drew blood, but Calon didn't bleed. His body just seeped what blood lay under the surface of his skin. Seeing her so frantic... I didn't know pain could have its own pain, but that's what it felt like.

When Toltan appeared beside her, Martol rubbed against him so hard, she almost knocked him down. Toltan returned it before he saw Calon.

Somehow, his eyes had never looked so heavy. "Martol. Is... is there..."

"No," Martol said. "No sign. He's gone."

"What happened?"

Martol panted, heaved hysterics. When her eyes found me, I almost wished Calon had killed me. It would have been better than seeing the layers of anguish in my mother's eyes.

Toltan bounced his eyes between us before settling on me. "Luna? What happened?" I couldn't form an answer. What would I say? Calon died trying to kill me? I couldn't get my own mind to accept it. How could I explain it to them?

"Luna! What happened?"

I tried to say something. I tried to make sense of it. Words never came.

So Rajor found his own. "I saw it all. Luna attacked him. They rolled into the river. When Calon tried to get out, Luna kept him down."

Jinta gave a growl that was low and rumbled, nothing like the usual puppy scratch. "Oh, come on, Rajor. You couldn't have seen it. You were with the rest of us."

"I saw it happen further upriver. None of you were there, only me. Luna killed Calon. I swear it in the name of Wolfor himself. He killed him like he tried to kill me. You remember, when he held me under the water? He did it to Calon!"

Toltan entered the death stance. Rajor, for the first time ever, stared back without fear. Toltan's ear turned my way, his eyes following soon after.

He brought his nose close to mine. "Luna. Luna, please. Say something. Wolfor's name, Luna, please speak to me!"

No words would form. I found nothing within while finding too much without. Toltan's pleading eyes, the stunned pack watching, Rajor's smug look, Martol still nuzzling the body of her pup... my brother's body. The same one that had tried to kill me. I didn't know where I was, much less where to begin.

"You see?" Rajor said. "He's so guilty, he can't even admit it. What's more, just look at Calon. Luna scratched him good before he killed him. You know it's true. Wolfor knows it's true. You can't deny it. He killed Calon to protect his place among the litter. Luna is a pup killer!"

At last, I found something. I glared at Rajor as if I could set him on fire. I'd warned him about harassing someone again, least of all me. Hair by hair, my fur rose, as did my lips.

My body shook from fighting the rage, and words finally came.

"Shut up, Rajor. You don't know anything. You have no idea what happened."

Rajor stood tall. "I saw everything, Luna. Your lies won't hold anymore. You killed Calon, just like you tried to kill me. You know I'm right."

That smug look, that arrogant stance, I'd had it. It was time to put Rajor in his place once and for all! I sprang toward him in full snarl. My fangs yearned to pin him under the ground. I had visions of him in great pain, and of him begging for forgiveness.

None of them had me doing either.

Before I got to Rajor, Toltan pinned me to the ground by the neck. I hadn't seen him coming, which meant my head was spinning. My sides hurt from landing, and my neck ached from the bite, but my insides were too hot to stop now.

"Let me go!" I said. "I need to do this. He has to learn his place!"

"Like Calon did?" Toltan said.

Anger turned to cold fear. "Toltan? Wha... what are you saying? You don't believe him. You can't."

Toltan's ears fell as his eyes closed. He looked back at the pack a moment, who looked at him like they expected something of him. When one of them raised his hackles, Toltan ticked his ears forward, then came back to me. When I looked into his eyes again, another, much older wolf, stared back.

"You've left me no choice, Luna. You have nothing to defend yourself with. Rajor invoked Wolfor's name. There's no other answer I can draw." Toltan turned to the pack. Silence fell like rain. "For... for this griev... grievous crime, there is only one punishment. Luna... Luna... is... hereby banished from the pack. He may not be allowed to run with us, or hunt with us, or to live within our borders. He is... he is... to live the remainder of his life... as... as a lone wolf. No wolf shall run with him again... ever."

Rajor stood smug as he'd ever been. The pack stood still. Every ear erect, every tail limp, including mine.

This isn't happening. Surely Toltan didn't mean it. It had to be a test, or some trick to mess with Rajor. He wouldn't do this. He couldn't exile me for defending myself.

Toltan turned back to me, looking no younger. I couldn't breathe. I couldn't think. Even my heart had stopped moving. It had to be a mistake, or a dream, or something other than what my ears had heard. I looked at each member of the pack, trying to find some sign, some shred of hope. The best I got was a pained falling of ears. The rest were merely blank. *Wolfor, please, tell me this isn't happening. He can't do this to me.*

"Luna," Toltan said, "you heard the sentence. Go. Be gone from here. Let us find neither scent nor hair... or face our fangs for the final time."

My heart stopped. It couldn't process any more pain. It couldn't understand how I could be among my pack and be totally alone.

"Toltan. Please. There has to be——"

"Go! Now. Before I am forced to end the life of another of my pups."

He meant it. Wolfor's fang, he really meant it.

I stood on legs I couldn't feel. My paws were so heavy, they may as well have been stones. I stared at my father like he was a stranger, but I didn't hesitate. I knew if I did, I'd watch his fangs tear into me. While I might have taken that over what I was walking toward, I couldn't do that to Martol. So I walked, and Toltan only watched. He would say nothing more.

Martol, however, would. "Luna. For as long as you live, remember I——"

Toltan snarled her away. I looked back at her, hoping to catch the rest. Instead, I found the snapping jaws of Toltan. I sprinted away before he acted on his threat.

I only saw my path enough to avoid running into something. My ears told me he wasn't there, but after seeing my own father try to kill me, I couldn't stop. My mind still couldn't even imagine such a thing, much less accept that any of it was really happening. I ran and ran, until my legs had nothing left to give. Even then, I kept walking. Blood and water were still drying on my fur. Between my fight with Calon and Toltan's pin, my tail was the only thing that *didn't* ache. None of it compared to the host of spines cutting into my heart.

He'd really done it. Toltan had banished me based on a lie. He was punishing me for something I didn't even do! How could he? I could still remember his nose touching mine before I could see. I remembered feeling his aura, his presence. I knew he would give his life to protect me. How could he do this to me? *Why* did he do this to me?

A long, deep howl echoed from behind me. They were mourning Calon. I tried to think some howled for me as well, but that only made it hurt more. My pack... my family... they would shun me now. If I ever came back, they'd kill me. Even Lonate.

I resumed my path away from my home. With my insides finding some measure of cohesion, I noticed that the forest had changed. It seemed darker than I remembered despite the sunlight. My ears found things they'd always ignored. And why not? Lonate and Toltan had always been there to protect me. Except they weren't anymore. No one would be.

For all my talk of wanting to be treated like an adult, right now, I might as well have been a newborn. I still wanted my mother's comfort. I wanted the soft warmth of her belly fur. The cool, wet touch of her nose. Her power lying beside me, ready to snap a mountain lion in two. I'd have given anything to be under Lonate's watch again. I wouldn't complain anymore. I swore I wouldn't.

My offer was met with Toltan's territory marker. I remembered him dropping it the day before. A short time ago, it was home. Now it was a place I would have to avoid, forever. As I walked by, I felt like a tree went through my heart. This was really happening. Nothing I said or did would change anything.

I dragged on for what felt like days. I had nowhere to go. No one to help me. I would have to find whatever I needed on my own. Every hunt, every meal, I would need to catch alone. But there was no chance of hunting today. My wounds had only just stopped bleeding. My legs protested every step I took, so running was out of the question. No, for now, I needed to find cover. Some semblance of safety where I could let my heart and body recover.

I set out looking for an old den I could expand, or a thick bush I could curl inside of. My search came up empty until a mockingbird fluttered over my head. My jaws just missed him, but as I glared at my near-snack, I saw an odd pile of rocks. It seemed to be a random pile in the middle of the forest, almost as if Wolfor had dropped it there.

Whether he did or not, even at a distance, I could see an opening. I walked right up to it, first sniffing the rocks and the area around them. The only scents were far too old to be from a current owner. A look inside revealed a tunnel that ran no more than the length of an adult. I could see it expanded after that, so I dragged myself inside. The tunnel ended in a small cavern that had a thin layer of dirt inside. The lack of paw prints further confirmed this den was unclaimed. I went against the far wall, and flopped on my side so my body could rest at last.

While I wouldn't call it comfortable, the den proved to be enough. The rocks were so thick and tightly packed, they'd provide all the cover I'd need.

They would likely keep the rain out too. Were I not alone, it would have been more than enough to raise a litter in.

That thought sent another spine into my heart. *Were I not alone.* As if I had a choice in the matter. I was a lone wolf now. My own pack... Toltan... they would kill me if they found me in their territory again. Even now, as my body felt a thousand times heavier, I couldn't process that thought. I ran the image of him snapping at me over and over, and it still seemed like a nightmare. It wasn't real. I knew it was, but it didn't feel like it. The only real thing I felt was the pain that had nothing to do with my wounds.

How could he do it? How could Toltan do this to me?

CRAACK!- cshoo-shoo

My ear's shot up. *That sounded close.* How close proved impossible to tell. A short sprint away? Just outside? The sound echoed around the rocks, hiding the answer. Despite my weariness, diligence forced me to creep outside. If that strange thunder happened often, I needed to find a new den fast.

I stopped just inside the entrance. My ears found silence, and my nose found less. Certain that at least the immediate area was safe, I ventured out so my nose and ears could get a better reading of my surroundings.

I flinched when chirping shattered the silence.

"Hunt done, enjoy the sun. Hunt done, enjoy the sun."

I followed the call and found a small bird sitting on top of the rocks. Like all mockingbirds, his body was dominated by gray, while his wings and tail were mostly black. As he preened a wing, the white splotch on the inside of each wing was shown, as was the white edge of his tail.

My ears perked as I wasn't so sure he wasn't the same one I'd almost caught a moment ago.

"Hunt?" I said. "What are you talking about?"

"Beasts of two legs. They came, hunted, and went. So much time was spent."

"Beasts of two legs? What are you talking about? Where are they? *What* are they?"

"Be aware, heed your fear, they bring death to all things near."

The bird fluttered away before I could shake my head into thinking again. *I should have known better than to expect a conversation with a bird.*

CRAACK!-cshoo-shoo

That was definitely close. Though not as close as I first thought. My ears followed its path clearly this time, giving me direction as well. Were I still with Toltan, I would have left to tell him...

The thought triggered a growl. *There's an irony.* Being exiled meant I no longer had to follow Toltan's rules. I could do what I wanted for a change. I could hunt on my own, explore as much as I wanted, play with anything that interested me. My banishment had given me my freedom. The more I thought about it, the more the idea excited me. So much so that I ventured forth out of spite. It didn't matter that Toltan would never know. All that mattered is that he would never have allowed it. *Show him to not believe me over Rajor.*

Spite or not, I moved slow and silent. Something my legs appreciated, since they still hadn't recovered. My head stayed still with each step, though my ears were frozen forward. I tested the air with my nose at each pause, finding stranger things the more I moved. Icky, stale scents like when lighting struck a tree, musty scents I couldn't account for, sweet and salty mixed together as if some strange nut had bonded with tree sap. *What am I tracking?*

The sounds ahead proved just as confusing. There was something that sounded like barks, yet these seemed to flow constant like howls, but also changed pitch mid-howl multiple times. The energy in the barks suggested joy, maybe. I couldn't find a single familiar sound. For all I knew, they were killing each other.

I finally caught sight of something in the distance. It looked like a gathering of half a dozen or so creatures, all standing tall on two legs. Their heads were bare, save for some fur on the top of their heads. Well, except for one, who had no fur at all. Their front... top... "paws," for lack of a better word, were also bare, but seemed devoid of claws. *So do the big cats, until they are loosed on their prey,* I reminded myself.

Strangest of all, they all seemed to have gathered around a fire. I had only seen fire once, and it was barely a flicker. This was a raging fire, yet it remained in one place, never growing. My head turned in confusion when I saw the creatures were holding their bare paws out over the flame. They weren't close enough to burn, I don't think, but still very close. *I suppose if one didn't have fur, gathering around a contained flame would be nice.*

Except they did have fur, or some kind of hide. Their legs, bottom paws, and bodies were covered in thick, colorful hides. My ears shot up when the two closest to the fire shed their hide like it wasn't attached. Their... skin? Fur? Whatever it was, underneath was still colorful, just not as thick.

Are these the two-legged beasts everyone's been worried about? They didn't seem that dangerous. I'd seen sharper fangs on birds than what these had in their mouths. There was the chance they were incredibly strong or fast, but I couldn't see anything that suggested a bite to the neck would be any less effective. If anything, it might be easier on these, for they had no antlers to put in my way.

I continued to watch as the sun moved across the sky. These creatures barked on and on, at times holding small rocks up to their ears and barking to no one in particular. *At least birds sing.* Finally, three of them left the group.

They each grabbed a long, thin stick that seemed oddly smooth, almost as if it were river rock embedded into bits of wood.

One gave a stick to another, younger member, who barked in excitement. Then they marched out with their sticks hanging on their backs. I followed close behind, careful to remain hidden and silent. They were going somewhere, and the young one held all the tension I remembered from not that long ago. This was his first hunt, and I was about to learn with him. Only difference was, I was there to learn how to *avoid* them.

The group trudged through the trees and brush, making quite a racket as they pushed through limbs and leaves. Either they weren't trying, or they were the loudest hunters the forest had ever seen. If so, they wouldn't be hunting for long.

Though I began to second-guess that when they made a path to the field of dead rats my pack had encountered earlier. The stone teeth had found more victims since then. A crow caught by the chest near Rolin's body, a fox killed the same way as my brother, and an older wolf trapped by the paw just as the other had been. Except this one was still alive.

One of the two-leggeds bumped the younger one's shoulder. *His kill? Good luck with that.* The young one barked eagerness, seemingly unafraid of the wolf's snarls.

Despite my age, I wanted to act. I could feel my legs bracing for more sprint, despite still not recovering from my last two. My shoulders rocked as I thought about who to go for. The leader, the pup, the other, didn't really matter. I could take any one of them. If not, I could easily distract them enough to let the wolf get away.

One of the beasts looked my way, but I merged with the shadows before he could catch sight of me. The beast watched a moment longer before looking away. I never lost sight of my quarry. I wanted to act, but I wanted to learn more. I'd never get to see how these things hunted in such safety again. Now alone without a pack, I had to know.

The younger beast had taken his stick in his paws. The wolf snarled challenge, but his flat ears and tucked tail betrayed his fear. The young two-legged leveled his stick, pointing it at the wolf. My ears perked to try and find—

CRAACK!-CSHOO-shoo-shoo

I hugged the ground, too startled to remember much. My eyes were locked on the two-legged, or rather, his stick.

What magic did these beasts control? The sound had clearly come from the stick, but Wolfor, what a noise. My ears were still ringing, and I was some distance away. I could only imagine what the other wolf was going through. He was still snarling, which surprised me considering his ears had to be bleeding from being that close to the noise.

My ears cleared enough to realize, that wasn't a wolf snarling. Too much rasp, not enough rumble, too high a pitch. Soon after, the rumble itself felt familiar, from a time before I could see.

I followed the sound to a mountain lion charging toward the two-leggeds. No, wrong, toward *me*. Its eyes were locked onto me as if I were already in its jaws. It snarled and roared as it ran. It had found a meal, and I had no pack to defend me this time. I stood frozen, too terrified to run. Even if I could, what was the point? I'd never outrun an adult mountain lion. I had no pack and no Martol. I had zero chance of survival.

CRAACK-CRACK-CRACK!-CSHOOSHOO-shooshooo-shoo

I felt years fall off of my life when the sticks of the other two-leggeds went off. My body shook so hard, I was certain they could feel it, which only made it worse. Yet the terror faded, or at least diminished, when I found the mountain lion dead in front of the two-leggeds. Their sticks were all level, as if pointing them at the big cat. As feeling returned to my body, I wondered how far the wolf had gotten during the distraction.

When I turned to look, the terror came back with friends. The wolf hadn't gotten far at all. He too was limp on the ground, his eyes were closed, and blood seeped from a hole in his forehead. *They did that. Their sticks... they... they...* I was shaking so hard, I could hardly breathe. Two great predators, killed by these beasts. I was still a pup. What chance did I have against them?

My paws edged, edged, then blew away as fast as my legs could carry me, despite their complaints at a third sprint. I didn't care. I had to get away. I had to escape to survive. I tore a path all the way back to the rock pile, swept inside, and hugged the inside wall. Even then, my body shook so much I worried I might bring it down.

"Wolfor," I prayed. "Wolfor, protect me. Please. I was innocent. I didn't... I didn't kill my brother. Please keep me safe. Shelter me as my mother no longer can."

For a second, I thought I felt something. A warmth, a breath, something, seeping into my fur, calming me.

I doubted it was real. After so much time with Rajor, I'd gotten pretty good at lying to myself. But for the moment, that lie felt a lot better than the truth I'd just experienced.

~~~

Chapter 4

"NEW DAY, NEW DAY, FIND SOME PREY?"

That bird is lucky he's too fast to eat.

I might not have minded being woken up like that if it didn't come with another reminder of my new situation. I'd gotten lucky with a few mice the day after I was banished, but the spoils of previous hunts with Toltan had finally faded. I needed a real meal if I was going to survive.

I stretched, yawned, and ventured out to find a calm morning with more birds chirping in the trees. The same mockingbird sat where he'd been the last couple of days, atop the pile of rocks, twitching his tail at me.

"Good morning, good morning," the bird sang, "a hunt will start this morning."

Where are those two-leggeds when I need them? Though he was right about one thing: a hunt was about to start. My first as a lone wolf. *Time to see what Toltan taught me, besides betrayal.*

It appeared to be not much. My nose found sweet tree sap and, *ew, skunk droppings.* I chose another path, finding nothing again, and again, and again. My "hunt" had become more of a wander as I tried to find anything. Then when it did, it was a territory marker I didn't dare violate. I turned away from that path and stumbled across a much better one. It was a fresh deer trail that was strangely familiar, though I couldn't say how. Curiosity, and a lack of other options, had me following the trail over log and thistle. Despite the risk, I wanted to know why this deer was so vivid to my nose.

I panted a laugh when I found it. Not only was it a foal, it was the same one Toltan wouldn't let my siblings and me hunt on our own. Amazing that it had survived this long alone. I laughed again when I realized I now had a chance to conduct the hunt I was denied. Well, most of it, since I'd be doing it without my siblings. *At least there's no Rajor.*

I stalked forward, trying to get as close as I could before it saw me. It was searching for me, but it was young. It didn't know what to look for. My paws flowed silently onto the ground with each step, my mouth drooling at the thought of such a meal. *My hunt. My kill.*

My legs filled with energy, and I used it. Once I got as close as I felt I could, my legs launched me into a sprint without a thought, as if they were separate from my body. The foal turned and ran, crying out for help I knew would never come. Just as I had no pack, so too was this foal without a herd.

I slowly closed the gap, my legs burning, but my stomach snarled for a meal, and I was determined to get it. The foal turned around a tree, pushing for all the speed it could find. I kept pace, too intent on eating to let him get away. After another turn, I pushed my legs to their limit, bringing me just close enough to snap at the foal's legs. Two snaps missed, then the third got hold of a leg. The foal cried out as it tried to shake free, but to no avail. I planted my paws and pulled, bringing him to an abrupt halt. He tried to pull away, but my fangs were too deep into his outstretched leg. Eventually, the foal stumbled onto its side in a mess of tangled limbs.

I released my hold so I could rush forward for the kill. An adult deer might have done better, but this foal knew too little. Its hooves didn't even slow me down. I found its neck with ease, and death came soon after.

I laid still, panting from the exertion before I asked my body to do anything more. *What a rush.* The chase had tested me even more than my fight with Calon, and I had a fresh kill to show for it. Too bad Rajor wasn't around. *Let's see him find an insult to counter this one.*

Once my insides had settled, I dug into my kill. As blood stained my muzzle, I went for the best meat. The lack of competition made the bits slide down with more joy than I'd ever felt. It was so warm, so fresh, so perfect. *Who knew isolation would change so much?* I didn't have to worry about anything but my own needs for a change. I didn't have to listen to anyone either. Best of all, no more Rajor to spoil a perfect day. It all felt so good at one point, I tried to swallow a hunk of meat as slowly as possible, as if I could meditate on it and all the feelings I had running through my blood right now. *Why is this bad again?*

Those feelings changed when I caught wind of other wolves. I heard them approach, then I saw them. My *former* pack, with Toltan at the lead as usual, walking straight toward me. Either they didn't see me or didn't care. I started growling before they ever got close. There hadn't been any markers. This was free territory. That meant the foal was my kill. My growl grew the closer they got. My hackles rose at the same pace, with my ears straight and forward without a hint of fear. *You won't take this from me. Not after what you did.*

Despite my age, my snarl echoed off the trees by the time they reached me. I noticed the younger litter behind Toltan, no doubt on their first hunt. For a moment, I couldn't help remembering the thrill of my first time. Back then, I didn't care as much about proving myself. Just being out on a hunt, with him, was enough. Getting the chance to go after a rabbit had only made it that much better.

The memory touched on Toltan's voice at the time. I remembered him telling me to dig, and how it excited me. It would have been my first kill, if only had Rajor had made an effort to catch it.

All at once, I felt my insides burn as I remembered what he did to me. How he had betrayed that memory. It caused my snarl to grow when Toltan stepped forward to match my challenge. I barked and snapped at him, and Toltan returned the challenge with equal volume, though somehow, his hackles didn't seem as straight.

I stood over the dead foal without the slightest hesitation. "This is my kill. You'll not touch it. I'll fight you with all I have should you try."

Toltan stared me down, and I raised my tail. Deep down, I knew I couldn't win a fight, but that thought was buried under the anger. Not to mention the sense that, in the end, I had nothing left to lose. At worst, Toltan would kill me, which losing the kill might bring about anyway. If I was going to die, might as well die fighting instead of starving to death.

Toltan kept his tail raised while the pack watched with nervous glances between us. Lonate, of course, stood with the pups as he always did. *He does his job well that one.*

Our stalemate echoed off the trees for what felt like days, neither one of us relenting. That is, until a yip from the pups drew Toltan's ear. Lonate had stopped one from wandering off the way he sometimes had to: with his fangs. While he'd stopped the pup, he'd also brought an end to the battle.

Toltan's snarl didn't fade, but he did step back. "I'll not risk my pups today. I've lost too many this year. Keep from our boundaries, Luna."

"And you from mine," I snarled.

While Toltan tried to enter his death stance, he never achieved the same rigidity he'd always held. Eventually, he led his pack away without a word.

I waited until they were out of sight to finish what I could of my kill. My stomach enjoyed every bite until it finally admitted it had no more room. The rest would be raven food by nightfall, but at least I'd gotten the best parts. Even so, there might be enough scraps later to keep me strong while I found other meals.

Now full, and far less terrified, I set about claiming my piece of the forest. I went right up to Toltan's latest marker, and left a few of my own droppings on my side of the border. A step I repeated more than once in the hopes that I might keep more of what I suspected would be prime hunting grounds.

It was after lifting my leg at another tree that my nose found something else. A dirty, icky scent like charred wood, yet musty scents followed. The latter I recognized from that first day of my exile. The day I saw the power of the two-leggeds. A part of me wanted to run, return to the whelp I became that night. The stronger side wanted to find them. If nothing else, to determine what threat they posed.

I moved forward, ears and eyes searching for them. After watching what they could do to a mountain lion, I couldn't afford to get careless. I moved in careful spurts, not advancing too far before I felt sure I had a clear path. My legs and paws were quick and careful, moving so smoothly I barely felt them. I wanted to find the two-leggeds, but I wanted to do so without being seen.

I found other wolves first. It appeared to be a small pack, no more than seven adult members. Probably split off, or the first litter of a mated pair, looking for a home of their own. They moved just as carefully, the wind blowing my scent away, keeping my presence hidden.

Not that they would have cared had they known. They, like me, had turned their ears toward a group of two-leggeds. My position allowed me to see them as well. They were moving through the foliage more carefully this time, though still not silent. The closer they got, more of the pack turned toward them, save for a single pup who cowered by the legs of his mother.

The two-leggeds settled by the trees while the wolves began to slink back toward the forest. The two-leggeds leveled their sticks, just like that first day. *Oh no.*

CRAACK-AK-AK CSHOO-SHOO shoo-shoo shoo

CRAACK CSH-CRAACK CSHOO shoo-shoo

Three wolves fell dead at once. Two more collapsed as well, whining agony for no apparent reason. Blood gushed from wounds born of nothing, as the two remaining wolves looked around confused. I stood frozen, horrified at the sight I couldn't pry myself away from. The pup ran toward me, with one of the adults following, trying to keep him with the pack.

CRAACK-CRAACK CSHOOSHOO shooshoo-shoo

The remaining wolves fell. One dead, the other whining so much she probably wished she were. The survivors tried to crawl away, but their wounds were too great. The two-leggeds advanced, stepping right up to the injured wolves. When they leveled their sticks, my ears flattened to reduce the noise.

CRAACK-AK-AK CSHOOSHOO shooshoo shoo

The pack lay dead. Decimated by the magic these two-legged things carried in their paws. No wonder they had no claws. Smooth sticks of thunder were all they needed to kill. I kept to the shadows, praying I'd go unnoticed. Their noses were tiny, so with the wind holding its direction, I had a good chance of staying hidden.

The two-leggeds barked excitedly as they examined their kills. The barking often grew right after one examined a wound in one of the wolves. After some time of this, the two-leggeds hung their sticks on their backs, then dragged the dead pack away by their paws. I watched them go long after I could no longer see them, to be sure they were truly gone.

I yipped in surprise when a bundle of dark brown-gray-silver fur plunged into my legs. I tumbled onto it, drawing much of the same from my attacker. My yip turned to a growl until I saw the attacker was the pack's pup.

He was even smaller up close. Either a runt or somehow younger than the second litter from my former pack. His fur was still one-half puppy-brown, the other half a coat of pure ash I felt certain would grow to dominate his pelt. The pup laid there, whimpering, shaking like a leaf in a windstorm. His ears were so flat, I could barely see them.

My insides sank when I remembered how I'd felt the first time I'd been around the two-leggeds' thunder sticks. And I'd only been a witness. This poor pup had been among them, watching his entire pack get wiped out. I could only imagine what he felt.

I shook off the pain of our collision before slowly stepping up to him. The pup stared at me as if I might attack him next but remained still.

I rubbed my muzzle against the pup's as softly as I could. "Hush. Hush. You're safe now."

His shaking faded until it stopped, though his ears never moved. "My... My... My moth... My... My mother..."

"Hush. I'm afraid they're all dead."

"C... Com... come back?... Those... things... they come..."

"No. No, they got what they wanted. They don't seem to care about us. Come with me. I'll keep you safe."

It took some coaxing to get the pup moving. Even then, he jumped at every sound. He nearly vanished entirely when the mockingbird flew over his head.

"Pup and pup still facing stuff. Pup and pup shall—"

My jaws snapped at the bird before he could finish. "Shut it, you! He just lost his pack. Even you have to understand some part of that. So if I hear one word, one tweet more, it'll be your last."

The bird landed on a low branch and sat there, silent. He watched us walk without so much as a flick of his tail. *Not sure which part worked, but I'm glad it did.*

I led the pup to my den, and let him settle in beside me. Poor thing tried for hours to regain his breath, half of it from tears he couldn't seem to shed. Time slowly peeled away his fear until all he had were the tears still building behind his eyes. I stayed with him, unable to provide anything besides a larger wolf to lay against.

At last, with wet eyes, the pup looked at me. "Are you sure? Are you sure they're dead? All of them?"

My ears fell in pain. "Yes. The two-legged creatures killed them. You're the last of your pack."

Tears began to flow at last. "No. No, they can't be. They... they..."

He sobbed into my flank, and all I could offer was a comforting rub on his head. My mind tried to wander, to consider what we now shared. It never got beyond the raw facts. We were alone, no pack, no one but ourselves now. The points came without emotion, not counting the sympathy I felt for the pup. It was as if some other voice were trying to tell me something, but it couldn't figure out how, or even what exactly.

I let him cry for as long as he needed. While he did, I tried to find that voice in my head, only to have it go silent. There was still a sense that it had something to tell me, but with it gone, all I could do was let the pup tire himself out. When he finally stopped crying, the sunlight in the entrance had grown a lot dimmer.

Much like the pup's eyes as they found me again. "Yours too?"

I tried very hard not to growl at him. It wasn't his fault. He couldn't know about the thorn his words were driving into my heart. Though it brought up an interesting question: which was worse? Losing them like he had, or being driven from them over a lie?

I kept my growl silent, but I could do nothing about the thorn.

"No," I said. "Something very different."

"Different how? What happened?"

"It's too complicated. Just know that, like you, I'm alone."

A tweet sounded at the entrance. "Lu-na."

I thought I got rid of that bird. That said, the bird had yet to say a single word before, even if it was sung in two syllables. It still didn't keep a soft growl from forming.

"Luna?" the pup asked.

I stopped growling for the sake of the pup. "My name. Luna is my name."

"Folar is mine. Thank you, Luna, for... for being with me."

Folar rubbed against me, and another thorn stabbed into my heart. The shadow of the mockingbird appeared at the entrance, and I knew I had to deal with him, again.

"Excuse me, Folar. I need to see what that bird wants. I won't be far."

I slid into the entrance, feeling the weight of Folar's stare. I tried to ignore it as I went outside and stood over the bird. He didn't leave, and for some reason I could never find, I had no urge to eat him.

That said, my hackles refused to stay flat. "Now what?"

The bird seemed to struggle to speak at first. In the end, it came out a song, but heavier than any song I had ever heard before. "Pup no stay, pup won't live, a fighting chance, you cannot give. Must run and hunt and live with kind. Home and den and love, he not here find."

I tilted my head at the bird, then glanced back inside the den at Folar. "Just what are you saying?"

"You know, you know, the pup must go."

"Go? Go where? His pack is dead. The only established pack is... You can't be serious."

"Must run and hunt and live with kind. Home and den and love, he not here find."

I had to swallow a dozen pinecones as I looked toward Toltan's territory. "Do you have any idea what you're asking?"

"I do, I do."

A cold wind, and the bird fluttered away without a sound.

I watched him go with falling ears, and I felt another pinecone lodge in my throat. Even if I ignored the risk of going back to my former pack, I had an opportunity to change my fate. Folar was so young, he might not have heard the law. Even if he had, it may not matter. He was already drawn to me. He might choose to ignore my sentence and stay with me anyway. We could do it too. The two of us could form our own little pack. We could make a life for ourselves. Maybe with a little luck, we could do even more.

The pinecones pricked at my heart, forcing me to cringe. The mockingbird was right. For all my talk before, I was still a pup myself. Folar had yet to catch a mouse, much less help me with deer. I would have to support us both, which given my age, was almost certain to get us both killed. I couldn't condemn Folar to such a death, no matter how much I wanted the company. *So that's why this is so bad.*

"Folar," I called into the den. "Folar, come with me."

Folar came out cautious, but unafraid. "What is it, Luna?"

More pinecones. *Tell me this gets easier.* "Just, follow. Follow close, and no matter what, do as I say."

Folar's ears fell, but his eyes remained on me. "Okay."

Folar pressed me for more details, but I never responded except to keep him moving. Each step grew harder because my mind couldn't stop thinking about it. *I don't have to do this. I could feed us both until he grew enough. I don't have to be alone.* The words were hollow. It had to be done, if only for Folar's sake. The best I could do was keep moving in the hopes of ending it quickly.

I timed a response so Folar missed Toltan's marker as we passed it. My howls would be ignored, so if I wanted to get Folar to the pack, I would have to be more proactive. We walked on in silence, approaching the hillside above the dens. As we got closer, I told Folar to stay low. A stance I copied in the hope of appearing submissive. Folar had no trouble there, as his ears were as flat as they could be. Mine would have been as well, except they needed to search the area for any members of the pack. If the reunion went wrong, I'd be meeting Wolfor before nightfall.

Yet luck was on my side, or perhaps on some level I'd had a plan. In any case, as he'd been since the first day of thunder, Lonate was sitting atop the hillside, watching the forest for who-knows-what. It was a chance to lessen the risk. I knew Lonate wouldn't kill me on sight. With more luck, I could leave Folar with him and be gone before anyone knew I was there.

I moved toward Lonate, smooth but cautious, ready to run in case I was wrong. Lonate sat alone like always, a stone sentry almost unmoving against the setting sun. That is, until his eyes and ears locked onto me and Folar. I froze with flat ears while Folar cowered under my legs. Lonate turned an ear back, turned back toward us, then he sprinted toward us without a sound.

"Folar," I said, "get ready, but don't run unless I say so."

"What's going on?" Folar said.

"Just sit tight and listen."

Folar hugged the ground as if he might melt into it. *If only we could.* I'd felt Lonate's fangs enough to know I'd never beat them. My best option was to flatten my ears, tuck my tail, and pray it was enough.

Despite Lonate's sprint, fangs never came. Nor did a growl, or a bark, or any sign of intent. Just a rush forward that stopped cold right in front of me.

"Get out of here, Luna," Lonate whispered. "Now! Go!"

I held my stance, trying to convince my body there was no pain. "Not until I'm finished." I rubbed my muzzle against Folar's, who was shaking as much as my body wanted to. "Come on. Out with you."

Folar emerged, though slower than a snail. Lonate watched with perked ears as this tiny wolf stared at him. Lonate tilted his head at the pup, then at me.

"Finished?" Lonate said. "What are you talking about?"

My ears and tail started to relax. "I'm bringing him to you, so he may..."

Snarls sent me and Folar to the ground. Toltan had found us, and unlike Lonate, his fangs were fully exposed as he charged our way. My instincts warred with thought. Every strand of fur said *run!* but I couldn't until I was sure Folar was safe.

Truth be told, I was too scared to move anyway. All I could think about was what it would feel like to be torn apart by my father. As for Folar, for all I could see, the young pup had turned to stone beside me.

Only Lonate moved, directly into Toltan's path.

"Toltan, wait! Please!"

Toltan didn't stop. Not until it became clear that Lonate wouldn't step aside. Though his position said challenge, his flat ears and tucked tail said otherwise.

Toltan still shook everyone's ribs when he spoke. "You know the law, Lonate. Any lone wolf that returns shall face the alpha's fangs."

"Even a lone wolf that's trying to help?"

Confusion silenced Toltan's snarl, though not his glare. "What do you mean, help?"

Lonate stared at me. I took it as my chance to explain.

"This pup is the last of his pack. They—"

Toltan snarled again. "What does that have to do with you?"

Ignoring me again, Father? I'll show you how smart you're not.

I stood tall, anger burying all fear beneath its burn. My ears came up, and my tail relaxed behind me. It was just shy of a direct challenge, though my glare came closer than anything.

"I am his escort. I am making sure he gets to you alive. Folar—that's his name, if you care—has done no wrong, committed no crime. He deserves the chance to live with a strong pack. Yours is the only one I know will take him. You said it yourself: pups are a gift from Wolfor. Will you really kill me while I'm trying to deliver a gift from Wolfor?"

Toltan's growl returned as the pack watched in the distance.

"Luna?" Folar said, silencing Toltan again. "Luna, what's going on?"

My anger at Toltan caused me to be far less gentle this time. "You're going to live and run with them. Don't worry. They're a good pack... mostly."

"But what about you?"

"Me? I was banished. They don't care about me anymore."

"But *I* care! You can't just leave me here. You can't abandon me like this."

A part of me tried to remind myself that he was too young to understand. The message was drowned out by pain mixed with anger, forcing a growl from me this time. I glared at Folar, desperate to put an end to the torture. When I did, Folar flattened like a leaf under a rock.

"Why not?" I said. "He did. All on a vow too easily taken as truth. Learn well, young one. Learn the pain so you can remind him of it the next time Rajor calls on Wolfor's name."

Folar stared at me in horror as tears filled his eyes yet again. I found another mouthful of pinecones that only made the rage burn hotter.

"You..." Folar stammered. "You don't... you... you can't..."

"I can, I will, and I have. This is your pack now, Folar. Go! Be with them, or be my next meal."

As much to end the encounter as anything else, I snapped at him. Folar screamed like the jaws had landed. He dashed behind Toltan in search of cover, still shaking. *Not the best choice, but it'll do.* With Toltan offering almost no reaction, I ruffed at them both before turning back toward my den.

I didn't get far though.

"Fine then!" Folar said. "Live alone. Be a great big sulky in your little rock pile. I thought you were a hero, but you're just what my mom warned me of.

Stupid skunks pretending to be wolves. Too full of their own fangs to do the right thing."

Pup's got some fire. Shame he was too young to run with.

I trotted away before Toltan decided to run me off for kicks, or some other created reason. I stopped at my kill, surprised to find it untouched, and forced down what my stomach would allow. I then took what I could carry back to my den. Once the meat was stashed in the hollow of a nearby tree, I slipped inside my rock pile.

The place felt empty now. In the span of a few days, it had gone from refuge, to home, to comfort, and now it was pain. I could still smell Folar's fur and tears. For a moment, I thought I could still feel Folar's fur against mine too. It had been so short I'd barely noticed how nice it felt. *A "stupid skunk," he'd called me? Great big sulky?* I wasn't sure about the skunk part, but I had to admit I laid my head on my paws, more than willing to think about the wounds I couldn't lick.

"Luna, Luna, back and fine. Ready, ready, hunt and thrive."

Not again. Should have snapped that bird in two when I had the chance.

I went outside to find the bird, as usual, twitching on top of my den, out of reach. I could only growl as the bird continued to chirp at me.

"Will you leave me alone?" I said. "I've suffered enough today."

"Suffered, yes, sad and true, but listen, wolf, and see. Look within, heart and soul, both are full indeed."

I rolled my eyes at him. Darn bird had no idea what it was talking about. Not that it should have been a surprise. Mockingbirds weren't known for intelligent conversation. They could certainly talk though, or at least sing.

"Just shut up," I said. "I'm not full of anything. Rajor took everything I had."

"Still have fang, still have claw, still have mind, so far I saw."

"Got no pack, got no home, and you, my friend, need to roam—before I eat you."

"Roam I have and roam I will; watch the humans sort their kills."

I couldn't help it. My head tilted at the bird, now curious. "What? Humans? Kills? What are you talking about?"

"Come, wolf, come. See, wolf, see. Learn what shares your territoryyyy."

It fluttered into the woods as it sang, leaving me with a growing headache. I couldn't tell what made it worse: talking to the bird at all, or even for a second thinking about following it. In the end, curiosity won, along with the dim hope of shutting him up.

I followed the bird's path with ears perked and eyes high looking for him, or for any danger that may yet hunt either of us. The bird flew around the branches of a tree, still chirping at me, always out of reach.

"Come, wolf, come. See, wolf, see."

Exiled, scared to death the first night, and now I'm following a bird. I'm going crazy already.

My pace slowed when I found familiar scents on the wind. The same weird, sweet and salty mix I'd found both times I'd been around the two-leggeds. I inhaled the forest through my nose to be sure I hadn't walked into them.

"No fear, no fear," the bird sang. "Humans not find wolf here."

Despite its song, I held plenty of fear. Enough to keep my insides tight and my legs ready to sprint anywhere *not* here. My ears remained up, however, as they could hear something moving around ahead.

I hugged the ground when I saw the two-leggeds. They were still in their colorful skins, though not as thick right now. They seemed to be collecting piles of sticks and colorful square rocks that held sloshing sounds as if they carried water. Another such rock clinked from within among the sloshing, which made even less sense. More two-leggeds were breaking apart what seemed to be a large rock, yet it collapsed as if it were a skin without a body. They worked this skin, and smaller bones or twigs, into another skin, which they carried over to the strangest rocks yet.

They were huge, very smooth, one bright red while the other was black, and both so glossy I could see reflections on almost every side. More red and some yellow were at the corners of both rocks. On the sides sat round, black rocks, with circular, bright silver middles. The two-leggeds were placing many items in the back of these weird rocks as if stashing them. Some of it appeared to be hides of wolves, foxes, mountain lions, and other animals.

What are these things doing? Do they hibernate? Do they use skins as nest material? Must they carry water into their dens? Why... The questions were stopped by a stare of confusion when the two-leggeds moved part of the rock's sides away, and then got inside. They moved the sides back with a *thunk*, sealing themselves inside. *What in Wolfor's tail...*

Grrrrrrr-vree-kic-kic-kic-VAROOM!

I didn't know if I should run, hide, or pray. Their rocks weren't rocks. They were some kind of beast that had eaten them. Except the two-leggeds had gotten inside willingly, without fear. Stranger still, I could see them inside, still moving around through sides that were transparent. They didn't seem to be in any distress that I could tell, nor were they crying out for help. After a pair of clunks I'd never heard before, the black rocks on the sides turned on their own, and the creatures left the forest with a great rumble. I watched them go, alarmed that the red corners of the rocks appeared to be glowing.

"Humans gone, humans gone, humans gone at last."

I stared at the bird, still straight-eared and barely moving. "Humans? So the two-legged animals are called humans. Do you have a name for those big... things?"

"One built tough, one runs deep, both run quickly through the streets!"

I didn't know a bird could go insane.

I walked away from my singer to investigate where the "humans" had been. Only charred wood and fine dust remained from the fire they had gathered around. Among the dust were parts of their prey, though being burnt as they were, I can see why they left them behind. Why they were so close to a well contained fire in the first place proved a mystery too deep to explore. I found strange seeds or fruits scattered around the area unlike any plant I'd ever seen. Some were hard, some soft and chewy, and a few looked like actual seeds, but were covered in something that seemed to melt in my mouth. The rest tasted some strange mixture of sweet, sour, or bitter whenever I risked eating one. With nothing but packed earth where their... dens?... had been, I ventured on to see what else I could find.

In a pile only just discovered by ravens were the skinless bodies of several animals. Every creature bigger than a rabbit was there. Moose, deer, fox, mountain lion, skunk, all were represented, but these few kills paled compared to the mass of wolf bodies that lay among them.

In some ways, the wolves were worse than the others. The deer, elk, moose, and other prey animals were at least missing a few heads and other body parts. I even found a dead rabbit with its paws missing, while some bodies were missing some of their meat, and many others also missing their skin.

The wolves however, were all without a shred of fur or a single tail. Only one was missing a head. The rest were just left there to rot for the scavengers. Those beasts didn't have the decency to eat them. They just took their hides and left them there. For a moment, I considered running at Toltan in challenge. At least then I could be consumed by the wild with some measure of dignity.

What are these "humans"? With their power, they could have any prey they wanted, yet they let so much go to waste in the worst way. They only took great care with skins, which made less sense than letting such good prey rot.

"So you see, little wolf," the bird sang. "See and learn and know. Humans, humans, may be your greatest foe."

Can't argue with him there. Then again, from what I had seen, they carried their power in their thunder sticks. Without them, I couldn't see them being a threat. All the same, I was glad to see them gone. I had enough to deal with without dodging them too.

I found little else before a howl rang through the trees. It was yet another new voice to claim parts of the forest not held by Toltan. Amazing, considering the many bodies left to rot without their fur. Hope sprung within me when I considered that maybe, just maybe, I could use this. Maybe I could change my fate.

I sprinted toward the call, praying I could catch them before they found Toltan. Already my pack were raising their voices to mark their section of forest. If any of them actually met these new arrivals, I would never have a chance.

Much like Folar's pack, they were a small group. An alpha pair, two more barely a year old, and four pups bounding behind them all. *Perfect!* I thought. *They'll need strength, even if it is young. This is my best chance to find a new pack.* I made no effort to hide my approach, crashing through leaves and breaking twigs. A sudden introduction could end any chance before it started. All ears turned my way as I emerged from cover, my ears low and tail tucked. Now was not the time for pride, deserved or otherwise.

"I greet you, fair alpha," I said.

The alpha male didn't even blink. "Who are you?"

I prayed he'd believe the lie, even as I hated offering it. "The last survivor of a pack killed by strange creatures. Please. I am young, but I learn well. Let me run with you. Let me add to your strength."

"A fine tale, pup, but it does not yet answer my question. Who are you? By what name were you born?"

"Luna. My name is—"

"Luna!" his mate echoed. "The pup that murdered his brother? You can't let him join us, Tona. He'll kill our pups too."

Tona's ears turned forward, and my heart sank.

"Step aside, pup," Tona said. "Word of your crime has spread far. You'll find none that will take you. You will have to live alone for all your days."

Pain gave way to a growl. *He can't do this. Rajor can't deny me everything!* "For a crime I didn't commit? Based on words three times repeated? What a fine member of wolf-hood you are."

Tona gave a snarl of his own, which his pack echoed. "Watch your tongue, pup."

"Or what? If you'll not have me, then you'll not have these lands. This is *my* territory. Pups or not, I will defend it. The risk you take is your own."

Tona's snarl shook the air, but his ears were back at his younger pups. He watched them and me, then his snarl faded. I raised my tail as Tona retreated with his pack, never turning away until they were well outside sprinting distance.

So be it. If I was to live alone, I might as well build a reputation as being a wolf to be feared. I left a marker where I stood before turning toward my den.

Right into Martol.

"I knew you'd be strong," she said.

I nearly jumped out of my fur when she spoke right into my nose. I looked around for a scent mark I might have missed, or for the pack coming to kill me.

"Relax, Luna," she said. "This is not my territory. Nor has anyone else come with me."

My insides weren't convinced of that yet. My brain bounced around itself, unsure what to think or feel. Some part of me wondered if she had been the reason for Tona's retreat, though my mind was too scattered to ponder that for long either. Once things slowed down internally, my ears kept searching while I addressed Martol. I'd had enough surprises for one day.

"Wh… what are you doing out here?"

"After I heard what you did for Folar," she said, "I had to find you. I had to talk with you, to say things I didn't get the chance to say."

I ruffed at her near another growl. *Now she wants to talk? Yeah, right.* "Like what? Lone wolves can't live anywhere near their original pack? No, I know. You've seen the light and are here to tell me all's forgiven and I'm welcome to return. That it?"

Martol's ears fell in pain I didn't understand or care to learn. "Luna, I don't deserve that."

"Don't you? You stood by and did nothing. You let Toltan take the word of a bully over mine. Don't deserve it? My sweet, sweet mother. You deserve far more."

Her ears fell further. Tears formed behind her closed eyes. "Do you think it was easy, for either of us? You didn't say a word, Luna. We had Rajor alone to speak for you."

"And you didn't find error in that? I'd just watched my brother die trying to kill me. What could I possibly say? Then there's Wolfor. We invoke his name, and suddenly we can speak no lie. Rajor knew what he had to do, and he did it. You had your chance to do the right thing. *You* didn't. Then you all watched as Toltan drove me from my home. Now I don't know how easy it was, but I have to say, it sure looked like you didn't mind."

The more I spoke, the more Martol's eyes tightened, and the lower her ears went. She was almost whimpering as tears snuck out at last. I wanted to say more, to be sure I had made my point, but I stayed silent. I knew she'd come out of it soon, and I wanted to hear her response more than I wanted to yell.

Her eyes opened to show a void where a wolf should be. My ears perked, wondering just what she had to say for herself.

"Toltan was right. I lost two pups that day. Goodbye, Luna. May Wolfor care for you as I no longer can."

She walked back to her home, still sobbing.

I stood on legs that felt like they'd turned to stone. I didn't expect that. I'd expected a fight. I wanted a fight. In an odd way, I think I *needed* a fight. Instead, I'd gotten a thorn in my chest the size of Wolfor's claw.

I stood staring after her, trying to understand what just happened. For a moment, I considered chasing after her despite the risk. She was only walking, so I had a good chance of catching her before she was back inside her territory. When wisdom, or more lies, silenced that plan, I forced my way back to my den.

It was an odd constant, my rock pile. It gave me strength to deal with what I'd faced so far. Though it couldn't protect me from what hit as I lay alone that night, for that was the problem. My den held just one wolf and always would. My parents didn't care, or didn't try. Other packs would be "warned" of me. No female would want to risk mating with a "pup killer." In simple terms, Rajor had succeeded in denying me anything but a life of isolation.

Worst of all, some of it was my fault. Despite what I told myself, I'd chased away my last connection. I'd shunned Martol like an enemy before she had a chance to say what she'd come to say. If I had it to do over again, I might have said something else, or maybe said nothing at all. Whatever the case, I now wanted that second chance. I'd give anything to get it, even as I knew I never would.

Tears of my own dampened my fur, and the walls of my den echoed with the first adult sounding howl I'd ever given. A howl so deep, so longing, one would think I was the last wolf on Earth.

Chapter 5

ANOTHER SPRING FOUND ME STRETCHING awake alone in my den. It was my third spring spent as a lone wolf. Two and a half years since Toltan had banished me from my pack and family. Somehow, a part of me knew, or guessed, which day was my birthday each time. The first one wasn't so bad, though the wounds were still scarring, so it wasn't great either. My second had a wind storm that howled through the rocks of my den and kept me unnerved the entire day. As I exited my den on my third, I wondered if maybe I'd get a decent day this time.

As usual, my luck wasn't that good. I walked out into a mist thick enough to turn the forest white. The dew on my fur shimmered, bringing out the now dominant silver. When the light hit it right, it also heightened the glow in the "silver sheen" of my hackles. They were now outlined by a small smattering of black that was even thinner as it touched my fur up to the middle of my back. The cool, soft air was soothing, making me feel light enough to fly. Something that always made it easy to sleep, except my stomach needed food, so I headed out in search of a trail.

The mist messed with that too. I would find a good trail only to lose it minutes later, or have it merge into a mess of other scents even I couldn't make sense of. A soft growl escaped with each lost scent, wondering if Wolfor didn't want me to have good birthdays. I didn't even bother chasing a rabbit when it streaked by. It had too much of a lead, and the way the day was going, I'd just end up with my muzzle planted in a tree.

I pressed on, mostly because there wasn't much else I could do. More trails went cold until, at last, I found one that was strong and fresh. Thick fox musk, no indication of any injury, but it was alone. Not the easiest of prey, but I had no better option. I followed the trail to the edges of my territory, into an area dominated by rocks on the side of a large hill. It looked like the aftermath of a rock slide, with many of the boulders half buried in dirt and grass, though it still reminded me of the pile I called home.

I followed the trail more with my eyes than my nose. It led me to the base of the pile, where I found a young red fox. It seemed to be digging at something, allowing me to hunker down and approach as carefully as I could. A slow advance, waiting for the right moment to strike. The wind was at me, so all I had to do was get a little closer.

I must have stepped on something, for the fox turned my way, ears straight up. Before I could decide whether to hide or lunge, it vanished into the mist faster than I'd ever match. My growl came with a sigh as I watched another meal slip through my jaws. *Should have known I wouldn't be that lucky today.*

Then a voice sent my fur on end. "Next time, try attacking before it hears you. That is the only way to catch a fox."

I jerked as the voice seemed to come out of the rocks. A deep, echoing sound that had my heart pounding like I was sprinting. Once that faded, I perked my ears forward as curiosity grew out of the shock.

"Who's in there?" I said. "Who, or rather what, are you?"

"I am old, I am wise," the voice replied. "I am the wise one. I am like you, young wolf: a loner."

I ruffed at him more because of his tone than his words. "Right. A rock pile is like me. I ask again: who's in there? Show yourself."

A figure walked out slowly. The mist made it a large shadow at first. Then it cleared into an old, mostly dark gray wolf, with brown touching his back, tail, and ears. Scars on his head and shoulders spoke of protracted experience, though it didn't say how good he'd been.

"Call me 'the wise one,'" the wolf said.

"Wise one?" I said. "Yeah, right. You're just an old wolf finding fun in tormenting younger ones. You don't know anything about me."

"Are you sure? I have lived for eleven years. I know much more than you do. Like how to catch a fox and suffer very little."

Yeah. This conversation is going nowhere.

"Oh, well, good for you. I'm only three years old, and I've felt the pain of losing everything I have. My home, my family, my heart. I know what it feels like to be shunned by everyone I once knew. You don't know anything about that."

The old wolf's ears flashed back, too quick for me to read. "Actually, I do."

I snarled at him with a glare to match. "You can't. I was falsely accused of killing my brother. For that, I was kicked out of my pack. Every wolf in these woods knows of me, and they shun me more than my own. I am cursed to live alone, forever. What do you have to say about that?"

The old wolf looked right at me. It was an odd stare that somehow silenced my snarl and forced my ears to listen. It reminded me of the many times, as a pup, I sat and listened to Lonate when he wanted to teach us something. He looked a lot like Lonate too, though that wasn't enough to drop my guard.

"I was banished as well," the old wolf said. "My life was a lonely one until a female showed her support for me. We mated and started our own pack. I was happy even though I thought it impossible. I made a difference in her life. No one else would have her but me."

I may have been listening, but I wasn't enjoying. "Get to the point, old one."

The old wolf didn't react. I almost wish he had. "Lone wolf or not, you can make a difference. It may be small, or it may be big, but you *can* make a difference. Just as I did."

My attention span had reached an end. This old wolf didn't know me. He had a happy end to his life. A mate, a litter or two no doubt, a life. I never would. My little rock pile would always be mine alone, of that I no longer had any doubt. The best I hoped for was to be left in peace for the remainder of my days.

If only the forest would let me.

"Whatever 'wise one,'" I said. "You old wolves are stubborn, so I won't argue. I'll leave you alone with your small difference."

The old wolf growled for the first time. *I think I'd rather have Toltan's death stance.* "I'm not done with you yet."

"Yes, you are!"

I ran off without another word. I'd grown tired of that old wolf. He obviously had nothing to offer that would help me, not to mention the fact that he scared me in *so* many ways. *By Wolfor, what a snarl.*

I still had to find a meal, and the mist was thickening. At this rate, I soon wouldn't be able to see anything, and my nose fared little better. Worse than lost trails, now I couldn't find *any*. It's as if all the animals of the forest had vanished. I spent hours hunting and found little more than enough mice to quiet my stomach for the time being. Even that took digging in fields, chasing around bushes, and more than a couple of thorns in my paws. More than once, I'd chase one right into a tree or bush hidden in the mist. I returned to my den when I could find nothing else, already having more than enough bruises for one day.

I laid outside my rock pile, fuming about my rotten luck. *Poor day of hunting, an encounter with a stuffy old wolf, a mist that matches my emotions—OW!—thorns still stuck in my paws. What else does the day have in store for me?*

"There you are!"

I jerked to my paws so fast, I swear I left fur behind. My heart was racing a mile a second as a snarl formed on instinct. I expected to find the old wolf had snuck up on me, but my snarl dwindled to a low growl when I found a beautiful female almost as big as I was instead. Her fur was a darker gray on her back that lightened down her flanks. Her legs, ears, and the top of her muzzle were a strong brown, while her underside was a soft off-white. She looked at me with a playfulness that seemed familiar, as did her scent.

I growled at her in challenge once my insides settled down. "Who are you? What are you doing here?"

The female tilted her head at me. "Luna. Don't you remember me? I'm Estrella. One of the 'younger pups.'"

Oh yeah, her. Should have known.

"Ah yes, the pup that won her litter in the den. I thought I told you once, I don't like surprises."

She turned her ears back at me. "Still the same stuffy thorn-in-the-paw. Well, I don't care. I've finally found you. Had me worried for a while there. All I could find were your scent marks."

Wolfor, kill me now. Her body had grown up, but it didn't sound like she had. She wiggled like a pup waiting for her first hunt. Her tail wagged from side to side, and for the life of me, I couldn't understand why. Worse yet, I had a strange feeling she wouldn't be easy to chase off.

"And now you found their maker," I said. "Good for you. Say hi to the pack for me. Now if you don't mind, I've had a rough day."

I laid back down, choosing to ignore her. That is until she moved to lie beside me. I growled at her, ruffled my hackles, made it very clear how *not* welcome she was. It didn't seem to faze her. If anything, she grew bolder. She wiggled herself close and gave no attention to my growing snarl.

"Luna," she said, almost scolding. "Cut that out. Don't you want to talk? You know, catch up, swap stories, anything?"

Being left alone would be nice.

"You want a story? Okay. I was kicked out of my pack, I found a den shortly after, I learned to hunt on my own, I learned about the humans, I just met an old wolf who I'm not so sure hasn't lost his touch on reality, I can't find much prey in this stupid mist, that is my story, *good night!*"

I flopped my head on my paws, hoping that would end it.

Estrella instead gave a gentle, annoyed growl. "Very funny. I want to talk to you in a serious manner. I want to know how you have been faring."

"Just fine. Now leave me alone."

I went into my den and curled up to sleep, except Estrella still wouldn't give up. She followed me in, pushing at me until I growled at her.

"Keep pushing your luck and you'll get a good look at your own insides," I said.

"Luna!" she said. "I want to talk to you. I want to know if you are okay out here. I want you to come back." Realizing she wouldn't leave until she wanted to, I lifted my head and stretched out. Estrella laid down beside me with a satisfied huff. "That's better. Now we're getting somewhere."

"If you say so," I growled. "I just want to get this over with so you will want to leave. Then I can be left in peace again."

"Not going to happen. I am not leaving until I get you to come back."

"Did you miss Toltan's lecture on pack law? I can't come back. I'm a lone wolf."

"Doesn't matter. You're coming back if I have to drag you back by your tail."

You stupid pup. You don't get it. I left the den, trying to put an end to it. When Estrella followed again, I turned around and snarled with my hackles standing straight up. Never mind the annoyance, now she was causing pain.

Did she think I was out here by choice? Of course I'd prefer to be with a pack, but desire and ability rarely coincide. I couldn't go back. The sooner Estrella realized that, the better off we'd both be. Besides, going back would mean facing my parents. After what they did to me, I wasn't sure I'd even want to go back. *Another lie?* Maybe, but it was reason enough to ignore the whole idea.

"Did you forget what happened?" I said through my growl. "I was kicked out, banished, forced to leave forever. If I return, I'll be killed. That's assuming I wanted to, which I don't. They don't care for me. They never have."

Estrella barely even growled as she remained firm. "*I* care. You're the only one that's ever beat Rajor."

"So what? What does that have to do with me?"

"He's our alpha now."

My snarl ended in favor of a ruff, and a backward turn of my ears. *That didn't take long. Toltan finally let the whelp push him aside.* I couldn't imagine what life with him on top was like. Well, at least life for the others. I knew what life would be like for me if I were still there, assuming I'd ever let Rajor beat me.

When I didn't respond, Estrella continued. "It happened last summer. He was finally able to take the position from Toltan. He and Martol are still alive, but Rajor now leads the pack."

So what? "My condolences. Doesn't change anything. I'm still a lone wolf."

Estrella whined, and my snarl was buried for good. "But I need you. Rajor is insisting I be his mate. He says since he is the leader, I have to be his. I don't want to be his, or anyone else's, but yours."

My growl was laced with a sigh. *No wonder she's so determined. She's lost her mind.* "I'm flattered, really, but in case you've forgotten, I'm an outcast. Why would you, or anyone, want me?"

Estrella growled for the first time. Much like that old wolf, it was a strong rumble that impressed me enough to drop my hackles. "I saw your strength when you stood up to Toltan and Rajor. I saw your justice when you punished Rajor. I saw your heart when you risked death to bring us a pup in need of a pack. Finally, to bind it all together, I have always had a thing for you."

All hostility vanished in place of perked ears. *Me? This crazed female has a thing for me?* I'd be touched if I wasn't trying to swallow a laugh. Or so I told myself when, in fact, I knew I *was* touched. Estrella had come out here, alone, in defiance of Rajor, to pursue an interest in me. It wasn't pure puppy love either. She noted things in me that any female would like in a mate. Young as she acted, hearing all that did breed a little warmth within me.

I hid that behind the ruffs as I turned my ears back at her. Flattery, while appealing, didn't change my status or my feelings.

"You have a thing for me?" I said. "Oh, well, that changes everything. Of course I'll risk my neck to come with you. Hey, maybe Rajor and I will even get to like each other."

Estrella's growl left no doubt about her feelings. "Luna! I don't deserve that."

Those words froze me. With them came the memory of Martol, shunned by me. Hurt, by me. I'd played that day over in my mind a few times recently, wondering if I'd been wrong to act so harsh. Just like then, I had someone who appeared to care standing before me. I'd cried that night. It felt like my heart had broken in two. I didn't want to feel that way again. Not ever.

"I'm sorry," I said, my ears back and my growl silent. "I didn't mean to offend you. But I can't go back. Rajor would kill me if I did. If not him, Toltan, to uphold the law."

Estrella stopped her growl, though she was far from backing down. "You don't know that."

"I won't risk it. My life is at least livable out here. That's a lot better than being dead. Now if you'll excuse me, I need to find something to eat."

I walked off and started tracking as best I could through the mist. I needed to think, and hunting was the best distraction I could come up with. *What could I say?* She had feelings I didn't share. Even if I did, if Rajor was the new alpha, what would he do if he found her with me?

What am I thinking? I thought with a huff. Like I really feared Rajor. His pack maybe, but him? No. Estrella was right. I had beaten him several times as pups. I can't imagine he'd gotten much better.

"Luna wolf has two tails, Luna wolf has two tails."

I grumbled at my mockingbird, but it came with an amused tick of my ears. *Can't figure out why he is still hanging around, or how he's avoiding trees in the mist.* It was thinning, but not much.

I looked behind me and, sure enough, Estrella was there, again refusing to leave.

I huffed in frustration while resigning myself to more of her badgering. "You don't give up, do you?"

She trotted to my side like she belonged there. "No. Nor should you. Come on, Luna, let me hunt with you. If you still want me gone afterward, then I'll leave."

"Promise?"

"In Wolfor's name."

Another growl escaped my control. "Careful how you use that. The last time I heard it, my life ended."

Estrella's ears flashed apology for the first time. "I understand. I'm sorry."

The mockingbird swooped over us, chirping like it was the first day of spring. "Luna, Luna, not alone. Luna, Luna, love has shown. Luna, Luna, good be known."

Estrella watched him with straight ears. "Friend of yours?"

I chuckled at the thought. *If only.* "Pay him no mind. He likes to run his beak off. Come on. Let's see if we can find a trail."

"Then follow me. I thought I heard moose earlier."

"Forget it. We'd never take one down alone."

"Humor me. Please?"

I knew better by now than to argue, so I agreed.

Estrella led me toward the river, looking toward Toltan's... Rajor's territory often. Be it for my sake or hers, I had to admit, the attention to her surroundings impressed me. Maybe she had some sense after all. I let her lead, noticing that she appeared to stop and check her ears rather than her nose. A rather strange thing for a wolf to do, but then, my nose had failed me so far.

When Estrella froze with perked ears again, I did the same to see if it bore any fruit. In the distance, I found the high bleats of moose, but something else I couldn't quite make out. Not birds, too steady for that, yet very familiar. We moved toward the sounds in spurts, checking our ears each time we stopped. We were getting closer, we just didn't know to what.

The sound trail led to where we could see the river despite the mist. It was still running strong like always, but even over the rush, I thought I heard a bear downstream, barking. *Wait. Bears don't bark.* I held my breath a moment to let my ears catch the sound more fully. Once I realized it was another pack I was hearing, I barked at Estrella before she moved ahead.

"Forget it. Whatever moose is out there is already being hunted. I'm not about to face a pack defending their kill."

"Have a little faith," Estrella said. "The river is closer than they are."

"And this is grounds for faith?"

"Wolfor is always watching. If we let him, he just might... there, you see? Check the river."

I rolled my eyes while doing as she asked. *Maybe it'll satisfy her enough to make her leave.*

I looked again, not believing what I saw. I could see figures on the other bank, the herd and their hunters no doubt, but in the river itself, struggling to stay above water, came a moose so young its antlers were mere stubs on his head.

"Have a little faith," Estrella repeated.

I turned my ears back while stalking forward. Darn female was still annoying, but she was right. We had ourselves a good chance at an easy kill.

I kept low and slow, taking great care to avoid the slightest sound. Estrella came close behind, not faring quite as well, forcing me to swallow a growl lest it give us away. *She's only a few moons younger, but she acts like it's years.*

I hunkered down behind a tree a short leap from the river's edge. I watched and waited as the moose dragged itself onto the shore. It rumbled and stumbled, drained by the swim, and perhaps injury or illness. Whatever the reason, he was a kill too easy to pass up.

When the moose thumped against a tree to stay on its hooves, I exploded into a sprint toward my prey, my jaws open and ready to strike. The moose heard me, but it was so tired that when it tried to run, it only stumbled more. When it turned to face me, it made the mistake of leaving its head up, allowing me to leap right into its jugular and sink my fangs in deep. The force of my lunge knocked the beast down, but I never lost my hold. Blood seeped past my teeth as my bite cut veins. The moose struggled, but it was too tired and too late. I held my bite, waiting for it to go limp in my jaws before I let it go.

"Not bad," Estrella said, "for a thorn-in-the-paw."

I think I'd rather have the bird. He at least was something I could pretend to ignore.

I tried anyway as I dug into the moose, thrilled to have a proper kill. Mice silenced the pains but never worked the same as a full meal. Estrella joined me for her share, and since she did lead me to it, I didn't stop her. Though I made a point of going for the best meat. The kill was mine, and Estrella was, at best, a lower pack member. A fact I had to remind her of when she tried to sneak away with a kidney. I snarled and bit at her until she dropped it with tail tucked and whined apology. She gave me a very dirty look, but praise Wolfor, she said nothing.

Craack! cshoo-shoo sho

Estrella hugged the ground with her ears searching for the sound. I flicked mine up until I realized they were nowhere close.

"They're baaaaaaaack," I said.

"They?" Estrella asked.

"Humans. They come every year to hunt, much of it wolves. They have some kind of thunder stick that kills whatever it's pointed at."

Estrella rose, though her ears kept searching.

"You sound like you know a lot about them."

"I should. They build their dens not too far from mine."

Estrella's ears and eyes shot up. "What?!"

I ruffed a stifled laugh. I shouldn't enjoy the moment, but it felt *so* good.

"Relax," I said. "They don't know I'm there. I've watched them each time, with a fair amount of humor, I might add. I've never seen animals act so strangely."

Sharp whistles mixed with barks in the same direction as the thunder. The barks sounded oddly wolf-like this year, but their presence at all held more of my attention. I stepped toward the barks to get a better sense of where they were. I didn't like the answer I got.

"Grab what you can carry," I said. "They brought dogs again. Not much for fighting, but they lead the humans to their prey. I'd rather they not find us here."

"I'd rather they not find us anywhere," Estrella said.

"Never, never find wolves here," the bird sang over head. "Luna, Luna, never near."

"He always do that?"

"Constantly," I said.

Despite my best efforts to shut him up.

We pulled what meat we could from the kill before retreating to my den. There we ate our fill in blessed silence and refreshing company.

I couldn't deny, it felt good to have another wolf around, even if she was crazy. I watched Estrella break a bone open for the marrow and wondered: just what was it about me that held her interest? She'd mentioned admirable traits, but enough to chase after me in the hopes of mating? The best question was mine, really. *Do I want her?*

Despite only being a moon or two behind me, Estrella seemed younger than her years, perhaps a little naïve, and definitely talkative. Still, she had fire I could admire. I wasn't sure about mating, but if she'd accept a place under me in a pack, I could see it working out well. Who knows? Maybe something would develop.

My ears turned back as I finished what my stomach would allow. *Maybe something would develop?* Wishful thinking and I knew it. It would never work. I was a lone wolf while Estrella was destined to be pack beta, if not alpha once she realized her own power. We'd never mix. Even if we did... we just wouldn't. *Another lie?* I didn't bother answering.

We stashed the remainder of our haul in the same old hollow under an oak tree I'd used over the years. Not that I had much to add this time. With two wolves feeding off the same portions of the kill, there was barely a snack left. *Better than nothing, I suppose.*

I returned to my den to find Estrella sniffing around it. I tilted my head, trying to understand why. When she saw me, she ruffed in amusement and looked at the rock pile.

"Not too bad," she said. "Although I somehow expected better. Seems like you could manage more than a cave inside a rock pile."

My eyes rolled. *Here we go again.* "It keeps me warm and safe. I need little more from a den."

"What about yourself? How little have you allowed there?"

"How little have I *allowed*? I've had to fight for every scrap I can find, *alone.* I'd hardly say I've allowed or not allowed anything."

"Yet you continue to live alone. Don't you get lonely out here?"

A great sigh was followed by a greater growl. What a stupid question. Of course I was lonely. That's the whole point of being a lone wolf. No pack, no family, no anyone. Just you, your fangs, your kills, and there is no way to change or overcome it.

The pain of that fact kept me from looking at her, as did my failing hold on my temper. Both combined made it near impossible to find anything to say. I searched the dimming sky for the moon, hoping, praying there'd be enough to brighten my hackles tonight. After the day I'd had, I needed something to relax me.

Estrella stepped up to my side and gave me a short nuzzle. "That bad, huh? I understand. You've been alone for three years. It's natural to feel lonely. It hurts when you're thrust from everyone you love."

"Silence!" I snapped, reaching my limit. "You think you know me? You think you understand what I've been through? My own father drove me away when I was just a pup. My pack has disowned me. Every pack in sprinting distance knows who I am and shuns me for it. You don't know me. You never will."

Estrella started to growl, then she swallowed it, although she couldn't stop her ears from coming forward, matching my challenge. "Because you won't let me. I don't care what others think. I'm here for you."

"I don't want you! I don't want anyone. I've lived well on my own, and I intend to stay that way. It hurts a lot less."

When Estrella tried to growl again, I didn't let it take root. I pinned her to the ground with a snarl until she whined surrender. I remained over her, still growling, making sure she knew not to speak again.

"Go home, Estrella. Go back to that whelp. Go back to a pack that still cares for you."

After I stepped off, Estrella remained on her side, pleading with her eyes. "Luna. Don't be like this. Don't push me away."

As I glared at her, for a moment, I thought about it. Her hunting skills didn't seem too bad, and her stubbornness could be an asset out here without a pack. Perhaps I could give her another chance.

Perhaps... I huffed at the thought. Despite my best effort, "perhaps" was not enough to make it feel right. No, I'd made my choice. There was no point thinking otherwise. "You made a promise. I now ask that you honor it. Get moving. Don't let me catch you in my territory again."

I walked away, not bothering to look back. I knew I'd find pain there, not just hers either. I went all the way inside my den, refusing to see anything. I laid inside, staring at the empty entrance, and the anger melted away.

I'd done it again. I had driven away another wolf. I didn't need to see her to know Estrella was crying. Perhaps she felt as alone as I did. Part of me didn't care. The rest wished I didn't feel at all.

But I did. I could feel the void of where she'd been. The joy of where the hunt had been, now replaced by my usual pain. I was alone again, as I knew I'd always be. As the pain churned in my chest, my head lifted in a long, low howl, as if I might somehow expel it through my voice. The deep tone echoed among the rocks, ringing in my ears and piercing into my heart. The expression helped in the moment, but it also reminded me of that which triggered it.

My ears perked when I heard a reply. It was faint, distorted coming through the rocks, and unfamiliar, yet it sounded much like mine. It also sounded young and still unperfected. I rushed out to find the source, but the echo had already faded, as had most of the mist, thank Wolfor. I listened hard for a moment only to find birds and breeze on the air. I checked the scents, still finding nothing. *Maybe I'd imagined it. They say isolation does things to one's mind.*

One thing my mind knew all too well were the excited barks of the humans. They were close. Close enough that I saw one of them stalking through the trees with a thunder stick in his paws. I hugged the rocks of my den as if I might melt into them. My eyes and ears were locked onto this one human while I tried to choose the best escape path.

I abandoned those thoughts when I realized the human wasn't coming toward me at all. He was hunting something else. With the rest of the human's pack hunting elsewhere, I couldn't help wondering what possessed this fool to go out on his own. Was he a loner searching for a mate? Had he gone mad? Curiosity beat out caution, and I followed him, slow and silent, in the hopes of finding an answer.

He moved well, this one. Were I not watching him, I might not have heard him. Why he'd made so much noise a few seconds ago added to my confusion. I'd heard of coyotes yapping as they hunted, but somehow, I didn't think that's what this one had been doing. My best guess was some sort of brag, or maybe an argument, had been the cause.

The human made up for that noise by advancing without a sound. I stayed with him, moving just as silent, my heart thundering at the fear of being discovered. Half of me rather enjoyed the stalk, testing my skills against the human's. I remained a smooth shadow far off to his side. Downwind, out of sight, and in total control.

When the human stopped, I hugged the ground in case he'd heard me. The human knelt behind a tree so smoothly, he may as well have melted into the position. It was a stance I had seen before. He had his prey in sight and was preparing for the kill. I looked where he was looking, trying to distinguish shadow from something real.

I found one wolf lying there, alone, staring into the forest as if searching for something. She was pretty. Her fur mostly gray on her back, with brown legs... *wait...*

"Estrella?"

I whispered her name as I recognized her fur pattern. My heart sank when I realized she didn't know. A human had her dead to rights, and she didn't know.

My sides started heaving indecision. *He's going to kill her.* I could see the human working with his thunder stick. A few seconds more, and she'd be dead. The thought sent me into a panic mixed with confusion. Why did I care? Why was my entire body tensing by the second? Why the panic? Why the fear?

Why am I still lying here?!

"NO!"

I left everything behind, my fear, my doubts, my caution. I tore through the dirt, hackles high and snarl thundering. The human would not have her. Not today.

The human looked my way, and I swear his skin turned white. He tried to point his thunder stick at me, then had to change his mind midway to put it in the path of my lunge. He stopped the bite with the thunder stick as he was knocked on his back with a thud. I put my paws on the stick, trying to push it out of my way.

"Estrella, get out of here," I yelled. "Now!"

I didn't look to see if she listened. I'd spared too much focus already.

The human had managed a stalemate so far. My hind claws found only his fur, or whatever lay on top of his legs, while my forepaws were busy keeping me on top. I tried to bite through the stick, but much of it felt hard as rock and tasted cool and tangy like nothing I'd bitten before. I could smell the human's fear, though, which made my snarl grow.

We wrestled against each other in a battle of wills. The human tried to push me off, or to get up, only to fail each time. I tried to push past the stick yet fared no better. Eventually, the human dropped the stick, thrusting one paw to my neck just behind my chin to keep me at bay. The other paw went to his waist. The human pulled out a short reflective rock, much like their red beast, but still bright gray. He swung it out wide and pointed the rock at me, which my instincts did not trust. When the human stabbed, I thrust my shoulder in its path.

A sharp whine echoed off the trees as the rock jabbed into my left foreleg. A searing pain tore around the wound, running up and down my leg. Instinct drove my fangs to the human's wrist. When they struck, I felt bone snap. Now it was the human crying out in pain. His other paw lost grip on my neck as it clutched for the wound. Before he could recover, I pushed past the human's paws and sank my fangs deep into his throat. The human gasped and clawed at me with paws that held no bite. He was mine now. A few gasps and gurgles later, the human lay dead beneath my jaws.

I panted pain and exhaustion as I released my hold. When I tried to move, more pain shot down my left leg, drawing a wince and another sharp whine. I lifted my paw off the ground, which seemed to help, then investigated the rock still stuck in my shoulder.

These humans, they do know how to make up for their weaknesses. While his paws had no claws of their own, this one rock had done plenty of damage. With great whines, I pulled it out and tossed it aside, trying not to think about the blood running down my leg. *So much for hunting.* Hopefully that moose would go unfound long enough for me to pick at it some more. If not, I may be in real trouble.

Yet, in that moment, my mind had something it cared about just as much. "Estrella?"

I looked around for the first time in search of her. I found the forest empty. *Figures.* The one time she actually listened to me is the one time I'd rather she hadn't. *Well, I wanted to be alone. Looks like I got my wish.*

I licked my wound as clean as I could despite the great protest it gave. I growled at the dead human, frustrated at what he'd caused. Then my stomach took its turn to sink. It wouldn't be long before this human was found by his pack. With such an injury, it was best I not be there when he was. That meant my wound had to go uncared for a while longer, and it was guaranteed to hurt.

Unfortunately, I had little choice. With a persistent whine, and a renewed fear of the forest, I limped all the way back to my den. I paused to lick the wound occasionally, but instead of soothing it, I only managed to make it bearable. The long limp home was agony. The crawl inside my den was even worse.

Still, I was safe, if only for now. Waves of pain, and exhaustion from fighting through it, kept me panting between bouts of licking my wound. The bleeding had mostly stopped, but it would take some time before I could do much with it. I didn't let myself ponder the question of how long before I could use it in full again. Though if it didn't seal properly, the question was irrelevant, assuming it wasn't already.

What an end to a busy day. Almost wish it weren't over. Been almost fun in an odd way.

Then an old voice came from outside the den. "I told you I wasn't done with you."

Me and my big mouth.

~~~

Chapter 6

I LICKED AROUND MY WOUND, glad to see it hadn't reopened. The old wolf laid beside me outside my den, watching patiently. He'd refused to leave, and I was in no position to force him off. At least the night had cooled enough to calm me more than I expected. A crisp breeze ruffled my fur, almost as if Wolfor were rubbing against me.

Maybe that's why I was still talking. I had started just as the sun was setting, and I hadn't stopped since. The words kept coming, detailing everything that had happened since we met, as well as what happened years before. The old wolf watched with patient attention, stopping me only on the rare times he wanted clarification. Even then, he was so polite, I couldn't find a reason to growl. Thus, my tale spilled from my mouth, as if I'd been holding it in my jaws all this time.

I eventually caught up to the more recent events after another check of my wound. "Once I realized she was gone, I limped my way here to find some measure of safety, and that's about it."

"About it?" the old wolf said. "Isn't there more?"

A growl finally formed out of annoyance. "No, not really." The old wolf didn't react at all. He laid there, staring at me while I pretended to care for my leg. *Guess he does know something after all.* "Okay, there is more. I felt something. When I saw her in danger, I went into a frenzy. I don't know why. I don't understand what I felt."

The old wolf tilted his head ever so slightly. "Compassion? Care? Attraction? Love?"

I shook my head, trying to shake the feeling from my memory. "No. It isn't possible. I have no heart. I buried it three years ago. My future is to live in that den alone. Just like you... wait, you said you met a female and started a pack. Where are they now? Did they kick you out too?"

The old wolf's ears dropped, and so did his head. I kept a huff silent out of respect, and more than a little fear of reprisal given my injury. When the old wolf's eyes rose to meet mine, another thorn pricked at my chest.

"Humans," he said. "Humans killed them all. First, my pups disappeared one by one. Then, as a final insult, the last of my previous litter panicked, and in trying to run away, he led them to our den. The last of my pack, including my mate, were killed before my eyes. I banished that pup out of grief before I realized the truth behind his error. I suspect he's a lot like you are now: bitter and alone. Rightfully so, given my own crime."

This time, I couldn't help huffing. The parallel was too strong. "Another Toltan. Too blind to see the mistake, too foolish to let the pain fade before you make it."

The old wolf snapped at me, to which I whined apology before he did more. "Do not lecture me, pup. Not until you've seen the blood of your pups on the fangs of another. Face that and act as you said, then maybe I'll let you tell me what one should or should not do."

I wanted to do so anyway, to give a snap of my own, but I had no ground to stand on, nor was there any cause for it. That said, my ears quickly returned to where they belonged: forward and alert. While I owed him the apology, he had not earned the right to be my alpha.

"I'm sorry," I said. "I can't imagine that."

"No, you can't!" The old wolf closed his eyes, and breathed until his growl faded. He ended with an amused huff before opening his eyes again. "Now I owe you an apology. You don't deserve that."

I started ruffing, very close to laughing. Seemed like everyone was telling me when someone did or didn't deserve something. Somehow ironic that, this time, the wolf that "deserved" something was me. The whole thing had to be a joke by Wolfor.

"You find that amusing, do you?" the old wolf asked.

If only you knew. "Forget it. It's just me. Nothing more than the wolf that I am."

"Oh? And what is that?"

I stared at him, still fighting a laugh. "You in a few years. A lone wolf trying to find some joy in a world that won't let him. Not that I care. I've made my peace with that. Solitude is what I am and will always be."

"Tell that to the human you just killed. Unless you really think that was just some blood rage that took control of you."

"Worth a try. I'm pretty good at lying to myself. What's another one?"

The old wolf turned his ears back while trying not to laugh. "Pup, you're going to drive me crazy."

A soft growl escaped my control, after which I didn't bother trying to soften my glare. "I'm not keeping you here. I'm sure that fox is still out there, and I'd just as soon be alone anyway."

"Is that so? Have you ever considered..."

Both of our ears shot up when a chorus of howls erupted close by. So close that, at first, I looked around, thinking they were right on top of me. I rose in case they were and winced when my leg reminded me of the wound. I tucked it against my body to remove the pressure and stop the pain, then perked my ears so I could follow the sound when they repeated the call.

"That's odd," I said. "There aren't any packs out there."

"Could be roamers," the old wolf said.

"Not likely. There aren't any packs there because that's where the humans build their dens."

The old wolf's ears and eyes shot up. "What? And you live here?"

Like I have a choice. Well, perhaps I did. Living so close to that much danger did seem to give me the solitude I thought I wanted. At least it used to, though now that it'd been broken twice in one day, I had to admit, the attention was starting to appeal to me.

Not that I'd ever tell the old wolf that. "They are not the cleverest of beasts, despite their power. Still, that doesn't explain the howls. Um, what are you doing?"

The old wolf was stalking into the forest toward the humans. He looked back at me with an almost devious tension in his ears. "I thought I'd see where those howls are coming from."

"Are you mad? Those humans see you, you're dead."

"Why do you care? I thought you wanted to be alone."

I would have growled at him if I wasn't so busy trying to answer that question. Estrella was at least someone I knew. This wolf had done nothing but annoy me since we met. Truth is, I would have been glad to be rid of him in any way possible. Yet some part of me didn't want to see the old wolf get killed.

I latched onto that and turned it into another of my lies. "The humans have killed enough of our kind. I'd rather not see another pelt hanging on the trees."

I don't think he believes me.

"First blind rage, now a touch of compassion. Better be careful, pup. One might think you actually care."

A growl formed again, more so because my feelings hadn't changed. Or because I didn't want to give the old wolf the satisfaction of being right. "Fine. You want to satisfy your curiosity?" I limped ahead of him, tested the air, and checked my ears to be sure we were alone. "Stay close, stay silent, and do what I say. The last thing I need is you repeating your pup's mistake."

The old wolf gave a nice impression of Toltan's death stance. "Careful, pup. I'll not have—"

"My name is Luna! If you plan to survive this investigation, I suggest you remember it. Now shut your muzzle and follow me."

My insides tensed, expecting fangs, except the old wolf didn't offer any. In fact, he didn't offer any reprimand at all. Not even a growl. If anything, the old wolf had lowered himself ever so slightly. I counted myself lucky considering my injury, then hoped I had some luck left for my next endeavor.

I led the old wolf toward the humans with frequent tests of scent and sound. I was not going to let myself get pounced on after surviving so much. That'd just be insulting. Or stupid, given the fact that I was heading toward dangerous hunters with a leg I *might* be able to use if I had to. Though if I did, I'd probably never get to use it again. Permanent damage, or starvation while it healed, would see to that. *Guess they were right. Solitude drives you mad.*

We moved like two shadows, picking our way toward light in the distance. My limp broke an otherwise silent journey, but even it was soft, and I had yet to hear any indication that anyone heard me.

Our pace slowed further when we approached the humans' dens, which still appeared to be smooth boulders that were oddly colored. Like the last couple of years, the humans were moving around these "dens," many of which seemed to glow from the inside. Shadows on the sides appeared to be the silhouettes of more humans within. I saw no sign of a fire, though I did see them gathered around one of their rocks that held two glowing stones inside it. I didn't understand those any more than their glowing sticks, other than it provided light the humans seemed to need. Poor creatures. So much power, yet they lacked the natural ability to see in the dark.

"I don't see anything," the old wolf whispered.

I scanned the humans' gathering area, looking for some sign of the wolves we'd heard. I knew I had the right direction, so where were they?

Some yips drew my attention to the side of the dens. There my eyes stayed while my brain refused to accept what they were telling me. There *were* wolves there. Five of them, not just among the humans, but interacting with them, rubbing against them with affection. Tails were wagging, an odd behavior in its own right, at the humans' mere presence, as if they were their parents. There were tales of wolves going mad, but this was something far beyond mere insanity. At least we had discovered why the barks from before has sounded so wolf-like. They *were* wolves.

The old wolf started muttering. "Vinsi? Harso? Marron?"

My ears dragged my eyes toward the old wolf. His eyes were transfixed on the wolves, and he was walking toward them. He moved slow, step after step, almost as if absorbed in a hunt. Except this was much more dangerous prey, and I nearly turned inside out in panic when I realized he wasn't going to stop.

I took a deep breath, then reached forward, grabbed the old wolf by the scruff, and dragged him down before someone saw him. My leg screamed in agony, but I held my breath, avoiding any noise beyond the rustle of me and the old wolf hitting the ground. Wolf ears turned our way, followed by human eyes. They pointed their light sticks out into the forest, shining beams of sunlight against tree and brush. I froze, too terrified to shake, or even be angry.

"Do. Not. Move," I said. "Don't even breathe."

The old wolf's voice was barely a whisper. "Luna. Luna, those wolves—"

"I said, quiet! Stay quiet or we're both dead."

The old wolf tried to move on until another human stepped out of a den with a thunder stick in his paws. The old wolf turned to stone, though I could feel his body tremble next to mine. I could only pray it wouldn't give us away.

The light beams scanned the forest, looking for us. I heard things scurry away, but I watched those beams with all my focus. Every time they came near, my heart stopped, wondering if they'd keep going this time. When the humans' wolves started to approach, I prepared to ruin my leg in retreat.

Then the humans started barking. Soft and firm at first, then with much more force. It was only then the wolves hugged the ground, their eyes up at their masters like they were their alphas. The humans grabbed them by a vine of some kind that was tight around their necks. Something I had seen on the dogs they'd brought before. For some strange reason, it appeared to be a source of control for the humans. However it worked, the wolves had halted their advance, though the humans were giving the forest one more look. I didn't breathe until they led the wolves back toward the dens, and the human with a thunder stick vanished into his own.

"We're safe," I said. "For now."

The old wolf rose with a shake of his shoulders. When he looked at me, he looked a lot like Martol the night she appeared to die within. The memory drew a twitch from my ears and a desire to look anywhere else.

"Luna," the old wolf said. "Those wolves. We have to do something."

The pain of my leg is probably the only thing that reminded me I was still alive. The rest of me was consumed by the question of whether or not the old wolf had lost his mind.

"We? What we? What makes you think... forget that. Why? Why do *we* have to *do* anything? Those wolves were submitting to the humans. Don't you understand what that means?"

"More than you can know. That's why we have to do something to free them."

I take it back. Wolfor's fang, I hope I am nothing like him in a few years. At least I'm still sane. "I return to my original question. Why does it matter?"

"Because those are my pups."

My ears shot up so straight it felt like they grew longer. "They're what? You can't be sure of that."

"Spoken like a wolf with no young of his own. Trust me, Luna. When you have a litter, you'll know them without trying. Their fur, their eyes, so many little things that to others mean nothing. But I tell you, I look at those wolves and I *know*, they're my pups. The ones that vanished before the humans killed my pack."

True or not, I couldn't deny the old wolf believed it. That certainty did nothing for my insides, or my concern that the old wolf had gone insane. The question was pointless, really. There or gone, his mind had been made up. That left me in search of an answer as elusive as that fox.

Why do I care?

The question bounced around my head, stirring an internal battle while the old wolf stared at me. I tried to ignore his eyes, but they wouldn't go away. There was a void behind them. An old shell where a wolf once lived. Just like Martol. That night returned to me as if it had just happened. Pain, fear, helplessness, it was all there, begging me to make it not so. The tears I'd cried that night broke me. Insane or not, I couldn't let him go alone. For reasons I could never find, I just couldn't.

"All right," I sighed at last. "All right. But if we're going to do this, we're going to do it right. We can't help them if we're dead. You say you recognize them on sight even after all this time? If they're anything like I am... was, it works both ways. They should know you by sight and scent immediately. The only way we can help them is if they help us."

Light returned to the old wolf's eyes for the first time. "So, what's your plan?"

"We wait. The humans always sleep inside their dens together. We must wait until they are all asleep. Then, we approach the wolves as quietly as possible from downwind. They must see us before they smell or hear us, or they'll alert the humans. If they do..."

"The humans will kill us," the old wolf said. "I've waited this long. I think I can control myself for a while longer."

"Please do. This is what one human did to me. I don't like our chances against six plus their wolves."

The old wolf growled, but stopped short of snapping. "They belong to no one."

I was surprised to hear my voice come out calm and almost soothing. "Until they remember you, they are part of the humans' pack. You above all know the power that bond holds."

The old wolf sighed with a forward tick of his ears. Neither of us said another word.

We found a comfortable spot behind a bush where we could watch the humans in safety. The two humans that remained outside the dens continued to growl and ruff at each other, oblivious to our presence. They held what looked like ice in their paws, yet there appeared to be some kind of brown liquid inside. While it looked like water, the scent that drifted on the wind was far too harsh to be anything I wanted to risk tasting. At times, they'd tap the "ice" together, which appeared to cause them some manner of pleasure. I could only guess they found the clinking sound amusing, or maybe they were playing some kind of game to see whose ice broke first. If so, no one ever won, because the ice never broke.

The only change in behavior came when one of the wolves came close to them. He repeatedly pushed his nose under the human's paw until the human rubbed behind the wolf's ears. The human barked softly, affectionately, to which the wolf responded by sitting still for the rubbing, even leaning into it as if to make it feel better. When the human stopped, the wolf would nuzzle again, or nuzzle the other human to get him to do it, or sit and stare, begging, until one of them resumed the rub.

Wolfor, I thought the humans were an odd creature. To see wolves acting in such a manner, I didn't know what to make of it. How could any wolf abandon their instincts enough to act like that? I wondered if our mission was little more than an elaborate suicide. If that's what the old wolf had in mind, I decided I'd rather go soul dead, the final state in which sick or injured wolves will cease to care for themselves. It's often more a final symptom of their injury or illness, but given a choice, I'd rather do that than charge into death as if it were a friend. It felt more respectable somehow.

Our chance to avoid death finally came when the humans gathered the wolves just behind their dens. There, they had something that looked like a giant spider's web strung between stiff, bare trees that created an enclosed space. All of the webbing was the color of stone and seemed to be about as strong based on how little it moved when a human pulled at it. Instead of breaking, they swung part of the webbing out to provide an opening the wolves trotted into without protest. Then the humans closed the webbing, trapping the wolves inside. I couldn't decide which was worse: the willingness to be confined, or the simple whimpers the wolves gave when the humans walked away. These were not cries of fear, but of longing, and short-lived ones at that.

Short as they were, they were long enough to force the old wolf to rise and shake like he had before. I watched him carefully, preparing in case he lost control again.

"Luna," the old wolf said. "Luna, what do we do now?"

I watched the humans work with their glowing rocks. Some took them into dens that had been dark, while others put theirs out. A second later, many of the dens that had been glowing darkened, beginning a process I had seen many times. *At least something is familiar.*

"We continue to wait," I said. "Just a little longer."

"But... but my pups..."

"Appear to be okay for now. Look at them. They're not afraid. Two of them are already settling in to sleep. Patience. We must be sure the humans are asleep."

The old wolf continued to shake but held his place. I kept an ear turned his way in case that changed, while my eyes watched the humans' dens for our chance. The silhouettes on the dens that were still lit moved around, rummaging for who knows what. Maybe they were eating cached meat, or mating, or fighting; there was no way to be sure.

The glowing eventually stopped within them all. I watched and waited as a few grunts sounded within. Then, at last, dead quiet.

Let's choose our words more carefully, I thought with a ruff.

I waited a moment more to be sure before rising myself. I winced as my wound shot pain up my shoulder, reminding me of my limitations while forcing my leg to tuck.

"I can do this alone, Luna," the old wolf said. "You've done enough."

I only hesitated because I hurt too much to think for a moment. "And if those humans wake up? You don't know them like I do. No, we started this together. That's how we'll finish it."

The old wolf just huffed, which frustrated me because I couldn't decipher the comment. Had he said something, at least then I'd have something to react to. Instead, I was left with a curious shift in my ears, wondering what it was he was saying.

I abandoned the search in favor of limping a wide arc around the humans' dens. I stayed among the trees and brush, never letting the dens out of my sight for long. When I heard clinking nearby, much like the sound the webbing made when it was manipulated, I froze. The webbing was obscured by a tree, but I couldn't hear any human barks, nor did any of the dens start glowing again. When the forest went silent again, the old wolf and I continued on our way toward his pups.

The more we moved, the more I wished I could hear something besides our paws. The forest was dea... *wrong word choice!*... completely silent, without so much as an owl screeching in the treetops. There was only the quiet grind of our claws in the dirt, as well as every beat of my heart. My ears were locked forward, my nose tested the air with each step of my good foreleg, and every hair stood ready to scream should they find anything. With any luck, it would be enough to avoid getting pounced on by anything, least of all the humans.

My ears perked further when they caught a rustling sound. My eyes dissected every shadow, finding only swaying leaves in the breeze. My ears said otherwise as the rustling continued, followed by the wind confirming the presence of other wolves nearby. While the scent was too weak to identify, it was definitely familiar.

As the noises came closer, it became a uniform snuffling, as well as a fair amount of snaps and rustles from barging through brush. Whoever these wolves were, they weren't very good. That said, I wasn't about to chance it. This close to humans, we couldn't afford the noise of a border dispute, to say nothing of my wound. I softly ruffed at the old wolf before hunkering down as low as I could get. The old wolf followed my example, though his ears also remained forward and alert.

Branches broke with loud snaps just ahead, while snuffles echoed across as if they were ruffing at each scent they found. *Guess the humans are heavy sleepers.* These wolves had to be on their first hunt to be making such a racket. I continued to hear them long before one came into view.

Definitely a young wolf, though not much older than I was, if at all. His fur was so smooth, so clean, it hadn't seen a lick of real strife. Otherwise, he could have passed as the old wolf's twin. His fur was dominated by dark gray, with brown highlights on his back, ears, and tail. Only difference was a brown vine tight around his neck and a slightly thinner build.

My head popped up as I realized I'd seen that wolf before. He was one of the wolves the humans had, except they were trapped by the webbing, or at least I thought they were.

Before I could doubt it was him, the old wolf stood up with a gasp.

"Vinsi?" he said.

This Vinsi, if it was him, stared at the old wolf without moving. His ears, still as stone, turned in the old wolf's direction. They locked eyes, and neither appeared to breathe.

Another wolf, much like the first but with no brown at all, came around a tree shaking his head. "Vinsi. Will you come on? If we're going to have any fun out here, we've got to get going before..." This second wolf became much like the first when he saw the old wolf. "It can't be. Father? Is that you?"

The old wolf struggled to breathe as tears formed on his cheeks. "Harso. You never did learn our traditions well. You must use my name so I may retain who I am."

Now it was the pup's turn to be short of breath. Whines lasted a second before both had their heads against their father's in the blink of an eye.

"Carlin," Vinsi said. "Carlin, we thought you were dead."

Pain of envy turned bitter and forced an amused ruff to escape my control. "Carlin. So, you *do* have a name."

Carlin allowed a moment to growl at me before returning to his pups. I looked away, not wanting to see warmth I'd never feel. I found the other wolves sliding under the edge of the webbing. As far as I could tell, they'd somehow dislodged the lower part, allowing them to slip under it and escape. The only thing that gave them away was a soft clinking of the webbing. *Clever wolves,* I thought with a chuckle.

The three remaining wolves looked around until they saw us. I worried they might alert the humans, until they too turned to stone for a moment. When a few tentative steps became a sprint our way, I scuttled in retreat before they ran me over on their way to their father.

These didn't wait to confirm. They were on Carlin like he was prey, except instead of making a kill, they whimpered, and whined, and nuzzled, and licked him all over. A yip or two sounded when one couldn't get to him to fawn over him. I watched the exchange, rolling my eyes at them. *And I thought Estrella hadn't grown up.*

Carlin took it with tears streaming from his eyes. He returned licks and rubs as best he could, though the flurry was beginning to die down. I found myself a place to lie down and let them be. I wasn't part of their pack. I never would be. Besides, they'd do too much to my shoulder anyway, though it was a lie I used to keep from leaving entirely.

Still, I had to wonder what it would feel like. To feel Toltan's fur against mine again. To have his tongue wet my fur. To hear his whimpers ring through my ears, straight to my heart. To be accepted, loved, again.

The mind wondered, but I knew I would never know. Not even Martol would give me that much anymore. As a lone wolf, no self-respecting wolf would have anything to do with me. *So be it.* Let them have their busy lives. Mine was just fine the way it was.

That lie didn't keep me from listening in, as if maybe I could join in anyway in spite of it all.

"Marron," Carlin said. "Altin. Tital. My pups. I thought I'd lost you all."

"So did we," Vinsi said. "When the humans took us, I thought for sure we were dead."

"But they never hurt us," Harso said. "In fact, they fed us. They cared for us, gave us dens to sleep in. Now we're a pack. We live and hunt together."

Carlin stopped his affection all at once. He grew still, then recoiled as if one of them had bitten him. He stood staring as if he might vomit at any moment.

"What are you saying? You're helping them hunt?"

"Of course," Harso said. "We're a pack. We help them hunt, and they keep us fed and healthy."

"You've been hunting wolves, Harso. *Wolves!* Don't you understand that? Don't you understand what they've done to you?"

"They've given us a home, Carlin. They're actually very affectionate. You'll see. They'll take you in too. They'll care for you like they did us."

I ruffed dark amusement. *Care for us? Yeah, right. Time for a reality check.*

"Excuse me," I said. "You aren't really that dense, are you? You've seen what they've done to wolves. You think he'll get special treatment? Uh-uh. They'll see him as another wolf, they'll grab their thunder sticks, and they'll kill him like they have all the others."

Vinsi gave a snarl I found impressive for a wolf raised by humans. "You don't know them. You don't know them at all."

"Oh no? My leg says otherwise. One of them threatened... someone I knew. I had to stop him. This was my reward."

One of the other pups raised her hackles with a growl. "That was you? You killed him? Do you know what that human meant to me?"

Carlin and I shared an appalled stare with ears so erect, they may never fall again.

"Marron?" Carlin said. "What are you saying?"

"I loved that human. He and I shared a special bond. Were he a wolf, I would have taken him as my mate."

I tried to stop that image before it became rooted in my head. I tried very, very, *very* hard, but I failed to keep it from making me sick. *A wolf mating with a human? Wolfor, kill me now.*

Carlin, meanwhile, was backing up, more on the verge of hyperventilating. "By Wolfor, what have they done to you? You're not even wolves anymore."

"You can say that again," I said, still trying to keep my last meal from coming back up.

Marron's snarl and bristling hackles left me impressed enough to wonder when I should start running. "You dare insult us? Come on then. Show me the quality of your fangs."

Humpf. Guess they have some wolf left after all.

Barks from behind drew my attention before I could respond. When I glanced back to check on it, I felt my heart stop. The humans' dens were glowing again. Worse, some were already outside. *Miss Hot Temper must have woken them up. As if I don't have enough to deal with.*

"Carlin," I said. "we need to go, now."

Carlin tilted his head at me, so I tossed mine toward the dens. When he looked back, his ears turned back in fear.

We turned to leave, but Marron jumped in front of us, still snarling fury "You're going nowhere. You took something of mine. I'll not let you leave without paying with your—"

Carlin rushed forward and bit at her neck with a snarl that shook my ribs. Marron yelped more in surprise than pain. She tugged and pulled, breaking free, but falling back once she did. Vinsi attacked as she did, but Carlin dodged right around him, landing a sharp bite on his leg that drew blood.

When the other pups went for me, Carlin appeared between them. His ears were forward, his hackles were on end, and his snarl was worthy of Wolfor himself. *Glad I haven't pissed him off yet.* His pups tried to match it, but their lower tails and ears said otherwise. As for Carlin, his tail waved straight up over him.

I looked over them to see the humans were still looking around as if confused. Their light beams scanned the forest again, while excited barks echoed from their meeting area.

"Carlin," I said, "we've got to get out of here. Those humans won't take long to find us."

"They'll only find me," Carlin said through his snarl. "You run."

"Excuse me?"

"You returned my life to me. Now I'm going to save yours. Get out of here. Get to safety."

I pulled myself forward, but my injured leg refused to allow more than a limp.

Yet that's not what stopped me. I looked back at the entire situation. I saw Carlin standing firm before his own pups, and I saw the humans gathering their thunder sticks. I knew what was coming. I tried to lie. I tried to tell myself I didn't care.

I failed.

"What about you? I can't just leave you here."

"Yes, you can!" Carlin said. "My life is here now. You have too much to look forward to, lone wolf or not. Now get moving."

"Not without you."

"I said *go!*"

He charged his pups before I could respond. Vinsi was knocked onto his side, and Marron was yelping in pain as Carlin sank his fangs into her leg. The other three bit at him, but landed only surface bites as Carlin snarled fury, drawing the humans toward the sound.

I didn't have a choice. Unable to fight, I winced through agony as I limped into the shadows before I was seen. Yelps and snarls followed as if the wolves themselves were right behind me. I couldn't tell which belonged to who, and part of me preferred it that way. The rest wished I couldn't hear them at all.

The wound reopened, allowing a trickle of blood to seep onto my leg. It couldn't be helped, as a short sprint had become a trail of agony back the way I'd come. I limped and winced all the way to, and inside, my cozy little rock pile, where I curled against the inside wall in a tight ball, wondering when my shoulder had decided to sympathize with my leg. The original wound was burning more than it had when I was first stabbed, requiring every bit of self-control I had to keep from whining at the sheer torture running up and down my leg.

"Stop him!"

"He's getting away!"

"Kill him!"

The calls echoed into my den, clear as if they were right outside. Snarls and yelps followed soon after. For a moment, it grew so loud I thought they *were* outside my den, or at least passing by. *Carlin must be one tough wolf to be fighting five younger wolves and still be alive to—*

CRACK!-CSHOO-shoo-sho

Crack!-Cshoo-sho-crackcrackcrack!-Cshooshoo-shooshoo-shoo

I flinched with each thunderbolt. My ears had long disappeared against my skull, while my entire body shook as if I were furless in a blizzard. I winced harder from the pain in my leg, which only added to my fear. I'd never fight off the wolves. Even if I did, the humans would get me instead. It seemed death was coming for me, and I could do nothing to fight it off.

I stared at the entrance of my den, watching, hoping, praying nothing would ever come through. Silence alone breathed inside. If I couldn't hear my own breath, I would have sworn I'd gone deaf, for the air lay still as if it were as afraid as I was.

The forest lay silent for what felt like years. Too long for them to still be working their way toward me. Too long for me to sit around doing nothing, even though the blood on my leg was still wet. I had to risk a peek, if nothing else, so I'd know what was coming.

I kept my ears forward as I crawled through the tunnel of my den. My breath shook as much as I did, but I kept going. I had to know if they were still out there. I stopped just inside the entrance, where I peered out at the forest, picking apart every shadow that moved. A few moved too steady to be leaves. Then they cast beams of light onto the ground ahead of them.

My body became another stone among the pile. They were coming my way. At an odd angle but... no. Not my way. In my direction, but their angle was too far to the side. I risked peeking my head out to get a better view of the group. The humans had their light cast far and away from me. Three of Carlin's pups were being led by a vine connected to that brown ring on their necks while another was being carried with great whimpers of pain.

Before I could find the fifth, I found something else. One of the humans was carrying another wolf, but this one made no sound, nor did he move, except for the flop of his paws against the human's body. I allowed another few inches of advance to be sure. I saw a body dominated by dark gray, with brown highlights on back, ears, and tail.

"Carlin."

I cringed in pain as tears I couldn't understand fell from my eyes. I tried to shake them off. I tried to tell myself I had what I wanted. I had my solitude again, free from that annoying old wolf.

My lies didn't work. Another wolf was dead. One I knew this time. One that didn't care who I was or what I'd done. He might have even joined me had I given him the chance. Now I never could. Another missed opportunity. Not my fault? I wanted to think so, but I never managed it.

I waited long after they were gone to limp outside, where a lack of scent and sound confirmed I was alone again. My heart stung, but I ignored it, for I had more pressing issues. I checked my cache for a meal, only to remember scraps being all that remained.

My injured leg twinged in pain, to which I gave a heavy sigh. I knew what this meant. I'd give it my best, but those scraps were all I would get before the end. As such, I decided to enjoy them. One last good thing before I starved to death. It helped fill the void inside too, if only a touch.

I returned to my den, contemplating my slow demise, whining at my injury as it complained about being disturbed. I settled against the back wall and cleaned the blood off of my leg until it had stopped bleeding again. It was all I could do really, since thinking about what it would feel like to starve churned my insides too much.

A howl echoed through the entrance, sending my ears straight up. This wasn't just some random wolf howling outside. Whoever it was, they had stuck their head inside to make sure I'd heard them. It was the only way to explain how loud it was.

Since it held no malice, I allowed curiosity to push me outside to find this other wolf. When I poked my head out, I didn't see anything except an empty forest and a hunk of moose laying in front of my den. *What in Wolfor's...*

"You going to eat that or not?"

I followed the voice, and my heart went to war with itself. Estrella, that stubborn female, was back. I wanted to drive her off, remind her I didn't want her. I wanted to nuzzle her, admit I cared, and enjoy the fact that she was there at all. I wanted to just take the meat and retreat back inside without word or acknowledgement.

Instead, I found the only question that somewhat satisfied all three.

"What are you doing here?"

Estrella proudly trotted up and sat on the other side of the meat. "Doing what you can't. I saw you fight that two-legged."

"Human."

"Whatever. I saw what you did, and what it cost you. Thank you, Luna. I never knew he was there."

I tried to keep my ears up, but they turned back anyway. "I... I just didn't want them to get another wolf."

Estrella glared at me with a gentle growl. "You're pretty determined to be a thorn-in-the-paw, aren't you? Well, I don't care. I'm going to take care of you, and there's nothing you can do about it."

I sighed with another growl. I knew her so little, yet I already knew that look. She was going to have her way, and no one, not even Wolfor, was going to stop her. *Might as well find a way to enjoy it while it's there.*

"Fine," I said. "Just try not to get too annoying, all right? I've been alone for three years, and I am not in a mood to have company for the rest of my life."

"Things change. I can wait."

Knowing her, she'd wait till the end of time too. I retreated back inside my den to find sleep after such a trying day. Estrella followed me in, food in mouth with a glare. My ears fell in case she decided to add fang to her reprimand.

"Sorry," I said. "Where did you get that anyway? Don't tell me you managed a kill on your own."

Estrella put the meat in front of me, then settled in beside me with a quick rub against my cheek. "I have my ways. Today it involved returning to your kill, and picking off what I could. The ravens hadn't found it yet, though an old wolf did. Almost had to fight him for it."

"This old wolf give a name?"

"No, but he kept calling himself 'old and wise,' like somehow that was his name."

My first bite almost got stuck in my throat, forcing me to gag and work to get it past the lump growing there. *It couldn't be.*

"This wolf. Did he have a lot of scars, with fur that was dark gray, with brown on his ears, back, and tail?"

Estrella tilted her head at me, and I didn't move. I didn't dare hope, even as my heart did with every strand of fur. Estrella looked up for a while, as if the answer was on the walls of the den.

"Now that you mention it," she said, "I think he did. Why? Do you... Luna? What's wrong?"

Nothing, nothing at all. I had closed my eyes as joyful pain took hold. *That stubborn old wolf. Should have known he wouldn't die that easy.* It had to have been his pup I saw, not him. I took deep breath after deep breath, trying to tell myself this was not joy I was feeling. That Carlin's survival meant nothing to me.

I got the edge of a laugh instead. I didn't even know why. I only knew quick bursts of panted amusement broke through, making it seem like I couldn't breathe, which in some ways, I couldn't.

"Luna! What's wrong?"

I ruffed in amusement again before returning the rub Estrella had given me earlier. "Nothing. I do know that wolf. In fact, just today, he saved my life. I thought it'd cost him his."

"And you weren't going to tell me, were you?"

"Nope."

Estrella turned her ears back, then growled, then sighed. "Luna, you are going to drive me out of my mind."

Now where have I heard that before? "You don't have to stay, you know. Living alone isn't so bad."

"You won't get rid of me that easy. Like it or not, I'm here, and I am not going away."

This much I knew without her saying so. A part of me even liked the idea, but it was overpowered by the years of pain. I had gotten used to living alone, even found a way to enjoy it. Now I had this crazy female who I'd never get rid of. Not until I healed anyway.

Except, just as I finished what I could of the meat, Estrella leaned against me. She fell asleep almost the moment she did, and I couldn't find a reason to move. I just watched her look so content, so peaceful, as if she trusted me to defend her from the world. I felt her fur against mine, the warmth of her presence, and her confidence, seeping through. Just her being there made all the thoughts I had in my head seem ridiculous.

The pine cone returned, only for it to melt when I inched my head down against hers. When our ears touched, she leaned into me again. I returned it, failing to convince myself I didn't feel anything. My second opportunity had given me a second chance. My third was still out there, perhaps waiting to do the same.

I barely felt my injury that night. Estrella's fur kept it hidden, almost as if it could help heal it. Try as I might, I couldn't lie to myself.

For the first time I could remember, I wasn't even sure I wanted to anymore.

Chapter 7

"COME ON, YOU THORN. No more moping. There has to be something out here."

I think I miss being injured.

My leg had healed in time for the onset of fall, though it felt more like winter. The cold at times bit through my still thickening fur, and that was without the wind and rain we'd had the last few days. Much of our prey must have had the same problem, for hunting had proven difficult, even for a healed wolf. That said, we would have to keep trying, or we'd have no chance of eating.

I stretched myself loose, then followed Estrella outside into dead quiet. Most of the birds had already migrated, including the mockingbird. Even the wind was still for a change. Leaves covered the ground as if trying to outdo the snow yet to come, yet the trees sported many more waiting for their turn to fall, not one of them green.

"Not a good beginning," I said.

"Have a little faith," Estrella said.

I wish I had your optimism.

I led the way along my usual hunting trails, winding through my limited territory. They had always produced enough game to keep me fed before. Today, however, every hole I checked, every bend I scratched at, not one had any sign of a meal. At one point, I stuck my nose inside a hole as if I might will prey to be there. I found it so long abandoned, there wasn't even an old scent left.

I pulled my head out and shook the dust off while grunting frustration. "Nothing. A whole family of rabbits just gone. That little bit of faith is fading fast."

Estrella tried to say something. Instead she just sighed.

Someone else spoke for her.

"I'm afraid that's my fault."

My ears perked toward a voice I knew all too well. The old wolf came from behind a tree, looking as healthy as ever, though his fur was just as bloodless as ours. *Not encouraging.*

Didn't change the swish in my tail to see he had survived. "Carlin, I thought you were dead."

Carlin tilted his head at me with a flick of his ear. "This matters to you? I thought you wanted to be alone." He looked past me, focusing on Estrella. "And now I wonder. Earned some forgiveness, have we?"

Estrella just about fell over laughing. "You obviously don't know him. He didn't *earn* forgiveness. I forced it on him."

"Quite a feat for one so young. You must be Estrella."

"And you must be Carlin."

I'm going to be sick.

I rolled my eyes, trying not to snap. *Just what I need. Estrella with a reason to talk.* I stepped out from between them before I got caught in the middle. For some reason, this killed their conversation on the spot. Estrella returned to my side, making a point of not looking at me. Carlin followed as well, not saying a word in the same way.

Then a sigh sounded from the old wolf. *Should have known he wouldn't stay silent.*

"Still carrying that wound, I see. You really going to do this?"

I stayed silent, partly because I wasn't sure what he meant. Maybe it'd be enough to get them to let me just hunt for a change. Free from distractions, conversations, and "old wounds." Carlin ran ahead and gave a short growl, forcing me to stop and lift my tail before he assumed a place in my territory that he did not possess.

Carlin only stood and glared. "Are you so intent on being alone you won't listen to me?"

"I'm not alone," I said. "Estrella and I run together now. We are as one pack."

I had to think to keep my tail up. *Where did that come from?* It felt so natural, I didn't give it any thought until I'd said it. The words felt good in my mouth. If only I could figure out what it had been, or when things had changed.

Meanwhile, Carlin's ears had gone straight up. His eyes had grown too. I didn't dare look at Estrella. I'd never shut her up.

"Well, well," Carlin said. "Estrella, you've managed quite a feat. I expected to find this one curled in his den, brooding about some rat that had bitten his tail."

My tail managed to go straighter, and my growl spoke of death lest Carlin say another word. "Careful, old one. My patience has limits."

Carlin stood still, tail level in that frozen look often seen before a charge, but a growl never formed. Instead, his ears and tail fell, though the tail never tucked.

"I'm sorry, Luna," Carlin said. "You're right. That was uncalled for."

I allowed my own tail to fall. I knew that further confrontation would bring me nothing, except a souring of the fact that Carlin had come away from that night much as he'd entered it. For once, I didn't try to tell myself I didn't find joy in it.

I stepped closer to say something, though I hadn't decided what yet. Before I could, I saw movement just past the old wolf. A patch of leaves that had been mud not long ago appeared to shift of its own accord. I moved forward to get a better look, ignoring my companions for the moment.

The patch of leaves had grown so deep, my paw sank to my ankle before I found ground. The trees above lay bare, save for a nest or two left from spring. I kept moving. I was only getting glimpses of movement, yet my nose could find nothing to account for it.

My ears filled in the gaps. When a leaf jumped in the air, seemingly on its own, my body froze while my ears kept going. They found familiar sounds of skittering and quiet squeaks. I recognized the sound just before I saw the first one sweep across the leaves.

"Field mice!" Estrella said.

I could hear Carlin's breath deepening beside me. Saw him lick his lips more than once too. I turned my ears back at him while focusing at Estrella.

"Have a little faith," I said.

"That's what I keep saying," she said.

I allowed a quick ruff of amusement. *Might get me to believe yet.* "All right, Carlin, you want me to stop living my life alone? Here's your chance. We work together, try to keep the mice between us, and we don't stop till our legs melt."

Carlin's jaws opened to show fangs wet with drool. "Just say when, Luna."

I allowed an amused ear flick, then licked my jaws dry. "Follow me in. By Wolfor, we're going to have a meal after all."

Leaves were cast into the air as we charged in. The first mouse never saw me until he was halfway down my throat. I swung a paw at another, and though I missed, Carlin didn't. He dug his head ear deep into a leaf pile, then came up with two mice going down in quick snaps. Estrella meanwhile was sending leaves back into the trees digging after her own. She stopped only to catch one mouse that tried to run past her.

More went sprinting toward the trees, and I tore through leaves after them. They tried to retreat under, but I jabbed my muzzle in much like a woodpecker, managing to catch a few. I shook the leaves off my face, then leapt nose first after another sound of more. My catches often came with twig or leaf, but it was worth the meal.

If one could call it a meal. The three of us tore the field apart, catching anything we could. We tried to keep ourselves spaced so the mice would stay between us, but with the chases and muzzle dives, the plan quickly collapsed. Carlin even caught my tail once as it twitched under the leaves while I lied in wait for a pounce. I brushed it off without a word and still caught my target, but the mice were finding holes or escape routes as fast as we were swallowing them. It wasn't long before the catches dwindled into none. We continued to try until we saw little and heard less. We remained still for a while after, hoping to find a few more. When the silence felt like it was crushing us, a unanimous sigh admitted we'd caught all we were going to.

"Any other ideas?" I said at last.

Estella turned her ears back to admit she had none. Carlin scanned the field once more before growling through a sigh.

"Rest for tomorrow," he said. "This forest will give us nothing more today."

"I think we can blame the humans for that," I said.

Carlin flicked an annoyed ear, which I took as agreement. "Whatever the cause, we're better off being fresh for our next hunt. Perhaps the three of us can take down a demon doe."

"Demon doe?" Estrella asked.

"She's huge for being a female. Has the courage of a buck twice her size."

"And a pair of hind legs to make up for the lack of antlers."

"I see you met her."

Estrella turned her head to show a swatch of fur missing from the back of her neck. My stomach churned when I remembered the day she came back with blood soaking her fur. She'd tried to downplay it, but I'd gotten her to admit that this "demon doe" had just missed a lethal blow. She'd gone on to describe a beast that sounded strong enough to kick down a tree. Between the wound and the tale, my stomach had churned then too. I couldn't bear the thought of another wolf getting killed trying to care for me

Carlin huffed at the injury. "You're one lucky wolf."

Estrella shook herself as if shaking away the comment. "Luck had little to do with it. I saw the kick coming. I just didn't expect it to be that... effective."

"Lucky, yet prideful. Interesting mix."

Oh, please don't...

"What's so interesting about it?" Estrella said.

Are the humans back yet?

With them not around to save me, I made my escape before the argument started. I trotted all the way back to my den so they could have it out on their own, half expecting them to go at it all day. *Wolfor knows Carlin is stubborn enough, and Estrella talkative. They might go on till spring.*

By the time the others rejoined me, the sun was just reaching the mountains. The temperature dropped as usual, though for once, the winds remained calm. Estrella flopped beside me while Carlin eased down next to the old tree where my cache lay.

"All finished?" I said.

Estrella held her head high. "Carlin seems to think I'm dangerous."

"Only to rivals," Carlin said. "I pity anyone trying to force themselves on her, or you, Luna."

"Not much chance of that," I said.

After all, I was still a "lone wolf." If it weren't for Estrella's odd reasons, I'd still be living the solitary life my banishment intended. The more I thought about that, the stronger my ruffed chuckle grew. *How ironic.*

"Something you'd like to share, Luna?" Carlin asked.

The chuckle eased, but the warmth didn't. "Just an odd chain of events. Look at us. Three wolves, living together, hunting together, each of us with a different reason for being out here away from our packs. I was banished for killing my brother, even though I never did. Estrella is here because she intends to be my mate and my mate alone. Carlin... why are you out here? You never did say what happened to you."

Carlin's ears flashed back, but the rest of him remained relaxed. "I was banished too. While my crime was real, it was also necessary for the pack's survival. You see, I killed my mother and two of her pups. She had caught the Rage Plague. She attacked everything, even went after humans. It threatened the pack, and my father couldn't or wouldn't act. I had no choice. I had to save the pack. When the pups showed the same signs, I killed them before they turned violent. Only Wolfor knows how I didn't catch it myself."

For a moment, I watched him like an elder teaching. Carlin looked back, his ears up and alert, no longer in pain. I had seen that look before only once. He was waiting to pass something on. His pain, or a lesson, I couldn't say, but for the first time, Carlin looked his age.

I only wished I had more to offer him.

"You had to know what it would cost you," I said.

Carlin turned his ears back again. "Small. My pack meant more. That is how it must be, Luna. The pack must come before the individual. Those with the blood of an alpha know this on instinct. You may find yourself in the same place someday."

I huffed anger. *That'll be the day.* "For a pack that cast me out? I think not."

"I didn't mean them, Luna. Though how odd that you did."

Now he searched me for something. I waited for a snide comment, or some other point yet to be made. Instead, Carlin hummed, then laid his head on his paws. His eyes closed the next moment, entering sleep as only older wolves seemed able to do.

"You make good friends," Estrella said. I tilted my head at her, a bit unsure. "Just noting how quick an old wolf is to lay his fur beside yours. I see why Rajor fears you."

"Fears?" I ruffed, shook the weariness from my fur, and headed for the river. Estrella alone followed. "He doesn't fear me. He hates me. Would probably like nothing better than to see me dead."

Estrella stood by while I drank from waters cold enough to freeze soon. "Why do you think that is?"

I growled at her. No, not her. I was growling at the thoughts she had conjured up. She and Carlin were trying to take me back to someone I thought I'd left behind: a lone wolf at peace with his fate. In some ways, I preferred that version of myself. Yet in other ways, I was glad to see it gone. While the certainty of my status had brought an odd sense of peace, I couldn't deny it felt good to have others around.

Even if one of them was an annoying female who, despite her gift of gab, was helping me face a few things.

"Does it matter?" I said. "He's an alpha now. He has his pack. He doesn't care about me anymore."

"I thought you said he hates you. Which is it?"

I thought about pinning her. I knew it wouldn't work, assuming I even could. "Whichever lets me sleep better."

I walked past her, hoping to end the conversation. Estrella stayed with me, not bothering to drink. My insides again warred with themselves, trying to decide what they wanted most. I wanted to keep walking, ignore everything she was saying and doing. I wanted to sneak a nuzzle or a lick, as a thank you for the same thing. I wanted to think this was really happening. That somehow, I'd gained what I thought I'd never have. I wanted to believe that it would last.

I wanted to want it too. Except I had so many old wounds, the worst being Martol's eyes that night, I couldn't help wondering if I really did. I had grown to like my solitary life. I had all the amusement I needed watching the humans, and things were certainly simpler when I only had to worry about myself. Yet it had always come with a constant ache, like an itch I had no way to scratch. The memory of the void where my mother had been made it that much harder. After doing that to her, and after how I'd treated Estrella the first time, I had to wonder if I had a right to silence that "itch."

I looked at Estrella, walking beside me, absolutely refusing to leave my side. Feeling that certainty, that fire radiating from her soul, began to melt away the doubt. I still couldn't decide if I deserved it or not, but I was slowly warming to the idea of finding out.

I had almost decided on whether or not to thank her when Estrella stopped with her ears straight up. Without question, I knew she'd heard something, and I perked my ears the same way to try and catch it. I found heavy rustling nearby, too much for some random creature running through the leaves. Even if it were, it could lead to a kill.

When Estrella looked to me for permission, I answered by trotting toward the sound. She followed as we returned to the leaf mounds of before, mouths watering at the idea of a real kill. When we got there, we instead found other wolves digging in the same leaf pile we had picked clean. The majority of the commotion was the pups bettering their skills. I couldn't recognize the distant adults, except for one who stood watch like only one wolf could.

Lonate had heard us long before we'd seen the pack. As far as I could tell, he hadn't said anything, but when I saw Rajor among the leaves, I felt my hackles ruffle. His adult fur hadn't changed much. Aside from a small amount of gray touching his body like a thin layer of ash, mostly on his back and underside, his fur was entirely black.

"Go get Carlin," I said. "I'll handle the rest."

"Luna—"

"I'll be fine. Go."

Estrella snuck in a lick before dashing off toward my den. I watched her go for a minute, feeling her lick dig into my heart. *Guess she's not so bad after all.*

I tried to imagine what Toltan might have looked like in such a situation. More than his death stance, there was no doubt he'd have the same stone glare I now cast toward Rajor. From there, I put every hair on end, forcing my body to turn stiff, sharp, and unwavering. When I stepped forward, my movements were smooth and exact, more like flowing than walking. I wasn't just claiming my space, I was announcing myself. I didn't try to stay hidden, for the whole point was to be seen as strong, as proud...

As *owner*.

"What do you think you're doing?" I said.

Though Rajor looked up at me, he couldn't stop his ears from reevaluating his position. I held my ground, refusing to be scared from my territory.

"Well," Rajor said, "what have we here? Come to kill another pup, dear brother?"

I stared him down, not making a sound. I didn't have to, as a rise in my hackles was more than enough to catch the attention of the pack. The moment they noticed, they began gathering the pups at a safe distance.

With them out of the way, I rose my tail with a firm step forward. "This is my territory. You will leave."

Rajor chuckled, though his tail still hadn't risen. "Says who? You are but one wolf. I have a pack."

"Changes nothing. These grounds are mine to hunt in. You will find no prey here."

"And if I say that I will?"

I glanced back when I heard Estrella and Carlin arrive. I traded a quick rub with Estrella, while Carlin ducked his head. Far from surrender, Carlin was examining the situation with the experience gained from his scars. His nose worked hard, and his ears were fully perked, watching the pack. Or so I thought, until I realized he was focused entirely on Rajor.

"Is this the brother you've told me so much about?" Carlin said.

I returned my own focus to the wolf in question before replying. "Yes. This is Rajor."

"How did a whelp like that ever make alpha?"

Rajor growled for the first time as his fur started to rise. "Careful what you say, old fool. My patience has limits."

Funny, I told him the same thing a little while ago.

Carlin must have remembered too, because he looked at me before turning his ears back, almost laughing. I ignored it while matching Rajor's growl.

"As does mine," I said. "You will not hunt here. Take your pack and leave. Do not violate my territory again."

Rajor's tail finally found some height, just not all of it. "Speaking of violations, do your companions know about your sentence? What you did?"

"Yes, we do," Estrella said.

"And we don't care about lies," Carlin added.

Rajor's hackles started to rise at last. "The only lies are the ones he's apparently told you. He killed his own brother as a pup. For his crime, he was made a lone wolf. He is destined to live alone, to never know the company of another wolf. You risk—"

"Shut up, pup," Carlin said. "We're not listening. Now I suggest you heed Luna's command before you feel our fangs."

Rajor now cast a glare close to Toltan's death stance, if not as intimidating. "Do not underestimate me. My position is mine by virtue of my strength. I go where I wish. I hunt where I wish. No murderer will dictate what I can or cannot do."

I allowed an amused ruff with a sideways glance at Estrella. I couldn't leave that there. I just couldn't.

"This... murderer... has chosen what mate you *won't* have. Why couldn't he also say the same about your territory?"

Lonate tried to remind him he had pups, but Rajor never heard him. He charged at me, ears forward and blood on his fangs. I rushed to meet him, but though my jaws were open, I kept my growl low. Rajor was sprinting, whereas I held myself to a fast run, preserving my maximum speed, waiting for the moment to use it.

When Rajor went for the side of my neck, I used that extra burst to catch the bottom of his neck before he got close. I had him up and falling on his back before he knew what hit him. Rajor sank ankle deep in the leaves, and I held him there in my jaws. He snarled fury, but no amount of pawing or turning found freedom. I let my fangs cut into Rajor's neck. Fresh blood touched my lips as I let my jaws close his windpipe.

I *didn't* let myself end it.

My body shook with fury of my own, my growl shaking both of us. It built into a fire within that grew hotter with each additional note. *He was a bully to all of us. He lied to get me banished. He denied me the life I was born to. Now he violates my territory. Lone wolf or not, this is my right. I'm defending my territory from an intruder. I'm killing a rival to my pack.*

Rajor managed to whine through a gasp. Then, his tail tucked and his ears fell back in submission. The two of us froze as if time itself were holding its breath. I breathed my snarl into him, while my fangs sat embedded in his neck.

So easy...

So right...

So unable.

With a great sigh, I released my hold, allowing Rajor to cough as he regained his breath. My jaws closed, though nothing about my display had lessened. I stood over my brother, fur and tail high, and with a glare that could split the world in two daring him to try something. When Rajor looked at me again, our eyes met, and we both held our breath.

His eyes, they feared me. More than any wolf had ever feared me before. Rajor's body shook like a leaf in the wind. He shrank into himself, his posture taking on that of a wolf half his size. It was everything I had ever wanted, and I couldn't stand it.

"You will not hunt here," I said. "Leave. Let your pack retain their alpha. Let mine live free of you."

I left him there without so much as a growl. As Rajor finally rose, I turned an ear back just in case he tried to attack again. I only heard the rustle of the leaves, followed by the paws of the pack heading the other way. I thought I heard him exchange words with Lonate, but they were Rajor's problem. I didn't care anymore.

When I returned to my own pack, I found Carlin frozen, stunned by something he'd seen, but his gaze wasn't for me. He was looking past me, past Rajor even, to something farther on. I slowed for a moment, wondering what held his attention while trying to decide how to ask.

Estrella stepped forward before I could. "*That* would be why he hates you."

I turned my ears back, trying not to laugh. "You're not going to let me forget this, are you?"

"Nope, because Rajor won't. You just beat him in front of his pups. That means something."

"Might not be over yet either," Carlin said. He sounded more distant than normal, probably the remains of his trance.

I looked back, expecting to see Rajor at the head of the pack.

Instead, I found Toltan and Martol approaching, alone. Neither held themselves very high, and both showed tattered fur not quite cared for. Were it not for the thick state of their ribs, one might think them soul dead.

Martol's eyes found me first. They hadn't changed since the day I took Folar to the pack. They watched me, as did Toltan's, for something they expected me to say or do.

I couldn't do or say much of anything. Toltan, I wanted to drive away, bite a notch in his ear if I had to. Martol, I wanted... I didn't know what I wanted. I was trapped in that night I saw her die within. The memory took hold as I remembered wishing so hard to get another chance, only to have it turn to hate the next day. The emotions couldn't sort themselves out. By the time they got close, the best I could manage was a harsh glare.

"Can I help you with something?" I said.

Toltan's ears never came all the way up. Martol's didn't move at all. Toltan spoke for them both.

"We were with the pups when you came out. We saw everything."

I ruffed pained amusement. "Really? How ironic. Not like you haven't missed things before. No, that's wrong. You have. Now all of a sudden, you see everything? Oh, I'm touched. From the deepest parts of my heart."

"Luna. Don't be like that."

"Why not? You weren't there to teach me better. You gave me other lessons, and I intend to use them."

I turned to leave, ready to be done with them. I might regret it the next day, but right here, right now, I wanted nothing more to do with the conflict their presence was causing within me.

"Luna!" Toltan again. "We deserve more than that."

I stopped cold. Pain lasted but a moment before it was replaced by rage. I felt everything within me tense for a kill as my fur bristled another wolf's worth. *Deserve? He dares use that word?*

I whipped around and cast a glare that would put Toltan's death stance to shame. "You deserve more? What about me? Did I deserve to get driven out by my own father? Did I deserve to live out here alone, shunned by any pack I met? Did I deserve to lose everything I had because you failed to listen to me?"

Toltan gained some years in his eyes, and his fur started to rise as well. "Do you think it was easy?"

"Seemed easy enough to me."

"Do you know the pain I suffered that day?! I lost one pup and was forced to drive out another."

"You didn't have to drive me out. You took the word of a known bully."

"He swore in Wolfor's name."

"You never listened to a word I said."

"You never *said* a word!"

I almost killed him. I wouldn't have stopped this time. My insides were so tight, I could barely growl, much less speak.

"What do you mean I never said a word? You didn't bother to listen."

Toltan's fur fell hair by hair. His growl faded even faster. He breathed so hard, I thought he might hack his lungs out. While I waited for a reply, I heard Carlin lead Martol and Estrella away. There were words there, but my ears never heard them.

Toltan had lost all aggression by the time we were alone. "Yes, I did. I listened with all I had. I searched for anything, the smallest whimper I could use. Why do you think I told you to talk to me? Luna, I had no choice. The only words you said were ones of rage. It was that against a solemn swear by Rajor. Before the pack, I... I couldn't protect you. Not without endangering myself, my mate, and my remaining pups."

Now he's just making excuses. "Endangering them how? You and Martol were strong enough. As for the pups, Wolfor's law—"

"Is a lie!"

Time froze. No, that's too much movement. Everything stopped. Even my rage ended for half a heartbeat that lasted a thousand years. I stared at my father, hurt beyond feeling, confused beyond thought, unable to be or feel anything.

"It's a lie, Luna," Toltan said. "The pack knew that. Even Rajor knows that now."

When time resumed, so did my rage. It took much of my returning breath with its fire. "You banished me over a *lie*?!"

Toltan tried to be angry. He even started to slip into his death stance. He never got there.

"I banished you because a pup that kills fellow pups is a danger to the pack. That's what the law is for. To keep pups from killing each other. To keep you and Rajor from killing each other. But if an alpha loses his position, his pups become a threat to the new alpha. That alpha then has the right to decide the fate of those pups. It happened in my last pack, Luna. The new alpha refused to risk it. He killed the previous litter to make way for his own within the pack. I couldn't let the same happen to mine. If I hadn't acted, I could have lost the pack then and there. I had to make a choice."

Oh, that makes it so much better.

"You chose them over me. What gives you the right to sacrifice me in the name of others?"

"My blood. Your blood. The blood of all wolves. The blood of an alpha. I couldn't save you. I could save them."

"You declared me a pup killer."

"I never believed you were!"

I stood frozen, not a hair moving, not a sound made. For a moment, I was pretty sure my heart stopped. Toltan, meanwhile, continued to grow more shaky the more he spoke.

"Not once did I think you were guilty. But, Luna, the pack would have never accepted the instinct of a parent over what they'd seen. They saw you try to attack Rajor. They heard him swear you killed Calon. Our traditions forced me to shun one of my own pups... and I have never slept well since."

A tree grew in my throat. Its roots silenced any hint of a growl left waiting for the chance to come out. I could see the tears rolling from Toltan's eyes. With each word, he aged decades, while the void behind his eyes grew until it swallowed him whole.

I never knew. I never understood. Martol always said, as alpha, Toltan had to make hard choices. Now for the first time, I could see just how hard some of them were. To think... I didn't want to think. I didn't want to remember all the things I'd wished on my own father. It would only lead to a place of deep regret I didn't want to go to.

I had to fight that tree down before I could breathe again. It took even more to find words. "How did Rajor become alpha?"

Toltan's ears found a new low point. "I couldn't fight him anymore. I tried for a while, even managed to raise a second litter, but I didn't have the will. Not after seeing you bring a packless pup to... he's grown strong, you know. Folar, I mean. Even caught Jinta's eye. Too bad Rajor probably won't let them have pups."

The last of my rage ceased to be. Nothing had changed. Despite the bitterness, the anger, the betrayal, everything was as it had been the day we first touched noses in the darkness of the den. Seeing Toltan's pain, I couldn't deny it anymore. He was still my father. His blood was still mine.

"She'll find a way," I said. "She never did let obstacles stop her." When Toltan didn't so much as raise his head, I rubbed mine against his. I forced his head to rise before I spoke again. "Follow."

I turned and went after Estrella and the others. I found them just out of listening distance, all lounging in the dirt. All except for Carlin, who had been working with Martol's fur, despite a very disgruntled look from her. A pair of snaps didn't stop him from making her fur look a little less messy. *I'll have to thank him for that sometime.*

They all rose when they saw me approach. Three sets of ears turned to face me. When I looked back, I found Toltan's ears were the exception, frozen in a lowered position.

I allowed my ears to ease forward. *So easy now.*

"My den's not far from here. It's not much but... you're both welcome to join me."

Martol left her pain behind. The wolf that began rubbing and licking me to death was whimpering like a pup herself. The moment her fur touched me, my heart shattered in joy. After so long of dreaming, of wishing I could feel her love again, I now had it several times over. I was her pup again, embraced by her protective aura. Her scent bled into my soul, reminding me of all the love I'd longed for. I couldn't feel a thing because all I could feel was her.

While I liked the emotion, I couldn't stand the act. Mostly because I was too old for it. Further still, because somewhere deep, there was guilt over how I'd treated her before. It started turning her rubs painful, for with each one, I imagined how much *she* had longed for it. It took me back to that night when my first howl was one of pain. The ache, combined with feeling too old for this, became too much to bear, despite the warmth filling my skin.

I pushed her off with a gentle growl. "Enough. I'm not a pup anymore. I'd prefer to be treated like the adult I am now. Please?"

Martol panted a laugh with a forward tick of her ears. "Fair enough. Thank you, Luna. You don't know what this means to me."

"Actually, I think I do. Come on." I rubbed against Estrella, then stopped at Carlin. "What about you, old one? Think you could handle running with wolves half your age?"

Carlin feigned insult. "Half? Why, I'm old enough to be your parents' great-great-grandfather. The wisdom of those years—"

"Is as rickety as your tired old bones."

The others stifled laughs while Carlin looked positively furious. Anyone could tell it was fake, though, given that his hackles hadn't even ruffled.

"Well," he said, "I guess I'll have to run with you. Show you just how *not* tired my old bones are. Think you can handle that, pup?"

I flicked an ear, looked at him as if thinking, then perked my ears in challenge.

"I have a better question. Think you can beat me to my den?"

I took off before he could answer. Carlin yelled something about not being fair, but I didn't care. I enjoyed the chase too much. More importantly, I enjoyed the idea of having a pack of my own again, complete with my parents.

I enjoyed it so much, I failed to notice the snow falling moons ahead of the norm.

～ᴜᴜᴜ⌐

Chapter 8

MY FANGS WERE WET WITH DROOL, drops adding to the icy powder my paws had vanished in. A thin veil of falling snow covered the surrounding forest, making the trees seem not just bare of leaves, but void of life. Seemed like the forest as a whole was like that, for we'd found precious little in our hunts.

While the forest might have given up, my pack hadn't. My ears perked forward to confirm that our many days of hunting, tracking, and praying had indeed borne fruit. We'd found her at last. A doe. *The* doe. Big as a buck with an attitude to match. She was stripping bark off a tree without a care in the world, almost taunting us with her indifference. And why not? She'd fended us off twice already. Mostly because of terrain, but escape was still escape, regardless of the reason.

Not today. We had her this time.

I looked toward Martol and Toltan to give commands. Before I could say a word, or even move a muscle, they both turned their ears forward. They glided through the snow around the back side, just as I had been about to tell them. I ticked my ears forward in approval while waiting in cover. I gave them as much time as I felt I could to get into position. The doe stripped off more bark in silence, unaware of the wolves inching closer before the sprint.

That is, until the doe turned her ears toward me. *I must have hit something*, I thought. At the same time, from the back side of the tree, came a thin foal. It huddled under its mother, who continued to stare at me.

"She knows we're here," Carlin said.

I swallowed a growl with a forward tick of my ears. "She does. Doesn't change much. She's the first prey we've seen in days. We can't let her get away."

"You have a plan, Luna?" Estrella asked.

"Not yet."

I couldn't tell if the doe actually saw me, but she did seem to be looking right at me. *Maybe she doesn't know about the others.* The question became moot as I decided that, with my cover blown, I would risk blowing Martol and Toltan's as well.

I told Estrella and Carlin to stay silent, then lifted my head in a long howl. When the doe's eyes didn't move, that confirmed everything. *She can see me. Changes nothing. The plan moves forward.*

Two similar howls sounded from the other side, both from separate angles. Martol and Toltan were responding, announcing their positions. The doe allowed only a glance their way before returning to me. I turned an ear in much the same way, giving me what I needed. I knew exactly where the others were. Now I just had to hope they could make this happen.

"Stay here," I said. "When you see me attack, go for the foal. Try to separate it from the mother."

"What about her?" Estrella said.

"My parents and I will deal with her. Don't howl when I call."

I made a big show of trotting out from my position. The doe's eyes followed me with every step. I moved on a wide angle, keeping my distance while getting into position. When she was staring right at me without a turn of her head, I stopped. I lifted my head in a short, deep howl. Two more sounded from the side, one nearby, the other more on the other side of the doe.

When the doe glanced again, I charged.

I let her see the full force of my fangs. I let her hear my snarl. I didn't let my eyes drift to Estrella and Carlin sprinting from the side.

The doe reared up and slammed her hooves into the ground, sending enough snow flying to distort my view, which brought a halt to my charge. I dug into whatever ground I could find to turn the other way as the doe advanced and reared up again. I felt her hooves brush my tail as they shook the ground I ran on. *That was close!*

Cries from behind drew both her and my attention. Estrella and Carlin were driving the foal clean away, with Toltan coming from the woodwork to assist. The doe forgot me and charged after them, ducking her head as if she had antlers. She leapt into the air with such grace, I swore she could fly.

"Estrella! Your tail!" Martol called.

Martol had come tearing around the tree, sending snow flying in my face as I tried to follow. Estrella looked over in time to roll on her side, avoiding the blows that pounded the snow around her legs. *Thump-thump-thump.* They continued to search for her. Each pound spurred me faster to prevent crippling injury to my packmate.

Carlin snapped at one of the doe's legs while Toltan continued after the foal. The doe changed from Estrella to Carlin. The old wolf turned and ran the other way as best he could, but he never got any traction. His legs sank so deep in the snow, he was more leaping than running. The doe didn't bother to chase him. She instead turned, lifting on her forelegs, and kicked both hind legs after him. One missed, then the other slammed into Carlin's shoulder mid-leap. His yelp echoed off the trees as he collapsed in the snow, then tried to crawl, still whimpering.

Martol sliced through the snow as if it weren't there. Her fangs went for a leg but found only air. I tore in after her while Estrella shook her fur clean with a snarl of her own.

The doe pounded the ground in front of me and Martol, keeping us at bay. Then cries from nearby echoed for a moment before being cut short. Toltan had caught the foal. The pack knew it, as did the doe by the turn of her ears. Before anyone could land a bite, she turned and kicked at me and Martol, forcing us to duck low or lose an ear.

Instead of preparing for another strike, the doe planted her legs and leapt away. I gave chase for a second before I saw her bound into the distance.

I stood glaring with a pant shaking my ribs. "She's a demon, that one."

"Never seen anything like her," Martol said. She drew my attention to where Toltan was dragging the dead foal toward us. "Looks like we got something for it, though. That'll hold us for a while."

"Not a long one. You two dig in, I need to check on—"

"I'm perfectly fine, Luna," Carlin said.

So he said, but Carlin walked with his right foreleg tucked tight against his body. I didn't want to think how much damage had been done. Though with him moving strong despite the injury, I couldn't resist teasing him about it.

"So, you're wise enough to catch a fox, but you don't know enough to duck under a doe's kick?"

Carlin gave me a dirty look with a laugh hidden beneath. "The snow got in my eyes."

"Sure it did. Come on. Eat your fill, all of you. What we don't finish, we take with us to the den. I doubt we'll find anything left of him by morning."

"Assuming he lasts that long."

He lasted even less. Split between five starving wolves, a single foal didn't go very far. We picked him clean down to the bones. I tried to give them more, but they all refused to eat the last few parts. They stared at me until I cracked into the bone to get at what little marrow there was to be found.

Carlin never winced or whined until he set himself down just outside the den, and even that was a minor complaint. I stood there watching, trying to find something to say, something to feel, other than dread.

"I am wolf," Carlin said. I tilted my head at him, confused. "Something my father used to say during harsh times. 'Let the winds of winter come. I fear not famine, nor blizzard, nor a horde of predators. For I am wolf. My power is matched by the many that stand beside me. My blood runs through them, and theirs through me. So long as they live, so too will I. Come what may. I have faced it before, and it has yet to touch me.'"

I ruffed with a backward turn of my ears. "So says the wolf with a broken leg."

"I'm still alive. That's all that matters."

I turned my ears back again. *Crazy old wolf.*

I turned to find Estrella, only to walk into a small branch Toltan had tossed aside. It landed on my head and somehow stayed put without so much as a wobble.

That's when Estrella found me.

"Look!" she said. "It's a wolf-moose!"

Martol didn't miss a beat following it up. "A wolf-moose? Should we eat it, or take it into our pack?"

They all glanced at each other, then said at once, "Eat it!"

Martol, Toltan, and Estrella all began chasing me around, half growling, half yipping. I ran away from them, begging them to spare me. I tried to convince them I had a mate and twin calves back home. It didn't work, probably because my ears were too well perked.

I tried to call out for my herd, but I never managed more than rolling growls or deep barks. The pack must have been tired, though, because they never got a hold of my leg. Not to say they didn't try. I had to dance over several bites that would make me their next meal for sure. I managed to stay ahead of them, and we bounded and yipped around the den several times while Carlin lay on his side, laughing his lungs out.

My own legs didn't last long, for they'd spent too much on the hunt. I had to withdraw and let my legs stop burning. Toltan and Martol shifted to Estrella, while I lay beside Carlin, panting fresh exhaustion. Carlin kept laughing until he ran out of breath. He panted for a while, slowly catching his breath, before turning toward me.

"You sure know how to make an old wolf happy," he said. "It's been a long time since I've seen a pack like yours. You've got it all. A close bond, loving members, a good location, and a fine young wolf leading them."

My ears fell as much in pain as to disagree. I saw some of it. I couldn't deny the bond, the members were there too, even the good location. But that last part? The "fine young wolf"? That I didn't see. Every time I looked, I saw an injured pup, still too proud to admit it. Not to mention far too naive to be leading anyone in anything.

"I'm not that good of a leader," I said. "You got injured in the last hunt."

"I got careless. It happens when you get to be my age. But you, you acted well. You went for the smart target, you directed a smart hunt, and you didn't make me feel bad for my error. You have a lot of potential, Luna. You just need to let yourself see it."

"Potential," I echoed. "Potential to lead wolves to insanity, maybe."

Carlin gave another huff I didn't understand. "Is that so bad? Look at them. We're in the middle of the leanest winter I can remember, and they're playing like newborn pups. If that's your fault, then I thank you for it. Look, Luna, who or what we are doesn't define our lives. It's what we do with those lives, the effect we leave on the world and those around us, that matters. Even a lone wolf can do good things."

"Don't you mean *great* things?"

"Anyone can do great things. It takes someone special to do *good* things."

He was getting annoying, yet I couldn't help feeling encouraged by his words. *A lone wolf can do good things.* Crazy? Maybe, but then, I had a pack of wolves who were playing in the middle of a harsh winter. If I could manage that, maybe I could manage more. Assuming, that is, we survived long enough to try.

"Hard to imagine me doing much when my pack is still starving," I said.

Carlin sighed with a backward turn of his ears. "Don't make me pin you, pup. The wilds will bring what they will. Your job is to face them with fur and fang and pride. The rest is up to Wolfor. Seems to me he likes you. Stay close to his fur. You'll meet your potential."

"If you say so."

"He's brought you this far. Doesn't he deserve the chance to take you farther?"

My ears flashed back equal parts anger and pain. *There's that word again.* Martol, Estrella, Toltan, they were all using it. Every time they did, it hurt, as if one word brought up all the years of pain, as well as the mistakes I'd made. I didn't like how often I'd heard it, more so because it always took me back to my first night alone and all the grief I'd felt that day.

Carlin's ears fell as well, as did his head for the first time ever. "I'm sorry, Luna. I didn't mean to—"

I rubbed my muzzle over Carlin's to silence him. "It's all right. Just seems like everyone is telling me what others deserve from me. I thank you. I still think you're a crazy old wolf, but thank you. For everything you've done."

Carlin only ruffed amusement and bit an itch.

The others joined us, all panting hard, but still panting the joy of the game. When I stood to meet Estrella, our eyes met, and we froze.

There was something there, something I couldn't name. There was tension in my ribs, a warmth in my heart, and a massive pinecone in my throat. I couldn't keep my ears up, and neither could she. We each tried to lick the other's nose, but it did nothing to break our hesitation. I swallowed hard, as much to be sure I could move as to try and clear that pinecone.

Martol gave a growl behind Estrella. "Oh, for goodness' sake." She pushed Estrella into me, her head landing on my shoulder. "Get snuggling already. The tension is driving me crazy."

My ears remained back, uneasy, terrified even. But I did as my mother asked and rubbed my head against Estrella's. She returned the affection, and it got deeper and deeper. All of a sudden, winter seemed to melt away. The nerves faded, and I closed my eyes so I could just feel her fur against mine. I felt her spirit, and her confidence, radiate all the way inside my soul. For a moment, she was all I was aware of. The forest, the pack, even my own fur had fallen away. There was only her and me. We never said a word because we didn't need to. Our scents had merged into one, as had our hearts. I had found my mate.

"Much better," Martol said.

My ears flicked forward, more amusement than agreement. I broke away from Estrella to find Martol and Toltan lying beside Carlin, trading playful nips like they used to when I was a pup. Carlin had his head on his paws just looking at me, not saying a word.

I suppose he doesn't need to, or maybe he's being kind for once. Whatever the reason, I didn't care. I settled in beside my mate, offering more nuzzles and licks of my own.

Crazy? Absolutely.

Chapter 9

THE LONGER THE FAMINE LASTED, the more my stomach churned. More because it was empty, or because of the state of my pack, I couldn't say.

I could count our ribs just by looking at them, which only made it harder to miss the roughness of our fur. Worse than that, every day I returned from a failed hunt, my eyes found Carlin. He saw we had nothing, and he couldn't hide his cringe. He also couldn't hide just how dim his eyes were. As for his leg, I kept telling myself it was still healing from his injury.

Toltan wasn't much better. Thin fur, thinner ribs, and not much light left in his eyes either. He'd tried and failed to move every day, and it worried me more than Carlin's injury. Add a near constant blizzard, and I spent the nights in terror of what I'd find the next morning.

When the storm finally broke, Martol, Estrella and I set out to hunt. I vowed we'd find something, anything, to keep them going. That vow got hollower by the minute, as the snow came up to my knees. The only scents I found were those of my pack. The trees were so bare and laden with snow, one had fallen under the weight, right where I'd pinned Rajor not that long ago.

I pressed on, using the memory of that day to keep me going. I ignored the pain in my belly, as well as the cold biting through my fur. *We can't give up. We can save them. We just need a little more time.*

A soft snap sent my ears up. I followed them to the source, and desperation forced me to ignore my better judgment when I saw her. Not as proud, not as well fed, but there she was. The demon doe. Her legs shook under her as much as mine did. Her sides heaved as if she'd been fighting all day. For all I knew, she had, not that I cared. She was my father's last prayer.

"Cut her off," I said. "Don't let her run this time. Do whatever it takes."

Estrella and Martol snuck behind her, drooling as much as I was, while I stood directly in front of her. The doe stared me down, anger burning behind her eyes. Anger at taking her young, anger at being a wolf, or perhaps just a promise not to go down without a fight. I tried to match it, but I spent more time keeping my emotions under control. I knew I'd never get in, so I waited for the others to make their move.

Estrella and Martol charged as one, hunger forcing growls deep in their chests. The doe looked back, leaned on her forelegs, and kicked back with all she had left. The first strike missed, Martol ducked under a second, then a third caught her in the side of her head. She crumpled in the snow without a sound, knocked out cold.

Estrella never stopped moving. The doe's kicks had all been for Martol, which allowed my mate to catch one of those legs before they could change targets. Estrella cracked bone with her first bite, then she held and pushed into the other leg. The doe tried to cry out, but she fell hard on her side, knocking the wind out of her.

My jaws were on her neck before she could regain her footing. I found her windpipe and blood vessels, and I tore into both, crimson blood staining the white snow. I kept digging, hunger and the need to save my pack ensuring she didn't escape again. The doe pawed at me, but her own hunger, and Estrella's work, kept it to just a last defiant act, before her eyes closed at last.

I panted over our kill, glancing at my mate to see her doing the same.

"Have a little faith," Estrella said.

Amusement colored both of our ears. The pain vanished, and in an odd way, I wasn't even hungry anymore.

Estrella turned to wake up Martol while I tore a chunk from the doe's side. I sprinted toward the den, feeling like a pup again. *This will do it. This'll bring life back into Carlin's eyes, and get some fluff in Toltan's fur. There will be more, enough for all of us. Maybe enough to survive the winter. We just need to make sure no one else finds...*

I paused when I saw two figures in the snow. I kept my ears up and my nose working as I approached, unsure if they were friend or foe. That is, until I saw Carlin's brown-tipped ears and realized it was Toltan lying next to him. *Stubborn old wolf. Couldn't let me go on the hunt without him.*

I trotted forward, carrying their dinner with pride. I dropped it between them, waiting for a tease that really meant pride or compliment. Except they didn't move. It was only then I noticed the layer of snow on their fur... on *all* of their fur. That never happens. No matter how carefully you move, a great deal gets dislodged.

"Hey," I said. "Wake up, you two. You won't believe this: we got her! We killed that demon doe. She... she..."

Rational thought found me, as did other thoughts I refused to allow or accept. *No, no, not now, not when I'm able to save them.* I tapped Carlin's nose and found it ice cold. As was Toltan's. I bit them, tugged at their scruff, bit so hard I broke the skin. Blood never came from either one.

"Come on. Come on. She's just over here. She's not far. Just a little... just a little more. Not far. Not... not... not..."

I lifted my head and howled. I howled until my lungs were empty. I filled them and howled again. Tears poured down my muzzle as I couldn't find the will to howl anymore. I could only stare, could only cry, could only lie, however badly. I couldn't face the two dead wolves I knew so well.

Footsteps sounded behind me. When I turned back, I found Estrella... alone... walking slow, with a limp tail and low head.

My eyes bulged. I couldn't breathe. I couldn't feel. I couldn't... couldn't...

"No."

Estrella's ears fell. Fresh tears trickled down her face when she saw Carlin and Toltan.

"She never felt it."

I stopped breathing. It hurt so much, I couldn't feel anything. I fell into the snow, unable to stand. I tried to howl, but I never even got my head up. The only sound I made was a raspy, barely audible whine. Tears would soon freeze on my fur as I closed my eyes, trying to turn back time. Trying to tell myself I hadn't lost them. The father I hated, the old fool that annoyed me, the mother I... I...

Warm fur brushed against my head. I lied again, even though I knew who it really was.

"I'm sorry, Luna," Estrella said. "But there's nothing we can do. You need to come."

"Where?" I sobbed. "To an empty den? To a place where just days ago, we were pups? How can I go back when their scent is waiting for me? When all I have... all I had, is here?"

"Because I'm here too. I'm not going anywhere, Luna. We have a kill now. We... We have to use it. Luna. Please. They deser..." She cringed and sobbed while I glared through my tears. I knew what word she'd swallowed, and it had me shaking in renewed grief. I once again was taken back to that first night, and it shattered my insides. All I could see was the void behind my mother's eyes. A void I had caused. The pain of that memory kept me from yelling at Estrella, which allowed her to recover enough to use the full attention I now gave her. "We can't let ourselves join them. I still need you. Please. Luna, please. Eat. Survive. I couldn't live without you. Especially now."

The tears flowed anew. It was over. I only had her now. Raw facts told me I had to move before I became another mourned wolf. While I might not have cared about myself, Estrella had suffered enough. I couldn't let myself add to it.

I forced myself to stand, my legs shaking as if they might shatter. Estrella waited for me to follow. No pushing, no words, just a gentle, watchful gaze, asking me to join her. Except I couldn't. Not yet. I had something else to do first.

I rubbed against my father one last time. I tried to ignore the chill of his body, instead trying to remember the first time we had touched noses. I hadn't been able to see him then, but I'd known at once who he was. If only we'd had more time. We might have returned to the father-pup duo in the den. Toltan might have grown proud of me. Now, I would never know... and neither would my father.

"I forgave you," I said. "I hope you knew that."

A breeze ruffled my fur as I joined my mate. I told myself it was something it couldn't possibly be. It made it easier to believe that despite all I'd lost, I still had a reason to fight on.

I rarely worried much about silence, mostly because, being a wolf, my presence had a tendency to cause it. But when one wakes up to it for several days straight, in the middle of an early spring, when howls celebrating birth should be ringing from every tree, silence becomes concerning.

At least the view was better than it had been. Despite winter usually having another moon to go, the trees had sprung to life, though still far from full foliage. Not that one could tell by listening to the birds. Many had arrived with the early spring and were announcing their arrival just as loudly as if the trees were in full bloom. Crisp beams of light filtered through what leaves were there, as if Wolfor was trying hard to melt the pockets of snow that refused to go away. Or maybe he just wanted to brighten the mood.

He didn't need to, at least not for me. Estrella lay beside me outside the den, still fast asleep. With the return of good hunting, her fur, much like mine, was full and smooth, without a rib to be found. I couldn't remember when she became enough to keep me going, nor did I care to find out. I only know that, because of her, I was still here.

Losing the pack had hit me hard, and continued to do so for some time after. But Estrella, my other half, had refused to let me stay in that state of sorrow. She kept me going when I was certain that demon doe would be our last meal. She let me cry when I needed to, yet never let me sulk alone, or for too long. As the hunting improved, she wouldn't let me see anything but the positive, and somewhere along the way, I learned how to do it without her help.

"Sunshine, all behind, prey, prey, it's time to find."

Now if we could just do something about that bird, life would be perfect.

And yet, I found myself laughing at him as Estrella awoke and stretched. I couldn't seem to get rid of that darn mockingbird. All the times I'd snapped at him, after everything that had happened so far, that one little bird was still there, perched atop the rock pile, singing at me. *Must have taken stubbornness lessons from Carlin.*

Estrella yawned, then nuzzled me with a soft whine of affection. "Good morning, thorn. Care to share the joke?"

"Luna, Luna, got himself a mate," the bird sang. "Luna, Luna, Rajor must really hate."

Estrella stared at him, looking almost disgusted. "Did you freeze your brain during the winter?"

"He's always been like that," I said.

"Frozen brain! Frozen brain! Frozen brain, I am!"

He glided over us, though never low enough to have a chance of catching him. Estrella tried anyway. She snapped at the air just under him, but the bird didn't even fly higher. He chirped at us as he vanished into the trees, joined by a female mockingbird that was rasping at him.

"Looks like you're not the only one that found a mate," Estrella said, fighting a laugh.

"Let's hope that's not her," I said. "Seems she doesn't care for his antics."

"Didn't stop you. Why would it stop him?"

I nipped at her, and she nipped back. Back and forth we went until we were laughing too much to close our mouths. I stood and intentionally bumped into her before walking toward the river for a drink. She, of course, countered with a gentle nip on my tail before following.

The once gentle flow, fed by the heavy snows of winter, had become twice as wide, and more powerful. The quiet rumble of moving water was like a gentle thunder now, at one point carrying an entire branch downstream. Luckily, that same strength had caused a flood at some point. It had created a small, calm lagoon, perhaps as big as our den, but only as deep as the hock on my leg. I waded in to see what fish I could catch, then settled for the drink I'd originally come for when I found nothing.

Then it hit again. A stray thought turned into a memory. Today it was Toltan giving swimming lessons. *"Keep your paws moving as if you're walking up a hill that keeps running away from you."* His voice echoed in my mind, and my ears fell. I stared at myself in the water, picking apart the wolf that stared back. Someone once said I had Toltan's ears and tail, though I could never see it. The silver sheen in my hackles, yes, especially when the sun or moon caught as it did now, but Toltan? He was never there. Not that it stopped me from looking.

"Luna?" Estrella said. Gentle as ever, yet worried too. "Are you here?"

My ears flicked up, then I snorted into the water, rippling my reflection away. "I'm here. I'm sorry."

"Don't. Don't apologize for feeling. I miss them too."

I cringed again, but only for a moment. "I can still feel him. His nose touching mine before I could see. Then I remember the last time I touched his, and I..."

Estrella thumped her head into mine. While the force made me adjust my balance, the rub warmed the rest of me, pushing the pain into the back of my mind. I returned the rub with equal warmth and affection as thanks.

"He'll always be there," she said. "Like he said, his blood is yours. The blood of an alpha. He lives in you and those that will follow. As does Martol."

"What about Carlin?"

I cursed myself the moment I said it. It was an uncalled for, snide comment neither she nor Carlin deserved. *I thought I left those behind.*

Estrella didn't seem to notice. "He left his mark too. That moment of pup play we just had would have made him proud, or knocked him on his side in laughter."

I panted a laugh myself. *Knowing him, he'd manage both.* "It's nice to know it's still there. The pup side, I mean. I thought I'd lost it when... well, you know."

"I know. Losing them wasn't easy for me either. But I was more worried about you."

"Afraid I'd become a permanent thorn-in-the-paw?"

Estrella's ears ticked forward with an amused ruff of her own. "Something like that."

In the moment, I hatched a plan. I had to work hard not to go down on my front paws. If I did, it would spoil the fun for both of us.

Though I would get to have fun first. "Well, I could always go back there, you know. Seemed like a nice place to be."

She fell for it.

"I won't allow it! You're my mate now. I can't have you getting all stuffy just because you liked it."

I held my act to the point of showing a fringe of challenge in my ears. "I see. So you control me, do you?"

Estrella matched my stance exactly. "In that regard, yes."

I ticked my ears forward, walked calmly behind her, waiting until I was a few steps away.

"Well, tough luck. You want to prevent it..." Only then did I drop on my front paws with a joyful pant. "You'll have to catch me first."

I tore into the forest as if sprinting after a kill, my tongue flapping with my stride while Estrella yelled after me. She sounded angry, but she couldn't hide the play in her voice.

"Get back here, you! I'm not finished!"

Perfection!

I wasn't done yet either. I leapt over fallen logs, broke through bushes, and sent a family of rabbits scattering like roaches. I'd have been laughing if I wasn't panting so hard. I made a wide angle turn back the other way, with Estrella still chasing after me. I wasn't sure how yet, but I had to get Estrella on her side in that lagoon. She'd probably light the water on fire, but I knew she'd be laughing about it as much as I would.

Except I never got there. A glint of light, too strong for snow, drew my attention. I stopped and looked at an odd rock that appeared smooth, much like the human's monster, yet this one wasn't much bigger than I was. It was a rectangular boulder just sitting there, with each side being flat like a slab of stone the river had worn down, and it seemed to have holes in almost every side.

I had forgotten Estrella until I yipped surprise when she tackled me. She bit at the back of my neck and shoulders, though her growl was purely playful.

"Tell me you won't go back," she said. "Tell me you'll never become a thorn."

I hated to do it, but I had to give her a real growl to make her understand I wasn't playing anymore. Her ears ticked back in apology, though her eyes searched for a reason.

"What did I do?" she said.

"Nothing," I said. "It's this."

I tossed my head at the rock, still looking it over. The holes in the sides were oddly clean, crisp, and uniform. It was definitely the same stone the humans used, though why they'd left it there was the more pressing question. They had a tendency to leave things behind, but not like this.

Estrella walked up to it, nose hard at work. I followed close behind doing the same, finding only what I expected: sweet, tang, musk, and that sharp, crispy smell their stone things seemed to have. Normal human scents, if there is such a thing.

"They were here, all right," I said. "Not that long ago by the smell of it. But I've never seen anything like this before."

"Could it be one of their dens?" Estrella said.

"Too small. Barely enough room inside for one, and they never sleep in stone like this. It's always that thin fur stuff."

"So what is... well, hello."

She was standing by the only open side to the rock. When I joined her, I found the inside was hollow, as I'd expected. What I didn't expect was the freshly killed rabbit stashed inside at the back.

"Now they're bringing their own caching places?" I said. "Can't these humans find anything themselves?"

"Apparently not," Estrella said. "Still, nice opportunity for us. After chasing you, I could do with a snack."

I sniffed at the rock again, then tapped it with a paw. It seemed solid enough, with little to no risk of collapsing on her. Not that it would be a problem if it did, being as thin as it was. Still, something about it didn't feel right. Humans didn't leave perfectly intact kills just laying around. Something else was at work here.

"Let's find our own," I said. "I don't trust anything human."

Estrella ruffed with a roll of her eyes. "Oh, don't be such a pessimist. It's not a thunder stick, and there aren't any humans around. I see no reason we can't take what's there."

"Nothing human is ever good for us. Leave it. We'll find our own." I turned to leave, and Estrella followed, though hesitantly. I grew worried when she stopped after only a few steps. Panic followed when she turned and headed inside for the rabbit.

"Estrella! Don't! You don't know—"

A snap and a clank followed as the open side suddenly closed behind her. She tried to break through, but the rock just clanged with each attempt. She tried each side, finding no give in any of the walls.

"You were saying?" I said.

Estrella growled from within. "Save the lecture for later. Try to push from the outside."

I pushed hard on all sides, including the one that had closed, but nothing moved. I tried my fangs, but the rock never even chipped, much less broke. Panic set in again as I banged myself against the sides, hoping I could do what she couldn't. I could feel the bruises already forming as I pounded into the sides of the large rock, but all that did was cause loud clangs to echo off the trees.

"It's no use," I said. "We can't get through, but there's got to be a way. We can't... I can't..."

"Luna!" Estrella barked. "Take a deep breath. Calm yourself. I'm not hurt, so I believe we're okay for the moment."

Barks sounded from the distance. Human barks. On top of their usual crashing, they were making a lot of noise as they approached from what sounded like a great distance. *I thought they were terrible hunters before.*

"Any other statements you'd like to be wrong about?" I said.

Estrella growled again, but I could see through the holes. She was breathing as hard as I was.

We both tried again, and again, to no avail. We pulled, pushed, bit, clawed, even tried to kick like that doe had. All we did was make the rock make a lot of noise. As the humans got closer, I found it harder and harder to breathe. I knew they'd be here soon, rounding a tree any moment now. I had to get Estrella out of there. There had to be a way. There had to!

"Luna. Look at me," Estrella said.

Her voice was so calm, so pleading, she was like Martol trying to calm me when I was scared, except there was a darkness to it. One that froze my body cold in fear. I found holes through which I could see her face, finding her staring straight at me, ears shifting. *Please, Wolfor, no.*

"You have to go," Estrella said. "Get out of here before they find you."

She'd barely finished her sentence before I snapped at her. "Not a chance! I lost my pack in the winter. I won't lose you too."

"There's nothing you can do for me. This is my time."

Breathing became harder by the second as my chest filled with pinecones. It didn't help that I could see tears welling in her eyes.

"I won't leave you," I said. "You're my mate. I can't live without you."

"Yes, you can!" she growled. "You have to. Dead or alive, I have to know you're out here living."

"I won't be alive. I won't have any reason to fight."

"You will because I say you will. Promise me, Luna. Promise me you won't die. That you will continue to hunt in this forest until you no longer can. Say the words. Swear it. In Wolfor's name, *swear it!*"

Hard to do when I can't catch a full breath. For a moment, I couldn't breathe at all. Tears fell like rain from both of us. The holes were so small, I couldn't touch her, but her eyes. They found me. They were pleading, asking, demanding one last act of love.

I heard the humans again. *Very soon now.* I found what I could of Estrella through the holes. Pain or not, I knew if I stayed, I'd die. If I left, I'd die within, but maybe then Estrella would face her end in peace. I couldn't deny her that. Not after everything she'd done for me.

I fought through the sobs, scrounging enough breath to speak.

"I promise. In... in Wolfor's name I... I swear... I will survive. I will live."

Estrella pushed her muzzle against the rock. Her nose squeezed through a hole, and I managed to touch my nose to hers. I stayed there, absorbing every drop of scent, every ounce of her soul, until she pulled away. It felt like a lifetime suddenly stolen.

"Now," she said, "get out of here. Don't make me watch you get killed. Don't you dare let Rajor beat you either. Not ever."

I could only turn my ears forward.

Rustling from nearby announced the human's arrival. *Out of time... forever out of time.* I allowed one last look inside at my mate before running off. I ran back to my rock pile, now so much emptier than before.

All of it, everything I'd gained, I had lost it all. My parents, Carlin, and now Estrella. I had nothing left, not even my rage. Just when it seemed I'd escape my fate, the humans took what little I had left, and I could do nothing about it. Nothing except one last gift for Estrella.

I lifted my head and howled, deep, long, and mourning. I was mourning a death not yet come, while saying goodbye to the last of my heart.

~∽⌇∿◡

Chapter 10

THE DEN FELT LIKE A MOUNTAIN NOW. Moons ago, it was home to a pack, even if we couldn't all fit. Then it held only two, with the love of hundreds between us. Now it was an empty cavern that still wasn't big enough for me to lose myself in.

Her scent was still there. Some of Estrella's fur clung to cracks in the wall. I'd even found a bit of a claw in the corner. *So that's where it went.* Estrella had bitten at her paw so long and hard, I worried she'd bite it raw. Then all at once, her head had snapped up, almost hitting the wall. She had ruffed victory, then gone searching for whatever had gone flying. With the pack's deaths still fresh at the time, I hadn't had the heart to ask what had been wrong. I now wished I had. At least then I'd know, and knowing might help me hold onto her a little longer.

A pained sigh escaped as it hit. I'd never know now. I'd never know a lot of things. How she'd be as a mother, how we'd fair throughout the years, how many times she and I would have to remind Rajor who was the better wolf.

How many years we'd have with each other.

My pain chased me out of the den. I had to get out of her scent, to get away from all the reminders waiting for me with each breath. Except she was outside too. Estrella had marked our territory just as I had. Her scent was everywhere, still pricking at my heart. I tried to escape her by the river, but there I found the memory of our first hunt together. Somehow, Estrella had known that moose would swim across. Luck? Skill? I never cared to ask. Now I would never know that either.

"Calm day of warm air, calm day free of care."

Only a bird would think of such things.

I didn't bother yelling at him. I didn't even turn an ear. I just flopped my head onto my paws and stared at the river. It still raged hard enough that I didn't think it wise to risk swimming. *Bet Rajor would.* I could just imagine him, jumping in with all his pride, declaring he had the strength. Then he'd slip below the surface, too fast for Lonate to catch this time, never to be seen again. It was the only thought I had that didn't hurt.

"Luna wolf is strong and proud, needs to eat or mate be loud."

"I doubt that very much."

The bird fluttered to a low branch, too high to catch as usual, but still in plain view. "Have heard her, have heard her, she has——"

"She has nothing now!"

I turned and glared at the bird. Were it easier to breathe, I would have put Toltan's death stance to shame. I wanted to be alone. I wanted to grieve, to be anywhere but here, where she still remained. I wanted... I wanted it to stop hurting.

At least it had a use. As the pain built, much of it turned to anger, which shook me clear to my claws. It would turn back to pain soon enough, but in the moment, it gave me the breath to try and acquire some peace.

"She's gone," I said. "Even you have to understand what that means. She's not here. She never will be again."

The bird did not stay silent, but his song was so somber, it was oddly soothing. "Luna mate also strong, Luna mate won't stay gone."

Just as fast as it had come, the anger left, leaving a hole the pain filled three times over. It filled my every hair, as if I were being eaten from the inside out. My ears fell as I cringed so tight, my head went numb. With the last of my will, I fought past it, hoping, begging, praying I could find a way to end the moment.

"Please. Leave me be. I can't stand the sight of anything right now."

The bird chirped one single beat, then turned and fluttered off into the trees. While I had no idea what it meant, a second of relief washed over me as, at last, I was alone.

But then, that was also the problem. So recently there had been a pack around me. My blood beside me in my parents, wisdom in Carlin, the future in Estrella, I'd had everything. Now I had nothing except pain so sharp, I thought about slipping into the river myself. It would be so easy. I'd let it take me like it took Calon. Like it tried to take Rajor when we were learning to swim. Were it not for Estrella, the promise she'd forced me to make, I absolutely would have.

A rumble in my stomach silenced all such thoughts. I needed to fill it, my cache was empty, and I'd made a promise. No matter how much it hurt, I couldn't break it. *She'd never forgive me if I did.*

But Estrella was there too.

While tracking a target along our favorite hunting trails, I would find her scent still lingering on a tree or shrub. I'd get lost in the memory of that particular hunt and would end up losing the current trail. Every time I tried to find it again, she was still there. A marking she'd left, or a tuft of fur, or the bones of an old kill, was enough to send the pain coursing through me. Worse was when I remembered her making that kill. Her movements were so crisp and precise, her jaws so strong, she'd only needed one bite. Then her approval, as I'd done my part to give her the chance to land that bite.

I turned away and pressed on. There had to be a trail I could find without her to get in the way. I tried going off our usual paths in the hopes I might get away from her.

In no time at all, I found the scent of fresh blood, mixed with pus to suggest a recently infected injury. Better still, this was deer. Likely an adult, by the size of the hoof-prints. A pack could feast on one. As a loner, it would feed me for days, assuming I could take it down.

The injury will solve that problem, I told myself, and I pressed on. A trot formed as the hunter within woke to enjoy the thrill. I'd get fresh meat at last, and it generated more energy than I'd felt in days.

It grew when I found my prize. There he stood, one male deer, younger than expected though still plenty big, and bearing a fresh wound on his hips. It didn't appear deep, but I could see and smell the signs of infection. It would probably kill him in a few days, but I couldn't wait that long.

Best of all, the buck hadn't seen me. He was too focused on forcing leaves down his throat, which was a struggle one could see with every swallow. *The infection must be further along than it looks. All the better.* I approached slow and quiet. I wouldn't need to do much to land this kill. A simple ear flick would be enough. Estrella and I had done this too many times for us to need words. She would get him startled, get him running, then this time, I'd be the one to...

I cringed so hard I thought I might slip into myself like a turtle. There was no Estrella, not anymore. The humans had taken her, just as the forest had taken my pack. She wouldn't be helping me, or even watching. The kill was mine to make, alone.

Stealth would get me in position, but to make the kill, I had to be quick. Except I couldn't even prepare that much. Preparing meant thinking, which meant remembering, which meant she'd be there again, which meant more pain. I couldn't risk it. I needed to take the moment while I had my emotions under control. I leapt into a sprint, intent on getting my jaws on a leg, a neck, or the hindquarters. Any one would lead to a bite that would lead to a kill.

The buck's ears shot up toward me. I didn't care. If anything, it was a good thing, for the deer tried to sprint away, putting a great deal of strain on his already wounded hip joints. While he attained a fair amount of speed, it was nothing like normal, making it easy for me to keep up. The times he tried to evade me were almost comical, as they were too slow or shallow to matter. *Estrella and I could take him in our sleep.* I thought about letting her have this one. She always enjoyed getting the kills on prey I chased. She'd love to tease me about being the one to reach up and catch such an easy...

I cringed as the pain hit again, reminding me that she wasn't there. Then real pain hit as my paw caught on something, drawing a yip of surprise as the sprint became a thump into the ground. My legs kicked out to stop me, but they only caused me to bounce instead. My side hit next, drawing one last yip as the hit emptied my lungs. My legs flopped over, continuing the momentum from the sprint, forcing my body to continue rolling. Again, I tried to find footing, and again, I failed to do more than keep me rolling. Another hard thump nearly knocked me out, after which my body went limp as it rolled and tumbled through dirty snow topped with dead leaves.

At last, I hit the ground without another bounce. My legs rolled over, then they stopped partway as I slid to a stop amid bits of tree and brush. My paws dropped to the ground, leaving me on my side, lying in damp ground bordering on mush, fur covered in wet forest debris, mud dimming the gray of my coat, my paw still stinging from whatever it had hit, and my body aching from the tumble. None of it compared to the void, both within and without. Pride held no meaning anymore, for without anyone to share it with, it had no place in my life.

I lay there in my pain, physical and emotional, for I don't know how long. Half a day? Several days? I didn't bother counting. I needed a warm rub, a wet nose, even a sharp fang to set me straight. I needed *her*. I needed Estrella's unending optimism, to feel her fur against mine. I needed to hear her growl, taste her breath, see the quiet swagger born in her bones. Yet even as she was everywhere, I knew she was nowhere. By now she was probably dead and rotting. No tail, no fur, just her skinless corpse left for the scavengers. She deserved better. *I* should have done better. Now I was paying for it.

I barely moved until my stomach cut through and reminded me, I *had* to eat. I didn't want to bother, but my heart wouldn't accept that. I'd made a promise that refused to let me go, no matter how much it hurt.

At some point, I collected myself onto my paws again. Things still throbbed, but I now knew there was no lasting damage. Though when I looked where the deer had gone, my heart sank. *There's no way.* I'd never catch something like that. Not when Estrella was everywhere to get in my way. Thus, I turned to find smaller, easier prey. While far less satisfying, considering I didn't care enough to clean my fur, it seemed like I didn't have much to lose.

Of course, I found her there too. I ended up at the same pile of leaves I'd seen before. The same one where I'd regained my parents. Except they were gone, and she wasn't. She stood there, waiting for me to dig in beside her. I could see her, even though I knew she wasn't there, which sent my heart into an all new quandary of pain. I couldn't feel, I couldn't hurt, I couldn't even cringe. I just wanted to fall and die.

A rumble from my stomach reminded me, yet again, I'd promised her. I swore I'd survive. It didn't matter that she couldn't enforce it. It hung over me as if Wolfor himself were glaring at me, borrowing Toltan's death stance to drive it home. I promised I would live. I had to eat to live. Therefore, somehow, I had to find a meal

Where I found the will to... forget it. I found it and kept my promise, despite the death it caused within.

～～～

Another day of small prey, just like all the others. It had become one of the many torments I now endured. First was the sensation of never being truly full. Then when I went home to my den, I was denied peace because, though I'd lost her a moon ago, Estrella was still there. My mind said her warmth remained, even though I could never feel it. The memories hadn't faded either, making it that much harder. Yet the promise I'd made held its own strength. Between the infernal bird, and my body reminding me of its needs, my bond kept me going.

Well, I've eaten what I can catch for the day, I told myself. *My body has what it needs. The rest of me...* I tried to tell myself it didn't matter, that I didn't care about the dirt still clinging to my fur. Not like I had much reason to clean it. With Estrella always getting in the way, I'd never catch much of anything anyway. At best, I'd become like Carlin in a few years' time, an old wolf without a pack, taking pleasure in harassing those whose youth I envied. *I wonder if I'll end up telling some other pup how to catch a fox.*

I cringed again, wondering if Carlin hadn't come back from the dead long enough to bite me. Become like him? I could only be so lucky. Carlin had wisdom to offer, a presence you couldn't help trusting. I would count myself lucky if I didn't end up simply cranky. *Who knew I'd think so much of him so long after he'd gone?*

I certainly didn't think much of my territory. Snow remained in patches large and small, while some trees couldn't decide if it was time to regrow, or shed what leaves they'd gained. It was as if the entire area was stuck in mid-thaw. At least the prey was still out in force. I couldn't go very far without sending something tearing for cover. It was nice to still feel feared, but today it had no basis. Half of it I couldn't catch, the other half didn't need to worry since my stomach had what it wanted for now

If only my heart could be filled as easily.

While I was staying alive, my "life" had become an endless routine without deviation. Patrol my border, mark it, hunt, sleep, hunt, sleep, patrol, mark,

112

hunt, sleep; to call it living would be generous. It seemed ironic that only now would the intention of being declared a "lone wolf" take effect. Then again, I'd tasted what life with a pack, as alpha even, was like. That wasn't supposed to happen. Lone wolves aren't supposed to ever know the company of another wolf. In truth, I wondered if they were supposed to survive as long as I had either. Now that I'd lost what I had, a part of me wished I'd never tasted any of it. At least then I wouldn't have the pain.

My routine had taken me back to my den once more. Though it still pained me, I was looking forward to returning to Estrella's warmth, imagined though it may be. Growls in the distance stopped me, despite my best effort to ignore them. I tried to convince myself they weren't my concern, that I was happy enough to be left alone. Estrella wouldn't let me, for my promise to her had included this as well. If ignored, these other wolves could get me killed, directly or indirectly, which would break my promise. Thus, I had no choice but to raise my ears to better catch the sounds in the distance.

I heard the menacing, threatening growls used to scare prey into making mistakes. Someone was hunting, deep inside my territory by the sound of things. If left unchallenged, they could take it over, leaving me less game to hunt, and more vulnerable to other rivals. I again tried to ignore it, then cursed under my breath when I realized I couldn't. At last, I surrendered and turned toward the sound to deal with whatever I found.

When the growls grew louder, I stopped, got a bearing, then moved more carefully. I kept my paws smooth and silent, careful to avoid detection despite how much I really didn't want to do this. My ears stayed forward in search of an owner, for I had to know who it was before I knew what threat they might pose. With a little luck, I might be able to ignore them as a non-threat after all.

Then the wind shifted, and it brought a scent I knew all too well.

I should have known.

I saw him soon after I recognized his scent. Rajor, once again violating my territory to hunt. He stood over a small buck that explained the thud I had felt. Impressive, considering he only had two other wolves with him. The whole thing brought on a laugh born of pity. *He must be desperate, or bold, to violate my territory after the last time he'd tried it. Well, let him have his moment.* I didn't really need the meat, and it's not like it could fill the void within me. Nor would a confrontation be worth the pain. Rajor would take some back to the pack, and then I would be alone again. *Fine by me.* I wanted nothing to do with my brother. I didn't even care that it'd be the first time he'd ever beaten me.

My paws stopped. I tried to move, but my insides refused to let me go another step. More to the point, *she* stopped me. Her spirit hung over me, reminding me she'd made me promise to survive, but there was another promise too. Not as direct, but no less binding. *"Don't you dare let Rajor beat you either. Not ever."*

Not ever.

I had been about to violate that command in the worst way. By allowing Rajor to hunt in my territory unchecked, I'd be doing exactly that without any resistance.

Yet the memory of that moment tore at me. It caused me pain that felt real, as if I'd been snapped in two. My eyes closed, trying to block the memory, and the pain, from entering. Instead I thought of how we'd handle it if she were here. How we'd make Rajor cower before us both. She'd probably scare him more than I would, depending on what kind of mood she was in. I could see it in my mind, and it made it hurt that much worse. It grew and grew, reaching a point where it felt like my flesh was melting from my bones.

Then, on top of that pain, rage. Rage at the humans for doing this to us. Rage at her for not listening to me. Rage at myself for my rage at her. It lit a fire in my chest that felt like I was being burned alive.

All at once, the pain and rage receded into my chest, where they became a tight ball of fury that could turn the world to ashes. The moment it did, I whipped around and charged. Every hair stood on end, and my snarl shook my own bones. My paws flew step by step as I went for my target, just as Rajor's hunting party was digging in. Their noses were buried in blood while Rajor went for the best meat. The rage grew even stronger, and I drove myself faster. Rajor would feel the full force of my blow. Penance for everything he'd done to me.

The hunting party turned their ears up toward me. Between my sprint and my snarl, even a deaf wolf would have known I was there. Except they didn't *see* me. Their ears were up, but their eyes were scanning the entire forest looking for me. Rajor seemed to check every tree and shadow, trying to figure out which one was me.

Rajor's eyes found me in time to see my fangs hit him.

My first bite was for Rajor's shoulder, and I didn't hold back. While my speed made me miss a solid hold, it didn't keep me from knocking Rajor clean off his paws. As Rajor hit the ground, my fangs went under the fur and tore flesh. While I didn't get much muscle, assuming I got any, Rajor's blood still wet my muzzle and drew sharp cries of pain. My snarl continued to shake us both as I tugged at my hold, drawing more pained whines from Rajor.

My jaws left him to go for the second wolf, who was too stunned to react well. She tried to jump away to evade, but the moment her forelegs left the ground, I pushed under them and sent her flipping onto her back hard enough to knock the wind out of her. I again punctured a leg with my fangs, this time leaving a gash just below the elbow, possibly cracking bone. The wolf tucked her tail and whimpered surrender when I bit at her neck enough to draw blood.

The third adult had a better reaction. As hard as I had tried not to, I'd ignored him. His jaws landed on my back, getting more scruff than real flesh. The wolf tried to push me down, but I twisted to the side so his push sent him sliding off to the side instead of down. The wolf moved with me, unable to take me down, but his hold remained. When another twist had the same result, I turned as much and as hard as I could to get my own jaws on his neck. I managed to tear out of the hold, wetting my fur with my own blood where fangs ripped through my scruff, but I was free to counterattack. My jaws embedded themselves in the wolf's neck, pushing him straight onto his side with a hard thud. The wolf snarled and pawed at me, but he could do nothing as my hold drew blood and made it harder and harder for him to breathe.

Rajor came charging in, forcing me to release and face him. Despite the snarl on his lips, his damaged shoulder slowed him. It allowed me to dance to that same side and plant my jaws right on Rajor's elbow without so much as a snap to deter me. I sank my fangs as deep as they would go, while Rajor yelped in pain as he tried to pull away. With one leg in my mouth, Rajor slipped and ended up on his side, at which point I traded my leghold for his neck.

I found a solid hold there, and I clamped down with all of my strength, drawing blood. Rajor wheezed under my hold. The male was still coughing from my last attack, while the female continued to cower. I had Rajor to myself. I had every right. I wanted it so badly. Rajor deserved to die for the pain he'd caused me. He was *going* to die. Right now!

...*Right now.*

...*It ends here.*

...He *ends here!*

...I... couldn't do it.

I heard Rajor whimpering. I felt Rajor's blood on my fangs. I knew how easy it would be... but my jaws never clamped tighter.

My fangs never drew more than surface blood. I shook as an almost physical battle raged within me. I wanted to end it, to end *him*. My hold refused to tighten. My anger... my agony... it wasn't enough to take that last step.

When the male recovered and began another charge, I left Rajor to knock him over again, putting new fang marks in the other side of his neck. I held him there until his tail tucked, with whimpers of surrender. There I stood, daring any of them to try again, shaking so hard I could hardly breathe. Any time one tried to move, I snapped a snarl their way, and they froze. When all three, even Rajor, refused to move, I turned to my brother. I put my bloodied fangs in front of Rajor's eyes so he could see them.

I was still shaking as I spoke.

"Test me again... and I will end you. Do you hear me?" Rajor shrank where he lay while his ears managed a very shallow forward tick. "Good. Now get out of here."

I snarled and snapped at Rajor's tail. Rajor rolled onto his paws and sprinted a short distance away, just ahead of the others doing the same. Somehow, I found myself happy to see they were all still able to do so, suggesting the wounds looked worse than they were. That said, my glare followed them until they were well out of sprinting range, and past my border. Rajor stopped there, turned toward me, and somewhere found the courage to be smug. Or rather, *look* smug. His tail announced his position, but his ears betrayed his remaining fear.

"Just remember your own place," Rajor said. "I won't hesitate to enforce your sentence should you violate *my* territory."

I ruffed and left. *Let him make his threats. The scars I gave him will keep him honest.* Besides, I was just beginning to get my body under control. The last thing I wanted was to start shaking again.

"Luna wolf still sharp in fang, Luna mate will—"

"SHUT UP!"

My voice echoed in the trees and made Rajor positively vanish toward home. I didn't care about him. Every ounce of pain-fueled fury was directed at the bird sitting on a branch overhead. It shook me so hard, I could hardly breathe. That knot in my chest was so hot, it's a wonder I didn't burst into flames. I didn't even feel my wounds screaming in protest at being pulled on.

"By Wolfor's fangs, shut up," I said. "You don't get it do you? 'Luna mate' is dead! She was taken by the humans and she won't be coming back. She'll never be coming back. For all I know, they killed her while she was still trapped in that stone... cave... den... I don't know what it was. Either way, she's gone, and I'd rather you not sing of her ever again... It hurts too much."

"Stone cave, smooth and holed? Luna mate may not—"

I don't know how I did it. I don't know if I could do it again if I tried

My legs launched me at the mockingbird. I summoned everything, every ounce of pain and fury, to jump up. I wanted him gone, maybe even wanted him dead. However it came, I wanted him silent.

The bird was so caught off guard by the jump, his flight was delayed. That delay allowed me to get close. Closer than I'd ever been. When the bird took to the air, I clamped down hard. While my main fangs missed, when my paws hit dirt once more, my front teeth held two of the mockingbird's tail feathers. Had he not taken flight when he did, I may well have been able to catch him outright.

I let the feathers drift to the ground as the bird chose a higher branch to rasp at me from. I ignored him, for I could do nothing else. My paws took me away toward my den, while my ears refused to listen to the bird as he sang at me. Chirps, rasps, long songs, my ears blocked him out all the way to my den. Yet before I could get inside, one sentence cut through.

"Luna wolf, I save you soon. Stay alive till next full moon."

I heard him flutter off as I slipped into my den. Estrella was still there, but she'd been there, and would probably be there forever. Really, I thought I should leave, except I couldn't. It was all I had left. The only reminder of what she meant to me, and why I couldn't simply fade like I wanted to.

I rubbed against the wall where her claw still lay, trying to remember the warmth that was there. It hurt, but it had hurt, as it likely would forever. All I had of her were damaged fragments of the life I had.

My stomach gave another rumble, which didn't make sense. I'd eaten well enough. There shouldn't be any reason for its protest. Best I could figure, somehow tasting blood had stirred it. It didn't matter, really. Whatever the reason, I was once again prevented from being alone with my pain because I had to care for myself. Even though my wounds made using the tunnel painful, my body, my promise, forced me out to hunt.

Except I didn't need to hunt, because Rajor had done that for me. I returned to his kill, now mine to claim. I chewed into it, further bloodied my muzzle, ate until my stomach refused to take anymore, but I never tasted it. It was a welcome change to the routine, nothing more. No joy, no victory, though the pain seemed to go numb as I ate. Either that, or maybe it had been so constant I had grown used to it.

Not that I really asked why. For the first time, the pain was less, which alone felt pretty good at the moment. Even so, I served my body by eating, then left it at that. I only hesitated when I noticed the broken feathers I'd pulled from the mockingbird. They were stuck in the ground, edges fluttering in the breeze. Two parts, that most likely meant an end. I'd never see Estrella again, that I'd come to accept. Now, perhaps, I'd be rid of the bird too.

Calm struck out of nowhere. I cringed, not from pain, but something closer to joy. Peace. I'd finally be getting peace, solitude. No more chirping or singing from the top of the den, no more reminders. I would finally get to sleep and hunt in peace. I'd finally be allowed to spend my life alone, as I was supposed to, with only my pain, my void, and my empty den as comfort.

I can live with that.

Chapter 11

DESPITE SPRING "ARRIVING" over two moons ago, it seemed like the forest had gotten stuck in mid-thaw. Patches of snow refused to melt, and trees continued to appear halfway between regrowth and shedding. A day of fresh snowfall only seemed to reinforce the standard. A crazy part of me wondered if it too was mourning Estrella's loss, while another part suggested it was nothing more than the seasons tormenting me.

Well, let the forest do what it will. It's still feeding me, so I guess I can't complain.

Things were certainly quieter without the bird. I still expected to see him on top of the rocks every morning, but he was never there. The feathers I'd pulled were gone too. With the kill I'd taken from Rajor picked clean by other birds, I had little left to take me back.

I also had little left to get in the way. Without the bird and other reminders, I had formed new hunting trails that reflected my change of choices. Estrella was still there, but she didn't get in the way anymore, for she'd never hunted there. I had no memories, save for those that lingered no matter where I went. I couldn't do anything about those, but at least now they didn't come up to bite nearly as often.

I also started spending less time in my den for much the same reason. The warmth had faded, the claw was gone, and though Estrella was there, that was the problem. I didn't want to be around her anymore. The only reason I went near it was because my caching spot remained too safe to abandon. Plus, like any wolf, I still had a need for a central place to call "home."

But I wasn't home tonight. A full moon glistened off the water, as well as my fur, as I lay by the river shortly after sunset, staring at my reflection. My hackles, the silver sheen Martol had spoken of, were glowing in the moonlight, absorbing it as if it might feed me. I didn't really think it would, but just as it always had, the glow calmed me.

I lost myself in the smooth blue light reflecting off of the river. I had begun to do so regularly during the brighter nights, for she wasn't there at all. Neither was Rajor, or Carlin, or Toltan, or Martol, or even Wolfor. There was just the glow, and me. The pain still throbbed, but I was too far away to feel it. The void felt somehow tolerable, or perhaps it too couldn't find me wherever the glow had taken me. Only here, with my sheen glowing, did I ever find peace. For this short time, I was able to shed the pain, let my wounds heal, and perhaps with enough time, find some measure of joy in a world full of torments.

While the pain wasn't able to find me, a chorus of howls did. My ears pulled my head up toward them as they echoed in the distance. They were far away, and few in number, but they were making their presence known all the same. Because I'd been lost in myself, I wasn't certain what the call was at first. Were they invaders, challengers, or simply passing through? Then they howled again, and the pain came rushing back.

Pups.

Only Rajor could stumble on a way to hurt me from a distance. These were not the howls of defense, or hunting. No, they were celebrating the birth of new life upon which to build the future of the pack. For the briefest of seconds, my mind wondered what it would be like to have that howl be for my litter.

That was all she needed.

Estrella would have been a strong mother, I had no doubt of that. I was also certain we'd be giving that howl ourselves by now if she were still here. Try as I might, I still couldn't convince myself I didn't want to know that feeling. To touch noses with my young like Toltan had for me. I wanted to share that tender moment with my pack, and my mate. To build my own future.

I never would, of course. She, and my pack, were dead. My fault? I had stopped asking. It didn't matter anymore. My fault or not, it wouldn't change the fact that I missed her. In many ways, I still needed her. She was never there, never would be again, even as she followed me everywhere I went.

A voice sounded behind me, shattering my thoughts.

"Wow. Martol wasn't wrong—"

I snapped around in a full snarl, tail raised high with every hair on my back doing the same. My fangs showed the intruder what they'd be facing for their infraction, then were covered when the wolf shrank like a turtle diving into its shell. She immediately whimpered surrender, to which I responded by lowering my growl. My anger faded to nothing beyond a glare when I recognized her, despite the many years since I'd last seen her. It was the larger-than-normal black tail tip that did it, though my little sister had become a largely white wolf, with gray thinly mixed in on her head, neck, and back.

"Jinta?" I said. "What are you doing here?" Her ears were slow to rise, though nothing else about her did, as she looked at me with the softest of whimpers. She was asking permission. The memory of the last time I saw her do that silenced the last of my anger. "You can get up, little sister. I won't hurt you."

Jinta rose so slowly, it's as if she were growing instead of standing up. Her head took even longer. I relaxed as much as I could, but said nothing, for I knew any attempt would come out stern, which would send her to the ground again.

After what felt like a day, Jinta's tail finally came out from between her legs. She stood tall, proud on her legs, no sign of fear in them, though her ears never quite came all the way forward.

"It's good to see you, Luna," she said. "You've grown as strong as I've heard."

"Thank you." I said the words, but there was nothing behind them. They were as blank as I felt, so much so that I wasn't even annoyed that she hadn't answered my question.

Jinta's ears shifted back and forth, as if searching for a sound that wasn't there.

"Where's Estrella? Is she hun—"

"Dead."

The sharp word perked her ears for the first time, while my glare regained some ire at having to even think about it. Were I alone, some memory of Estrella probably would have returned to torment me again. Having someone to focus on somehow kept her at bay for the first time.

Jinta's ears fell in a cringe I knew all too well. "Luna, I'm sorry. I know what that must feel like."

My growl made a comeback. "No, you don't. Now I ask again, what are you doing here?"

Jinta cringed again, and her tail started tucking. "I need you. You're the only one who can match Rajor's ability as alpha." I huffed. *Great, another idealistic female. Not this time.* I turned and walked away without a word. "Luna! Didn't you hear me?"

I kept walking. "Rajor is your problem, not mine."

Jinta stayed just behind me, keeping up without breaking my authority. "You care more than that, Luna. Folar wouldn't be alive if you didn't."

I stopped, then huffed and huffed until it turned into an odd, panted laugh. *Guess he really did catch her eye.* "Folar? All I did was point him toward his only chance to survive."

"You're being modest or blind. You *brought* him to us, at great personal risk, I might add."

"Toltan wouldn't have hurt me. He did enough of..."

The pain hit harder than it had before. I whined as if I'd been bitten, feeling a sting as if Wolfor himself were biting into my heart. All I could see was Toltan's body. All I could feel was his nose, ice cold, nothing like I remembered. I had forgiven him. I had! Yet there it was, another snide comment about his part in what Rajor had done. *If only she were here.* I could lose myself in her and let the pain pass. Of course, her absence was why it hurt so much.

When Jinta rubbed her head against mine, I snapped away and snarled as if she'd bitten me. For all I felt, she might as well have. She too recoiled, but only long enough to see I wasn't going to attack her. From there she stared at me, not saying a word, her ears up and alert. Then her eyes, soft as a morning breeze, deep as the sky, and holding as much plea as they did courage, found mine. Not a hair was raised in defense or challenge, nor was her tail tucked in fear. She stood as a pillar of a wolf. A fine hunter, in desperate need.

My ears fell. This was worse than her asking permission. She reminded me of *her*. Estrella. A calm beauty that held a fire many would miss. Only this time, she needed me, and that wasn't possible anymore.

"I can't help you," I said, somehow avoiding more whines. "Not without her."

Jinta, for the first time I could remember, did not back down. "You have to. We've lost Rajor."

My ears shot straight up as shock swallowed my pain whole. *I can't be that lucky.* "You what? I didn't wound him that badly."

"Luna, he's not dead." *Drat.* "But he's... he's not the same. He's lost his nerve. I worry what will happen when he loses the pack."

"Penance. That's what."

I moved on, making it all the way to my den without hearing a word she said. I was too busy thinking about Rajor. *I wonder what would happen to him if he did lose the pack. Would he become beta? Pup-sitter—no, that's Lonate's job. Omega? Now that* would *be fitting. Would serve him right if he were run out himself. Then he'd have to fight me for territory. Maybe I'd insult him further by making him my omega. Wouldn't he love that?* I laid beside my rock pile, almost tasting the fun I'd have with him.

Jinta, meanwhile, had not given up.

"Luna! You can't sit here and pretend you don't care."

I finally acknowledged her with a sarcastic turn of my head. "Can't I? That's not my pack anymore. Besides, Rajor can't be that bad if he's had pups."

"Those aren't *his* pups."

My ears perked in shock once more. I know what I heard. Rajor's was among the voices howling to celebrate the new litter. More to the point, it was his voice starting the call, as was the alpha's place. If they weren't his pups, whose were they?

"I don't understand," I said. "I thought you said he was still alpha."

Jinta sighed, growled frustration, then slowly laid down near me. Each step was a request for permission, which I never denied. I never did anything except watch and admire. Jinta wasn't as big as Estrella, but she had a similar smoothness to her. Yet even now, I could tell she had a softer, gentler side about her. Best suited to a loving mother... or sister.

I didn't say anything, of course. Voicing such feelings would send me after Estrella again. For the first time since she died, I was able to think of her without being bitten inside. I didn't dare mess with that now, and yes, I wanted to know what was going on with my old pack.

Once comfortable, Jinta spoke as softly as she moved. "Rajor is still alpha, but he never stopped Solas and Carfen from bearing pups. Every litter the pack has borne has been theirs."

"Non-alpha pups aren't unheard of." I said it, but even I knew how feeble that excuse was.

"Only in times of great game, as it was when you and I were pups. That's not now. Rajor has no mate of his own, but his pack has pups that aren't his, and yet he's still alpha. You know that can't last. That's not the worst of it. Rajor... he's not the same since the winter."

My head turned in honest curiosity. "What do you mean? Did something happen?"

Jinta again cringed in pain. "He lost half the pack, Luna. Kills just couldn't be found. With each death, he became more and more subdued. Then we lost the litter. Every pup from last spring died. Seeing so many of his members starve... it hurt him like I didn't think he could hurt. He's lost all the fire, all the nerve he used to have."

"This is a bad thing?"

Jinta growled at me, looked ready to bite me, really. I huffed it off, though my ears fell a touch in retreat. Mostly because I knew I deserved that bite and then some. After all, I'd lost just as much, if not more. I knew what Rajor had to be feeling. Then again, perhaps that's why I snipped at it. To acknowledge Rajor's pain would mean remembering my own. I had finally started to forget it. I didn't want to bring it back now.

Jinta looked ready to continue, but new howls sounded in the distance. Rajor's pack again, but different. This one was the long, deep howl of mourning. More interesting was how Jinta reacted. I saw her body relax, though it was more like it dropped than released tension. I knew that look all too well. Something about the howls distressed her, so much so her ears fell in equal pain.

Then Jinta glared at me with a perfect recreation of Toltan's death stance. It, and his memory, forced me to drop my ears in submission, if only a little.

"Do you know who they're mourning?" she said. "They're mourning the pups. The pups Rajor couldn't provide for. The lack of game in this forest meant a weak litter, and a weak mother to care for them. The first two came out dead. I left after I heard only two of the seven survived. I'm guessing they lost more."

I don't know where it came from, but a hot anger lit within me. It burned deep in my chest, though I didn't know at what, nor could I find a cause. It was just there, fueled further by my disgust for it. On its tail came a wave of shame that flattened my ears. I knew the pain of loss, very recent loss at that. If Estrella were there, she would have said the same, after she bit me. She would have reminded me how hard it was when I lost my pack. To ignore Rajor's pain would mean ignoring my own, and as much as I wanted to, I couldn't do either. I had to be the wolf Estrella expected me to be. Except it wasn't that easy. There was a lot of pain to push past, and the anger from nowhere didn't help things.

Jinta's glare hadn't weakened, though her ears had started to nervously shift, which only made it that much harder for me to find some mental clarity. She was out here, looking for help, or... *wait... what* is *she after?* Jinta had never really explained her goal, and it proved to be a good thing, for it gave me what I needed to push the anger back. True, it left the shame and the pain, but I'd gotten used to both lately.

"So, what do you want me to do?" I said. "I can't go back. I'm still a lone wolf."

The calm, gentle sister I knew instantly replaced the glare. "I'm not asking you to. I'm asking you to let me join you. Rajor's pack will implode if he doesn't snap out of it."

"He may still. He has a lot of pride."

"Perhaps. But I'd still rather run with a brother I can trust and parents that I love."

My ears fell in the hardest cringe yet. She didn't know. *No, of course not. With her pack in such turmoil, how could she? She'd only asked about Estrella.* I wondered if perhaps that's what I was angry about.

Jinta was here, looking to run from the turmoil in her pack, not knowing the turmoil I had in mine. She didn't know what had happened, and she needed to. She wouldn't understand if she didn't. I cringed again as I remembered the day I lost them all. It was the only way I could bring myself to tell her, not that it made it hurt any less.

Nor did it keep my voice from shaking. "It's not possible, little sister. You can't run with them."

Her glare returned, and it hurt worse than the memory. "And why not? Are you so proud you can't let—"

"They're dead." Shock took over as Jinta's breathing deepened. *Tell me this stops hurting.* "So is Carlin, the old wolf I'm sure you heard about.

They're all dead. The hunting... I couldn't save them. It's just me now, and I can't help you."

I stood and started to leave, only to stop when I heard her whine. A soft, pain-filled whine, just like the one I'd given myself that day. Hearing it from my little sister made it cut as deep as the loss did. It also took me back to our puppy days, when a game was ruined because her pain had been real. Just as it was now. Yet I still couldn't help her. I could barely help myself. She deserved more, but she'd never find it with me.

That said, I did turn around to face her. I had no idea what I was going to say, but I never got the chance. Jinta was looking at me, her eyes trying to tell her it wasn't true. I could see all the pain I'd felt in her eyes, making my own wounds hurt that much more.

After breaking in two a thousand times over, all I could offer was a very soft, "I'm sorry."

Jinta took deep breath after deep breath, at times swallowing as if she might swallow the pain. *It doesn't work*, I thought, for I'd tried to do the same many times already. Seeing her pain only refreshed my own, which froze me in place as it replaced my blood. More than ever, I needed Estrella. I needed my other half, but all I could find was the void.

As the breaths came, Jinta gained more composure. Through my own pain, my ears managed to perk, impressed. I would have said she'd be too soft to fight through all that, but she did. Her ears rose, her fur lay flat, even her eyes grew brighter by the second. It wasn't long at all before she stood without any hesitation. She faced me full on, a rock I'd never seen her be.

"If you can't help me," she said, "then help my pack. Help me find a kill I can take back to them. There may yet be pups we can save."

I wanted to refuse. Spending time with her meant spending time with anyone. I'd just gotten used to an empty den. The void had become as much a part of me as my fur, but I couldn't swallow the lie. I couldn't convince myself their plight meant nothing to me. Had it been anyone else, it might have been different, but Jinta? My little sister? I couldn't say no.

"Follow." It's the closest I could come to yes.

I led her along my new paths, following trail after trail that went out of reach, or straight up cold. Even areas that usually produced a reliable source of rabbits were bare. I knew this happened on occasion. Even in the best of times, there were those days where prey just couldn't be found. Except this time, I had a desperate sister following me. Every cold trail and empty den caused my heart to sink lower. Despite my best efforts, I was letting her down.

Odd that I cared, really. Despite the fact that I was helping Jinta, I knew what I was really doing was helping the same pack that betrayed me so long ago. And yet, I couldn't lie to myself about this one. Jinta was right. I cared. More than just the fact that I was helping her and my other siblings by helping them, though that made it easier, it mattered that I was helping the pack survive. Now *why* it mattered, or anything beyond the fact that it *did* matter, proved impossible to find. I couldn't even imagine what Estrella would have thought about it. Of course, failing so often might have altered that some.

Who am I kidding? What did she always say? "Have a little faith?" She wouldn't stop that now.

I didn't either. I continued on my usual trails, digging through more than one snow patch, looking for a rabbit or two still huddled for warmth. Through it all, Jinta never voiced concern. She simply followed, assisting where she could.

That is, until I ignored a trail I might otherwise be glad to find. Deer, quite sick by the scent of the pus, yet still too big for me to take down. I had no intention of risking another tumble like the last time I'd tried, nor did I want Jinta to see me like that. So I passed on by without so much as a dream.

This time, though, Jinta stopped.

"I think you're losing your touch, big brother. There's a prime target this way."

"Not for me." I didn't give it any more thought. I'd rejected the idea, so I didn't even feel the need to protect my pride.

"Come on, Luna. You and I can take down one half-dead deer."

I stopped, sighed, and tried very hard not to be angry. She didn't know. She didn't see me the last time. More to the point, she didn't understand whose place she'd be taking.

That said, I tried and failed to come up with a reason she'd accept. Curse her. She was always softer, but rarely wrong. In some ways, it was worse than Estrella. Estrella was stubborn, even when she was wrong. Jinta didn't have to be stubborn. Being right was enough.

"Fine," I sighed. *Might as well get this over with.* Either she'd be right, or she'd see me covered in mud like the last time.

I checked the scent again before following the trail, not that I needed my nose. The deer had left plenty of broken twigs or knocked-off tree bark to lead the way. The scent made sure I still had the same target, not much else.

"Luna," Jinta said, "I know you lost a lot, but is that all there is?"

Really? Mid-hunt, you ask about my emotions? I kept moving as if I hadn't heard. "Don't know what you mean."

"You didn't used to be this hard, and you were more eager to hunt the prime prey than Rajor was. Why didn't you want to chase this one?"

Because she's still here. "You wouldn't understand."

"Because you're a lone wolf? Luna, I've taken down prey like this *alone*. That's not good enough."

I stopped and tried to figure out if I was fighting down anger or pain. Might well have been both. Whatever it was melded into an uncomfortable, burning mixture that made me wish for the void. It hurt less.

"Do you want to talk or hunt?" I said, my voice shaking from one or both emotions. "I can't do both." The part I kept to myself was, "not without her."

I looked back to glare and found Jinta's ears and tail in full submission. *I hate seeing her like that.* Gentle as she was, Jinta was too strong to submit so completely. It didn't look right on her. Still, she'd made the choice, and I was glad to be without the distraction... and the reminder.

My frustration spurred me to break into a run along the trail. Part of me thought I needed to follow the scent, but this deer had shown signs of being too disoriented to stray much. I slowed to check a log, a bush, or a scraped tree to be sure it was still the same deer, but such stops rarely lasted long.

All the while, Jinta never said another word. Not until—

"There it is!"

I stopped and looked to find the deer more off his path than I expected. It was also a lot younger than I expected, little more than a foal really. It must have been injured while playing, or simply got unlucky and caught a severe illness early on. Whatever the reason, it was still stammering along, rubbing against pretty much anything near him. Would probably be dead in a few days on his own.

Have a little—

"Shut up," I muttered. I'd gotten this far without her getting in the way. I couldn't afford to be lost in her again. I could almost hear her voice, and I buried it. *She's never coming back. It's time I left her behind in order to hunt at will again.*

A soft whine came from Jinta. I saw her submitting again, and my stomach dropped.

"Not you, little sister," I said. "I... never mind. Just perk your ears up. Please." They rose slowly, but they rose all the way, as did she. "Better. More your place. Now, swing around and make sure he doesn't get away. I'll make the kill."

Jinta ticked her ears forward, then vanished into the trees. I was surprised to find that once I lost sight of her, I lost sound too. She'd always been a fine hunter, but I never knew she could be such a ghost. If Rajor didn't pull out of his current state, I had to wonder who besides Jinta could challenge him for control of the pack. *Bet she'd revoke my sentence if she did.*

I shook my head as if to shake the thoughts away. Even if she did, it wouldn't work. I'd lost enough wolves in my time. Better I stay alone. It would hurt a lot less.

Another lie, and you know it.

Perhaps, but for now, I'm okay with it.

Certain that Jinta was in place by now, I made my move. I didn't care if the deer heard me. My prey was too far gone to do anything about it. I simply charged in, paws moving like the wind, jaws open, panting in excitement and exertion. I had my target. I knew where to go.

The foal's ears turned my way, then it surprised me by finding a fair amount of footing to make a run for it. Even so, he didn't get but a few steps before his illness slowed him down. He still had some speed though, so I went for the easy kill. I got close behind, my prey too busy running to kick. My jaws went up, caught a mouthful of flesh around the genitals, then I stopped and pulled. The flesh stayed, but the deer tumbled to the ground, too winded to cry out. Blood stained the ground, and my muzzle, as I slowed my chase. I'd already made the kill, it just hadn't hit yet. The deer struggled to stand, but he never did. The blood loss alone, combined with his wounds or illness, claimed him in a matter of seconds.

Jinta appeared from behind a tree just ahead of me. *Had she been there all along, or simply ended up there during the chase?* I was curious, but didn't ask, for it didn't really matter.

"For a lone wolf, you remind me a lot of Toltan," she said.

I cringed at the thought, more so at his memory. *I could only be so lucky.*

"You have your kill," I said. "Take what you can carry and be on your way. Your pack needs you."

Jinta outright shocked me by standing firm with a glare worthy of Toltan's death stance. Just like him, no one could doubt just how very unhappy she was. Despite my indifference, I had to wonder if I dared risk her wrath either. *Is this the same wolf that was asking permission just a moment ago?*

"They're your pack too, Luna. Calon was the last of our litter to die. The rest still live. *My pack* carries the same blood we both do. The same blood you do."

"And I have seen too much of it on the ground," I said. "Besides, they wronged me. I owe them nothing."

"They're your blood! Rajor can't protect them."

"That won't last."

"Even if it doesn't, the pack deserves a strong alpha. *You* deserve—"

I snapped into full snarl. That word again. I'd heard it too often by too many who weren't there anymore. Any time I heard it now, it hurt

128

as if I were torn apart. Sister or not, I couldn't take hearing it again. Not from anyone.

Especially when it forced me to use it myself.

"I deserve what? A home? A family? I had both until Rajor took it from me. He deserves whatever happens to him."

"Even if that means losing more of the pack?"

My snarl faded as her words cut deep. I couldn't lie, not about that. Carlin once noted that I still spoke of them. Yes, it mattered. It mattered that more of my siblings might suffer or even starve. I cared about them, even after all the pain they'd caused me. But they were still led by Rajor. They stood by him instead of me, which meant I still couldn't go back.

No matter how much I might want to, I couldn't go home.

"Take your share and go," I said. "There's nothing more I can do for you."

I left without another word. She said something, but I never heard it. I left her behind like I left my former pack. I could do nothing for either of them. I could barely do anything for myself. Although I had to admit, I did owe Jinta for one thing.

For the first time, I could think about Estrella without inner torture. I missed her, and would always miss her, yet she hadn't gotten in the way this time, nor had she kept me from an easy kill. I'd even run with another without so much as a twitch. Had I been too busy missing her to notice when she'd stopped getting in the way?

I wondered for a time, then shed the question like a tuft of fur. Whatever the answer, it wouldn't change anything. I would always miss her. The void in my heart would always be there, but it would no longer stop me. I had made a promise when I lost my mate. Now for the first time, I felt like I might actually keep it.

Chapter 12

ESTRELLA WOULD BE PROUD. Wouldn't matter that I'd caught it with an injury away from its herd. Fact is, I had taken down a full-grown buck all by myself. The first one since my hunt with Jinta. I'd missed more than a few, almost got killed by three others, but I kept the faith, and here I was, eating my fill. She'd have been proud of me for holding onto hope that long. Even prouder for making the kill. The thought stung, but after feeling it for three moons, it didn't hurt as much as it used to.

At least the forest had decided which season it was in. The snow had finally surrendered and melted for good shortly after Jinta left. The trees made up for lost time, bursting thick bushes of leaves all around. The songbirds were back too, singing even louder the joys of spring. A spring not quite half gone, but it's the thought that counts.

The mockingbird wasn't among them. *Guess almost getting killed finally drove him away.* Strange, really. After wishing I could get rid of him for so long, now that I had, I found my days even emptier than before. My heart sank every morning when I looked for him on top of my den and found him still missing. For some reason, every time I thought about him, my heart was pricked by the same regret attached to the memory of chasing off Martol. As if it were another chance tossed aside.

In the end, it didn't matter much. I could do nothing about any of it now. Besides, being alone meant fewer reminders. Estrella was still there, but she didn't get in the way anymore. Nor did the reminders send me cringing when they came. They still stung, but they didn't keep me from eating my kill. Thinking about how Estrella would react even made it feel warmer. I didn't care about my blown chances, for I could do nothing about them anyway. Save for the mockingbird, they were all dead. As for Jinta, while I may not have been as gentle as I should have been, I had a hard time seeing a lie in why I turned her away.

When the wind changed, I found a familiar scent I cared about. Rajor was out there, with his pack. My ears perked toward the scent and found quiet growls and the soft padding of playful paws. The fact that I could hear them told me they were very close, which meant closer to my border. *Surely he wouldn't dare... wait... it's Rajor. Of course he would.*

I left my kill to see just how much Rajor was pushing his luck. I neither hid my approach nor rushed to challenge, instead going for a simple trot to check the situation. Turns out, Rajor wasn't pushing his luck at all. His nose was pressed against a tree I had marked just that morning. Behind him stood more of the pack, including this year's litter, if one can call two pups a litter. Didn't keep Lonate from standing guard between them as if any leaf could carry a threat. *That wolf was born to watch pups.*

The rest watched Rajor when he froze, his ears perking and his eyes searched around. I watched and waited, curious of what he'd do. Lonate, of course, did his own searching while keeping the pups in line.

Rajor lifted his head, tested the air, and looked out into the forest again. My ears turned back in case I'd missed something myself. Rajor ruffed, then turned to lead his pack along, walking the edge of my territory, but never crossing it.

When he stopped to examine another marker, I couldn't control myself anymore. The chance was too sweet to pass up. I walked toward him very proud and stern, claiming my territory. Lonate saw me first. His eyes and ears locked onto me, concerned about what I'd do, likely because of the fresh blood on my muzzle. He had no reason to fear, as I had no quarrel with any of them. I just wanted to have some fun with my brother.

Rajor was too busy sniffing to notice Lonate's attention. I didn't let him get the chance.

"You don't need to worry," I said. "You haven't trespassed yet."

Rajor's head and ears snapped toward me. I could see him swallow a growl like a hunk of meat he hadn't chewed yet. His ears were straight up, but his tail refused to rise. *Priceless.*

"What do you want, loner?" Rajor said.

Pure distaste, no hint of fear, he sounded pretty good, so I let him keep the credit earned. "Just checking on my borders. You needn't worry, Rajor. I have no quarrel with you today. Be on your way."

Rajor glared, and he growled, and he knew better. He turned away without saying anything more.

I tried to leave too, but Lonate's voice caught me before I could look away. "Where's Estrella?"

I couldn't stop a cringe. Unlike Rajor might have been, Lonate had only been curious, which left no reason to be angry. *Didn't Jinta tell them?* The two together almost made it worse, for the wound was still too fresh.

For the first time I had ever heard of, Lonate forgot the pups, and stepped toward me. He crossed the border, but I didn't say anything. It wouldn't have been worth it.

"Luna? Where is she? Where are Martol and Toltan?"

Another pinecone jabbed into my throat. *Jinta, why didn't you tell them? It would hurt so much less.* I couldn't form the words. It hurt too much. I could only stare, my head low and my eyes watering.

Rajor approached as well. My hackles rose, but I waited for him to make the insult before I pinned him for it. Assuming I could find the breath to fuel the charge.

"Luna?" *Is he... crying?* My ears focused on him. "What happened? Where are they?"

Anger at Rajor, however hollow, broke up the pinecone. I lifted my head and tail lest Rajor push his luck too much. Not that it dried my eyes any.

"I guess Jinta didn't share what I told her," I said. "They're dead. Martol and Toltan died in the winter. So did Carlin. Estrella... she was taken by the humans. I try not to think about what they did to her."

I waited for it. My legs tensed for the lunge. I saw the spot on Rajor's neck where I would cut into it again. I wouldn't tolerate his bullying, not about this. Yet Rajor stood there, silent. He swallowed a few times, seemed ready to speak, but closed his mouth before sound escaped.

Finally, he turned to the pups. "This is the price for being a lone wolf. It is the reason you don't want to be one or associate with one."

Was that... reverence? Compassion, even? My tail fell as confusion replaced my anger. Rajor wasn't saying crimes, just "lone wolf." His tone held even more respect. A part of me said it was the buildup to the worst insult ever. The rest waited to see what he really had in mind.

A pup asked, "Do you mean he's responsible for the others' deaths?"

Rajor said firm and clear, "No."

What?!

Rajor looked at me, no hate to be found, his tone turning soft... apologetic?! "I only mean he couldn't provide for them, as the pack can. This is not his fault. Only what he is. That's why being declared a lone wolf is the worst a wolf can suffer... and the hardest sentence an alpha can ever impose. Remember that."

I wanted so much to be angry. I *was* angry at Jinta for forcing this on me, yet I was too confused to act on it. The bully I grew up with was... I couldn't tell what he was. Rajor had several ways he could sting me jumping down his throat, yet he hadn't taken any of them. If anything, Rajor had lifted me up in an odd way. *Is this my brother?*

Before I could decide what to think, fast chirping sounded in the trees. I'd heard that call before. *Surely it couldn't...*

"Lone wolf he is not, strong pack Luna has got."

I forgot everything, almost forgetting Rajor was even there. I followed the sound to my little den bird fluttering onto a low branch. As always, never low enough to reach, but still there. I couldn't help it. I panted a soft laugh, triggering a sour tension in my chest. I'd wanted him gone, and then when I got my wish, I regretted it. Now he was back, and I couldn't be happier, or sorrier for how I'd treated him.

"What are you doing back?" I said. "I thought I'd chased you off for good."

"Like the sun and rain, I shall remain, flying near you, help your pain."

"I don't know about that, but I can't say I'm not glad to see you. Where have you been anyway?"

"Searching, searching, I did go, found, found, yours plus more."

"Yours plus more?" Rajor said. "What in Wolfor's name are you talking about?"

"He means me, Rajor."

My heart stopped while my ears tore toward the sound I couldn't believe was real. I found two wolves, but I only saw one of them. My body turned to stone, in a permanent perked position, while my eyes took her apart hair by hair. Even then, I could hardly believe it. I stared at her for a thousand years longer, trying to be sure I wasn't hallucinating.

Estrella, my mate, she stood there proud as ever. From nose to tail, the same as three moons ago, right down to the calm and cool confidence she exuded with every breath. Well, strong, alive, and back within reach.

Then her voice carried across to my heart. "Aren't you going to say anything, thorn?"

I ran so fast, it felt like I had burst right out of my fur. Twigs flew, I cut my paw on something, and I didn't feel any of it. The entire world consisted of one wolf I desperately wanted to jump into. The other wolf retreated just before I plunged into Estrella. I knocked her up and onto her back, licking, rubbing, and whimpering like a pup, all while unable to breathe.

I spent the next lifetime absorbing her back into my soul. Her warmth, her aura, her affection, and especially her ego. She was there, right *there*, where I could feel her fur and smell her breath. It was real. *She* was real. By the grace of Wolfor, she'd come back.

It was some time before I stopped whimpering enough to speak. Even then, it barely counted as speech. "Estrella. How? How did... forget it. I don't care. I just... I... Oh Wolfor!"

Estrella had been rubbing and whimpering as well, though nowhere near as hard. "I missed you too, Luna."

Tears streamed. My heart felt so warm, I thought summer had come early. I leaned into her with everything I had. I'd been so sure, so certain I'd never see her again. *I should have known better. I should have guessed even the humans couldn't keep her from me.*

"Luna," Estrella said softly. "Luna, I'm happy to see you too, but would you mind if I stood up?"

I ruffed a laugh while stepping off of her. Estrella rolled onto her paws, shook her fur clean, then nuzzled against me again.

A young voice reminded me we weren't alone. "Doesn't look so terrible to me."

One of the pups. It forced the memory of Rajor's presence to return. *There goes that tender moment.* Yet when I looked back at him, his ears were just coming up from a cringe. I perked my ears to listen to his response while also preparing for a fang-filled reprimand.

Rajor returned to his pack while Lonate rejoined the pups. Rajor traded a quick nuzzle with one, glanced my way again, then back to the pups.

"Come," he said. "You've seen enough for one day."

"But we want to hunt," a pup said.

"Soon, young one. Your time will come soon. Now follow."

Rajor led them away without a word or so much as another look my way. Estrella and I watched him go long after we couldn't see him anymore. *Was that really Rajor?*

Estrella broke her stare first. "Did something happen while I was gone? Rajor was almost... respecting."

I turned my ears back when I failed to find an answer. "If it did, I missed it too. I've never seen him like that. What does it matter? You're back. We're a pack again."

I looked past her to get my first real look at the other wolf, who was standing at a respectful distance. His back was mostly an ashy pelt, but his underside was a crisp and pure white like nothing I had ever seen. He didn't have a black tail tip either, yet strangest of all were his eyes. They were as brightly blue as his under-fur was white. I had never seen an eye color like that on any animal. Even newborn pups too young to see didn't have eyes that bright.

"And you brought a friend," I said. "A... blind friend?"

Estrella panted a quick laugh while tapping her nose against the new wolf's muzzle. "His name is Tilhack, and he's not blind. Just different."

"How do you mean?"

"I'll tell you later. We've had a long journey, and while I see you've eaten recently, we haven't. I'd like to hunt before sitting for a long conversation."

I drew myself up with pride. *Time to repay the gift.* "No need for that. I've got a fresh kill already. I took a buck down all on my own. Haven't eaten much of him yet."

Estrella's ears perked forward, as did the other wolf's. "A solo kill of that size?" Estrella said. "Well, Luna, I have to say, I'm rather proud."

I laughed. *Can I call it or what?*

⌒⌒⌒⌒⌒

"He's a what?"

I stared at Tilhack, trying to understand what Estrella had just said. Okay, Tilhack's eyes were a color I'd never seen, and his underside was a purer white than normal, but he still looked wolf. Even his scent spoke more wild than pet.

Yet Tilhack himself barely flinched when he confirmed it. "The proper term is 'mutt,' but yes, I am half 'domestic dog.' Husky, to be exact."

I felt my head spin. If I weren't lying beside Estrella, I would have worried I might fall over. A wolf mating with a human's pet? What would drive a wolf to such desperation? Then again, I couldn't see anything other than a wolf lying there. Tilhack had submitted to me while we ate without any direction, so his instincts were intact. His aura had felt just as wild, so the fierceness was likely there as well. I just couldn't get my mind to accept that half of his blood was the same of those that once hunted with the humans. Though after seeing wolves take their place, the idea of a wolf mating with a pet seemed almost trivial.

"So how did you two find each other?" I said. "And what happened to you while you were gone? Why did it take three moons for you to get back?" Estrella cringed, and her ears fell further back than they'd ever gone. She looked at me with heavy eyes, pleading with me to do something. I couldn't tell what, which sent my ears perking curiosity. "Was it that bad?"

"It's best left behind, Luna," she said, her voice a soft whisper. The calm confidence nowhere to be found. *What did the humans do to her?*

I wanted to comfort her, but something about her demeanor suggested she'd shy away if I tried. "That's not what you said when you came looking for me a few years ago."

"I had no taste of what you'd faced a few years ago. Please, Luna. Leave it be."

"How can I when it's clear it hurts you? How can I sit and do nothing?"

"Luna," Tilhack said, firm to get my attention, though his ears remained soft, respectful of my position. "Leave her be. You have no idea what kind of pain she's been through."

Oh, I've got a pretty good idea. "All the more reason I should know, so I can help her."

"Trust me, you don't want to know. You can help her by letting her lick her wounds in her own way. She gave everything to get back here, to get back to you. Be the wolf she told me about. That will be enough."

The wolf she told you about wouldn't hesitate to share her pain.

My insides warred like never before. Here was my mate in obvious pain, and the best way I can help is to let her suffer? I couldn't accept that because I'd been there. I'd needed comfort. Being without it turned me bitter in the worst way. Now Estrella sat in need, and they expected me to let her be? How could I do that when it went against everything my blood cried out for?

Except every time I tried to do something, Estrella's eyes stopped me. They still held that plea, much as they did the day I thought I'd lost her. I couldn't ignore that either. Not after whatever she went through.

In some ways, I wanted the void back. At least that was something I could work with, or at least endure. This... my mate was in pain, and she didn't want me to help. What do you do with that?

I rose to my paws, latching onto the only lie I had that could help, if only for a short time.

"That carcass won't be there for long," I said. "I better see what I can pull off of it before the birds get there. You two rest up. Sounds like you've had quite a journey."

"Thank you, Luna." Estrella said, still quieter than normal for her.

It only spurred me faster away toward my last kill. I needed to get away, to get my mind realigned with recent changes. Estrella was alive, and back with me. I couldn't be happier. I had another pack member on top of that, strange though he may be, also great. Yet Estrella also carried scars she wouldn't share with me. She knew I cared, she had to. So why wouldn't she let me care *for* her? What did the humans do to her that would make her reject me? Had they taken her from me after all?

The thought of that stopped me cold. *What an idiot!* She didn't want me to press for details, perhaps she wasn't ready to snuggle quite as much, that's all fine. *I can respect that. I may not understand why, but I don't have to. As Tilhack said, I need to be the wolf she expects me to be. That's not a wolf who would run from the confrontation. I'll respect her wishes, but I won't abandon her.*

I turned around in a huff, now confident I knew what I was doing. *I'll go as far as she'll let me without forcing it.* I'd needed that in my younger days. Now it was my turn to offer the same to her. She'd get me however she wanted me.

When the wind shifted to blow their scent at me, my pace slowed as Estrella's scent filled my soul. *Oh, how I've missed that.* Tilhack's scent was there, but I barely noticed it. I was too busy feeling Estrella slipping into me as she only could on the wind. I stopped in the shadows, staying hidden so I could have my moment before giving Estrella hers. The void needed to be filled, and her scent would do that.

Except my ears heard something else.

"We really should tell him," Tilhack said.

My ears perked, too curious to not hear what might be the cause of all this. I moved like a ghost until I could see them. Tilhack was standing near Estrella, who hadn't moved. She was too busy getting her ears back up.

I heard even more pain in her reply. "We can't do that to him. I can't... I can't do that to myself."

"He deserves to know."

"He *deserves* to have his mate back. You don't know him like I do. Telling him will only damage him. Like it damaged me."

Damaged her? What did the humans do to her? And how could it possibly damage me?

Estrella remained withdrawn. That is, until Tilhack rubbed his head against her, not in submission, but affection. She perked almost at once, soaking in his rub as she did mine.

"I wish there was something I could do," Tilhack said. "I feel like I owe you."

Estrella still didn't push him away. "You owe me nothing. You did more than enough."

"I still don't like seeing you like this."

She sat up, and my insides sank to the ground when she gave him a deep rub all her own. "Thank you. It's not possible, but thank you."

What in Wolfor's name is going on here? Has she replaced me? But she... she fought to get back to me... she escaped... and she defied Raj... but yet she... she's back... but she's... and him... and him! My mind went in so many directions, I couldn't find one long enough to follow it.

A ruffed chuckle from Tilhack drew my attention once more. Enough that I found anger growing, directed at them both, but mostly him.

"I wonder if I'll ever find someone like you for me," Tilhack said.

"You will," Estrella said, the comforting, soft voice I had heard so many times before. "As I said before, I'd chase you if things were different. I'm sure another female will feel the same."

"Are you sure they aren't?"

That was it. I couldn't allow it. I left my position to walk hard and fast toward them as my hackles bristled. Tilhack was treading on my territory, on *my* mate. That does not go unchallenged.

"No, they're not," I said, not quite a growl, but still glaring.

Both heads snapped toward me. Estrella's ears were straight up, shock, surprise, and worry all in one. So were Tilhack's, until he had a chance to see me in all my fury. After that, he sank into the ground, ears gone and tail merging with his underside. He whimpered surrender, enough that I almost let it be enough.

Estrella, however, barely flinched beyond her initial surprise.

"Luna, calm down. There's no harm here."

"Not yet," I said, though further from a growl than I had been. Estrella dropped all shock and met my challenge with one of her own. As usual, I knew better than to ignore it. I stopped my approach, dropped my hackles, and let my ears tick forward in approval. "Now there's the wolf I know."

"I haven't changed, Luna," Estrella said. "Nor have my feelings for you. You are still my mate."

"Am I? Looked like something different from my point of view."

"Your point of view is wrong! Luna, why do you think I came back? You are the only wolf worth the effort."

"And him?"

"*He* saved my life. *He* helped me get past human territory alive."

"And that matters because I wasn't there to do the same?"

Estrella backed down for the first time. Her ears softened ever so slightly, though her glare didn't. It went further as she cringed in pain, the same pain she'd returned with.

Tilhack stepped forward before she could come out of it. "Give her time, Luna. It can't all be shared at once. You can't understand what she went through."

Try me! "Oh no? Yesterday, I was convinced she was dead. I only felt the void of where she'd been. Then a moment ago, the void was gone. I didn't feel anything except her presence, and yours too. I felt the warmth of a pack."

"And now? What do you feel now?"

My mind went blank. Utterly, totally empty. A thought would last a few seconds before being swallowed by the new void within. *She is there, my mate and... she was dead yesterday, but... I have a pack now, what...* I couldn't hold onto anything. Even my anger couldn't survive. Panic alone survived, spreading into an ever-growing void of nothing within. *I have to... something.. but I... she... I... he... pain... her...*

I turned and ran. I didn't have a chosen path, I didn't even know what direction I'd turned. My body just… started running. I didn't see anything around me. My mind was still so blank, so empty, the only thing there was panic. Pure, terrified fear coursed through me. As I was sprinting away from so many things, I couldn't find one to settle on.

Estrella. My mate. She's not dead after all. She'd eaten her fill of my kill, expressed her approval of my skills... Tilhack. A new member. Strange, perhaps, but bearing something in him I'm sure will add value to the pack... The two together... Have they replaced me? Estrella said she didn't, but what I saw... And what about her pain? Why won't she share it with me? I'm her mate! It's my duty to—

My paw caught on something, drawing a yip of surprise. *Not again.* The thought lasted but a second, until my body thumped into the ground. The rest happened as it did before, as if time had taken me back to relive it once more.

My legs kicked out to stop me, but I bounced off the push and kept going. I hit the ground hard, flattening my lungs in one last pained yip. My legs flopped over, continuing my momentum from the sprint, forcing my body to continue rolling. I sent my paws out to try and stop me, and again, they only served to keep me rolling. My head glanced off a rock, almost knocking me out. I went limp as I tumbled over an embankment, into the last of the flood-made lagoon. Just enough water to not be mud, but not enough to drown in.

My legs flopped over my side, propelling my head out of the water onto a sandy shore. Then it was over. I came to rest on my side, laying half in the lagoon, fur covered in dirt, water soaking the side I lay on, my paw still stinging from whatever it had hit, and my body aching from the tumble. I hurt in more ways than I could count, though my mind remained blank, which only gave the physical pain more space to occupy. Nothing else was there. I couldn't think, I couldn't feel, I didn't even understand where I was. It was as if I was floating alone somewhere. My thoughts couldn't last long enough to find a comparison.

All I could do was lay in my torment. Half a day? Several days? I couldn't think enough to keep track. My body hurt too much to try, and my mind was still too empty to settle on any single thought. My eyes closed as I tried to find sense in the chaos within, yet all I found was more of the same.

I heard a soft splash first, but before I could tell for sure, something appeared beside me. A body. A warmth that coursed through my blood, lying beside me, its head leaning in to rub against mine. Then, a soft whine all at once drained my mind of everything but one thought.

"Estrella."

"Shhhh," she continued to rub, even as I couldn't find the will to return it. "Just rest. Let yourself feel the pain. It's the only way you can shed it."

"But... but Est—"

"Hush! Hush, my thorn. I'm here now. You're not alone. You never were."

I pushed my muzzle to meet hers. She licked mine in return.

There we lay. Half a day? Several days? We would never know or care. Her fur was against mine, soft, a little wet, but still warm. I could feel her presence, smell her, wet fur and all. Her soul merged with mine, and I lost my pain in her, even as I let myself feel it. I didn't move, but Estrella busied herself with cleaning my fur. *How could I have thought for a second she'd replaced me?*

At last, I pulled myself upright. I rolled onto my paws, shook myself dry, and returned to rubbing against Estrella.

"Thank you," I said.

Estrella only returned the rub, not yet standing. "I'm always here for you, Luna. Anytime you need me, I'm here."

"Yet you won't let me do the same. Estrella, we're mates. We share the joys *and* the burdens. How can I do nothing while it's obvious you're in pain?" Her ears fell, and she cringed again. I cursed myself for even saying it, then laid beside her again so I could rub my head against hers. "Forget it. I shouldn't have asked."

Estrella sighed, then snorted as if angry. I halted my affection in case it was me. She instead stared at me, deep in thought. "You deserve to know."

A ruffed laugh escaped me. That word. Used so often, never without sting. I had used it myself to announce my anger. Others used it when I'd mistreated them. To hear it from her with such pain behind it... it only made it worse.

"I deserve to have my mate back," I said. "If that means letting you heal on your own, then I will, but I can't not care. Not about this. I can't not be here, as you have been for me."

Estrella looked at me, ears up and eyes searching. Just like Jinta, she was asking permission. "Then you don't want to know?"

I rubbed against her again. "Only what you wish to share."

She returned it, and I felt nothing else. "Thank you. Come on, thorn. I told Tilhack to stay at the den. He's no doubt worried about us."

We rose together, both shaking ourselves loose. I leapt up first, then traded playful nips when Estrella was more graceful doing the same. She bumped into me as we walked back home, still play-nipping at times.

"You need to hear what happened," Estrella said.

"Only if you need to tell it," I said.

"I do." She stopped, bit an itch, sighed, and nuzzled my muzzle before continuing on. "The humans never really hurt me. I was taken to what Tilhack called a 'zoo.' Not sure what it is, but I was trapped in a small space. I think they wanted me to think it was like home. For a time, I couldn't get out. I spent my days being fed old kills and watching humans as they stared at me, as if I were a stick to play with. At first, it was torture. Then I... after so long... I... I started to adapt."

There was more there. Something painful, or shameful, she didn't want to share. I also knew she kept it hidden for a reason. I wanted to know what and why, but I'd promised to let her tell only what she wanted to. I couldn't go back on that now, so I kept silent as we approached the den.

"Then your bird came in," she said. "He reminded me of who I was. I... I found... I found a way to escape. I made my way out of the 'zoo' into a large area full of massive human dens. Dens as tall as the shorter trees, paths full of those huge rock beasts you told me about. I have to admit, I've never been so afraid before. I had no idea where I was, or what I was looking at. Somewhere in my escape, I'd lost your bird too. That's when I found him."

We arrived in time for her to indicate Tilhack, who was cracking into a bone in search of any remaining marrow. He stopped when he saw us. His ears perked up, again asking for permission.

I ticked my own ears forward. "It's all right, I ate my fill. You can have it." I settled in nearby, with Estrella lying down beside me. "Estrella tells me she met you right after her escape."

Tilhack ruffed in amusement while abandoning his bone. "More like *I* found *her*. I saw her streak across the paths where the rock beasts run. I thought for sure she'd get run over. Instead she slipped into the space between human dens. She looked hurt, and alone, so I risked contact. Thank Wolfor she didn't snap me in half."

I turned to Estrella first. "How did you get hurt and still manage to escape?"

Her ears fell in a cringe. I prepared to withdraw the question, but she answered it anyway... mostly.

"It happened... just... just as I escaped. The injury was minor, nothing life threatening."

I flicked a curious ear, but said nothing. Again, she had permission to share only what she wanted. A stare from Estrella at Tilhack made it clear he knew, but was being told to keep it quiet. I thought about asking him later, and rejected it almost at once. *It is Estrella's tale to tell, not his.*

And yet, Tilhack took over the telling. "Once I learned where she'd come from, I jumped at the chance to get away from the humans into the wild. My mother, my wolf side, had told me about it, and I'd wanted it more than anything. Especially after she was killed by a rock beast."

"What about your father?" I asked.

"He was a pet whose owners left one day and never came back. He managed to escape the den before he ran out of food and water. After a while, he turned wild, met my mother, they mated, I was born, and then he left for a hunt and never returned. Probably killed by another rock beast, by the humans, or by Hitlark."

"Hitlark?"

"A pure wolf that also lived in the area. He did not care for pets, and cared even less for mutts. Another reason I left. Anyway, I helped Estrella get away from the human dens and helped her navigate through more human territory on the way."

"How did you know which way to go?"

Chirping announced the answer before either of them could. "I search, I find, I lead, I save, to meet the promise that I gave!"

I found the bird where he'd always been, right in the middle of the rock pile, too far to reach as usual. I thought about trying anyway, but after almost succeeding, I decided not to do that to him, or his apparent mate sitting beside him.

Tilhack, meanwhile, growled annoyance I knew all too well. "He's right about that. He helped Estrella get out, then helped us get away from more humans after that. Took us a long time to get here, but he kept us moving in the right direction."

"As in, he kept you on course?" I asked. "Or he kept you going in the hopes he'd shut up?"

"Both," Estrella and Tilhack said.

I panted laughter. *I can imagine. After a few moons straight spent listening to him, I'd become Rajor's omega if it meant a few days of silence.* Instead, my mockingbird had used that charm to lead Estrella and Tilhack back to me. *I never knew he cared that much.* It made me regret some of the rather violent dreams I'd had about him over the years.

I shook them from my mind while addressing the bird directly. "I owe you more than I can ever repay, yet all I have to give is my thanks."

"Luna thanks like worm and seed, Luna thanks is all I need."

Tilhack again growled while cringing as if he might squeeze something out of his head. "Bird sang so much about you two, I'd give a lot to never hear either one of your names for a while. Uh, no offense, Luna."

I again chuckled. *Bird hasn't lost his touch.* "None taken, Tilhack. Believe me, I understand. That reminds me, though. Now that you're here, what do you plan to do? This forest is not what it used to be, and I don't know how your mixed blood will be received by the other wolves."

"Why do you think he's with us?" Estrella said. "We won't care. We'll take him in, give him a place. His heart is as strong as ours, even if his eyes aren't 'normal.' He'll make us stronger."

I cast her a reprimanding glare. It softened some as fast as it came, yet the message remained. Though my mind tried to go blank again, I wouldn't let it this time. I had no intentions of tumbling a third time.

That did not silence my anger however. Estrella had made an important decision without asking me how I felt. As much as I cared about the emotions she was dealing with, I couldn't ignore that she'd stepped out of line. She'd made a hard choice without even letting me voice my thoughts on it. Mate or not, neither of us could do that. *That's how pups get banished over false swears.*

Estrella let her ears soften, though she also returned a confused state of her own. *She won't understand if you don't tell her, thorn.*

I let my glare fade further. What came out was as much plea as reprimand. "Don't forget your place."

"I didn't think I did," Estrella said "I thought I was your mate."

I took a breath to settle myself. *Fair point, however...* "Mate, yes. Alpha, no. We can't make snap decisions without the other being involved. That's how I ended up out here. Toltan made the decision alone. We can't make that mistake."

Estrella's ears flashed back for a moment. I thought it a no until her ears ticked forward immediately after. She'd had her eyes closed in stress or pain, which sent me again cursing myself for acting like... *like a stupid thorn-in-the-paw.*

Tilhack rose before Estrella came out of her cringe. "Don't let me come between you. If you don't want me, then so be it. You deserve to have her more than I deserve a pack."

I growled, then had to ruff at Tilhack before he could finish a turn to leave. *Yet again, others say what I do or don't deserve.* I had to have been cursed to always hear it, or maybe Wolfor liked to use it to get my attention. I preferred the former, for the latter scared me in several ways.

Tilhack didn't move. His eyes and ears were locked on me, waiting for me to attack or something. I breathed deep for a moment to be sure my mind was clear before addressing him again.

"Let me decide what I do or don't deserve," I said. "Can you do that?"

"If that's the way you want it," Tilhack said carefully.

"Then sit your tail down, and go back to your bone. I worked hard for that kill. I deserve to see my pack enjoying it."

Tilhack panted a quick chuckle while his ears ticked forward. He took my advice and cracked the bone wider in search of more marrow.

Estrella flicked an amused ear at him before returning to me. "I'm sorry, Luna, for all of it. I didn't mean to disrespect you like that."

"You make it sound as if you broke my tail," I said.

"Didn't I?"

I rubbed against her to make sure she believed me. "No, but you have to understand, yesterday I thought you were dead. I had begun to move on. Now here you are, alive and well, carrying scars of your own, as well as a new member I know nothing about. You can't expect me to adapt to all that in such a short amount of time."

Estrella sighed, but didn't stop rubbing against me. "You're right, but you also can't expect me to just know. As you said, we're mates. We share the joys and the burdens. I can share mine with you if you'll share yours with me."

"I think I can do that, so long as you remember your place. You're my other half. Your place is beside me, defending me from harm, and allowing me to do the same. We can't do that if we won't talk about big decisions with each other."

"I don't remember you asking to add Carlin to our pack. Is this so different?"

I cringed more at the sharpness of her point than his memory. "Fair enough. Although I don't remember you resisting the idea either. But that doesn't matter. From now on, we check with each other. Agreed?"

Estrella rubbed her head against mine again. "Agreed. Can Tilhack stay?"

"No."

"Luna!"

"Just keeping your ears sharp."

Chapter 13

NEVER THOUGHT I'D BE GLAD *to find a new scent on my border.* I ruffed contentment after sniffing a pile of wolf droppings that were neither mine nor Rajor's. Another pack had found a new home. Between the harsh winter, and the constant threat of the humans, it was a welcome sign. It made the recent return of my own pack feel that much better. Like things might finally be turning in the right direction, and staying there, for a change.

"Found something, Luna?" Estrella asked while Tilhack sniffed at the marking.

"A touch of hope," I said. "If you haven't noticed, there aren't many foreign wolves these days."

"I have noticed. Can't imagine what happened to them."

Crack!-Cshoo-shooo

Estrella and I turned our ears toward the sound, as did Tilhack after he took cover behind us. I couldn't tell if he'd been startled or just wasn't used to it being that close yet. Then again, with their escape being so fresh, I could understand him being extra cautious too.

"There's your answer," I said. "That and the harsh winter either killed them or drove them off."

Estrella sighed with shifting ears while I walked along our border in search of a trail.

"Makes you wonder how long this new pack will last," she said.

Tilhack snapped up with his ears perked forward. "Not long by the sounds of it. Is that a pup?"

I perked one ear, then turned both when I heard whimpers through the trees. Like Tilhack, I couldn't determine the wolf's age, just its pain. Instinct drew my paws forward in search of the owner.

"Luna?" Tilhack said. "What are you doing? It's not our territory."

"It's not anyone's territory if that's all that's left of the pack," I said. Tilhack's ears fell, so I flicked my tail across his nose. "Relax. This is how we do things in the wild."

Tilhack only ruffed in reply. *Good enough, I guess.*

The whimpers weren't fading, but they were moving. I tried to find the source of the sound among the trees without going any further in than I had to. I caught a glimpse of movement behind an oak tree and stepped closer with Estrella just behind, watching for anyone coming close to us. The glimpse became a pair of adult wolves walking between streams of daylight. Or more correctly, a male limped while a female leaned into him to keep him going. *Too bad she and I are taken,* I thought. She was impressive. Smaller than Estrella, but something about her suggested a quiet strength that was familiar. Much like her larger-than-normal black tail tip that reminded... *wait...*

"Jinta?"

My ears perked up, as did Estrella's.

Tilhack tilted his head at us. "Who is Jinta?"

"My sister," I said. "What is she doing out here? And who's the male?"

I watched, trying to evaluate the situation without being seen. The border marking wasn't hers, nor anyone else I knew, which kept me from further violating the territory. Either Rajor had lost control of the pack, or Jinta was running with someone else. Either way, running to her now could put my own pack at risk. No matter how much trouble she might be in, I couldn't take that chance.

That said, I didn't see anyone else, pup or otherwise. Of course, that did not mean they weren't there. The part of me requiring caution wanted to leave them. My blood refused to. *Not until we know why the male is limping, or until a challenge is issued.*

Another pain-filled yelp echoed as the male collapsed. I watched on while Estrella and Tilhack watched me for instructions.

"I can't," the male said between pants, his voice almost familiar. "I can't go on."

Jinta tugged at him, trying to get him back up. "Oh yes, you can. I didn't split from Rajor's pack to give up on you now."

That's one answer. At the very least, Jinta was with a new pack now. Still, something in the male seemed incredibly familiar. His voice, to a point, though his fur was the biggest pull. It was a pelt of nearly pure ash, with his underside more a brownish cream, yet still ashy. I had seen that fur pattern before, but the memory was so old, barely a fragment remained.

The male protested again. "Jinta, I can't. My leg won't go anymore."

"Then carry it! I'm not leaving you. We live and die together."

My heart stopped. Something was chasing them. Something that had them running scared enough to keep moving despite the male's injury. I didn't hear anything else, and the wind was blowing the wrong way to carry any clues. I could only guess they were running from a rival pack, or perhaps another predator, like a bear or mountain lion.

"Jinta, get out of here," the male said. "If you don't leave, the humans will get you too."

Questions answered.

"Humans?" Estrella said. "Tell me they're not the same ones we just got away from."

With the wind still at our tails, we only had our eyes and ears to help us find any sign of the humans. We found nothing until we heard a loud *thwack*, followed by birds squawking as they were scared to the wing. Our eyes followed the commotion, where we found a pair of humans with thunder sticks. One of whom, whose head was utterly bald, I recognized as a member of the pack that came every year. *Should have known better. Humans don't do quiet.* The other, I didn't know. He was so young, I guessed this was his first hunt, possibly even the bald one's pup. Whatever their relation, they were traipsing through the forest as they'd always done: loudly.

My hackles bristled, as did Estrella's. She was the first to growl, but I was the first to move. A trot became a run, a run became a sprint, a sprint became a snarl-filled charge. I would not allow this. Not this time, not to my blood.

The humans heard us too late. The bald one only had time to see me leap into his neck. I dug my fangs deep, tearing flesh with repeated bites. The human gasped and gargled as we hit the ground, blood covering us both. He didn't last much longer. The second human had turned my way, only to have Tilhack tackle him from the side. His first bite tore out the human's throat. His second snapped it before he could bleed to death.

I turned to check on Jinta and found Estrella already there, having more luck with the male than she had. Jinta, meanwhile, was shaking her head for some reason, though I heard Estrella say something about a long story. Perhaps Jinta, like me, was needing to readjust to the idea that Estrella wasn't dead after all.

As for her companion, I saw for the first time the gash on his right foreleg, fresh blood staining a coat I still felt I knew. *No wonder he couldn't run. With a wound like that, it's hard to do much of anything. Especially if it's half as fresh as it looks.*

Estrella had him standing, but he still refused to step forward. *That needs to change.* As much as he needed to, we couldn't let him wait for the wound to seal.

"Come on," I said. "We can't stay here."

Now the male moved. He stopped me cold when he turned around to snarl at me. He winced with tucked leg while his glare bore through me. A glare that suggested he was ready to kill.

"I'll go nowhere with you. You didn't want me before. Why would you want me now?"

My confusion at his timing silenced all other thoughts for the time being. "Never wanted you? What are you talking about?"

"Don't you remember me? Don't you remember the pup you rescued only to abandon the same day?"

My ears perked in shock. I mentally bit myself for not remembering or recognizing his voice, even if it was different as an adult. His pelt hadn't changed much as he grew. Toltan said he'd caught Jinta's eye. Seems little Folar, not so little anymore, had done more than that. He'd grown strong within the pack. Strong enough to give me pause despite his injury. Were danger not likely close by, I might have spent more time admiring the adult Folar had become.

Instead, I turned my ears back at my choice of words. I prayed they'd pacify Folar long enough to get to safety.

"All right, I deserve that, but you don't have a lot of choice right now."

"Don't I?" Folar said. "You told me to learn the pain. Well, I have. Enough to know I want nothing to do with you. Now leave us alone, or face my fangs."

Folar perked his ears forward, raising his hackles and his lips. I couldn't believe it when I realized he was serious. Despite the certain presence of humans, he couldn't let go of that day, even for a moment.

Folar's challenge vanished when Jinta bit just below the wound. He yelped in pain, then turned to fend her off. He growled again while she only glared at him.

CRAACK!-cshoo-shoo

There was no blood, thank Wolfor, but fur from under Folar's neck flew off like a dozen tufts of sheddings blown away in a wind. He'd come that close to dropping where he stood. I didn't wait for the human to try again. I grabbed Folar by his scruff and pulled him, yelping and trying to escape into the best cover I could find. It turned out to be a thick log covered in moss, but it would have to do.

Folar was still snarling despite the cringe holding the rest of his body. *Just what I need with humans around.*

"Shut up and stay on my tail," I said. "These humans are noisy beasts, but they can be tenacious too."

Folar's glare remained. "You can't—"

"Shut up!" Estrella, Tilhack, and Jinta all said with a snarl turned his way. Folar became half the size he was as a pup. He tried to be angry, but he didn't dare risk that many jaws.

I perked my ears into the forest, but I didn't hear anything, not even a bird. Either this human was actually stealthy, or he hadn't moved. I couldn't risk either, so I prayed Wolfor was with me when I decided to make my move.

I tossed my head back toward my territory. I stalked forward ahead of the others, but my ears were trained behind us, in search of the humans. We kept to what shadows we could find, skittering between bushes when we couldn't. Folar whimpered with each step, but neither Tilhack nor Jinta would let him stop a second time. Nor would Jinta let him put his injured leg down to use it. *Smart wolf.*

Our group snuck through the forest for as long as Folar kept moving. When his steps came on shaking legs, I knew we'd gone as far as we could. I found an area thick with trees that kept the sun from shining there, creating a deep shadow the humans could easily walk past. Folar laid inside a crease in a tree, then whined and cringed at his wound. More so when Jinta began to clean it for him. I held my vigil in the direction we'd come, more disturbed at my thoughts than the blood on my muzzle.

Luck. That's all it had been. Luck we'd been there, luck Jinta and Folar were still alive, luck the humans were the prey instead of us, luck Estrella and Tilhack had escaped their grasp. I was getting sick of it. Sick of always running, never really sleeping, getting wrapped in terror every time I heard a thunder bolt. I could live with predators. I could even accept becoming prey, but these humans? They were just killers, and I'd had enough of them.

Estrella joined me while I watched the forest. My mind was elsewhere, considering the most outrageous of ideas.

"Any sign of them?" she asked.

I breathed stress before tapping my muzzle against hers. "I think we're safe for now. How's Folar?"

Estrella looked back, then flicked her ears when Folar yelped again.

"I've seen pups with stronger wills. I can't believe Jinta thinks he's worth mating with."

"He's actually doing... wait, mating?"

Estrella ruffed brief amusement. "You losing your touch, thorn? I can smell it on her. Jinta's pregnant. That, and the way she's caring for him, well... I'd think by now you'd recognize that kind of care."

I ruffed agreement, and felt myself turn stern. *My little sister? Pregnant?* I couldn't imagine it somehow. Not that I doubted Estrella. If she said Jinta was pregnant, I believed her. It made what I was thinking become not just easy. It became necessary.

"Guess I am a bit distracted," I said. "Anyway, I wouldn't judge Folar yet. The humans' thunder sticks don't always kill you. Maybe the magic doesn't always work right, I don't know. I just know I got a wound like that once, and it hurt worse than three broken legs for some time. He should be better by morning. I hope he is. We're going to need him soon."

Estrella became grave, even guarded, as hairs rose in response. "Need him for what?"

"To end this. We can't keep going like this. Wolves have lived here for generations. Now these humans seek to wipe us out? I won't allow it. We have to end this. We have to drive the humans off."

Estrella's ears went straight while her eyes grew. "Luna! Have you lost your mind? The humans have thunder sticks and who knows what else. We're just wolves."

I allowed an evil glare at the thought of them doing the running for a change. "Exactly. We're wolves. Our territory stands threatened. By Wolfor's fang, I will see it defended."

Estrella ears went straighter, appalled at the idea. The look faded into deep thought when I didn't relent. How could I? I'd seen too many wolves killed, I'd heard the thunder too many times, and I'd felt its bite. Now they'd come that close to killing my sister and her pups. As the resentment grew, so did the feeling that I should have done it years ago. This forest, this territory, it belongs to me, to my kind. I'd had enough of letting the humans violate it unchallenged.

Estrella's ears kept twitching, no doubt fighting with some unpleasant thoughts. I could see the weight of those thoughts when she turned her ears toward a more silent Folar.

"It won't be easy, Luna," she said. "The humans carry a lot of power and they know it."

I stared her down, trying to make her believe as I did. "We only have to drive them off. A united pack snarling death should do the trick."

"I'm not so sure. Convincing them we have more may not be possible without a scuffle. We'd lose lives if we took them on. You sure it's worth that?"

Yet again, something answered for me. A chorus of howls echoed from the forest. Not Rajor, not a new pack, not even wild wolves. I knew those voices too well to think otherwise. Only one pack sounded that disorganized, and to call them wolves was an insult to all wolves.

I turned to Estrella, now fully committed. "Those are the pet wolves I told you about. Carlin's pups? If the humans can force us to abandon the wild, what else might they do? That's assuming they don't just kill us. I won't be killed by some thunder stick to have my hide carried off for who knows what. This is my forest. This is my territory. I will not allow this violation any longer."

"Then you know where I'll be," Estrella said without hesitation. "I've followed you this long. I'm not about to abandon you now."

"Don't forget me," Tilhack said. I hadn't noticed him come close enough to listen in. "New or not, I care about her well-being, about both of you. If you're charging into battle the humans, I won't be far behind. Call it proof my wolf blood isn't just red water."

No need for that. He'd already proven a natural ability to hunt. So much so I almost wanted another harsh winter to see him shine like I felt sure he could. *I bet he'd cut through the snow just like Martol did, if not better.*

But a fine hunter means little in a territory dispute. Against other wolves, maybe we'd have a chance, but humans? The five of us would need to show a lot to scare them off. A larger pack would guarantee it. Unfortunately, only one remained, and they might be more dangerous than the humans.

"I've never doubted your blood, Tilhack," I said. "That said, we need more. A pack our size, though fierce, may not be enough to scare the humans. To do that, we'll need more bodies, and I know only one place to find them."

Tilhack tilted his head. Estrella sighed deeply.

"You do remember the risk that brings?" Estrella asked.

Intimately. "I know no other way. They stand threatened more than we do. No matter our past, Rajor has to listen to reason."

"I'm not so sure about that, Luna."

"I am," Jinta said. She stood behind Tilhack, glancing back at a still wincing Folar. "As I said before, he hasn't been the same since the fall. More so since the winter."

"What do you mean?" Estrella said. "What happened?"

"You don't know?"

"I've... been away. Luna hasn't had a chance to tell me much."

"He lost half the pack to starvation, including last year's litter, and much of Martol's original pack. He's been a shell of himself since. I think he'd be agreeable to facing a threat that could wipe it out for good."

Or he could be bitter about so much loss, he might finally decide to have me killed.

"Only one way to find out," I said aloud. "We'll wait here a bit longer, let Folar's wound stop hurting. I'll check our trail, make sure the humans didn't follow us."

"You shouldn't go alone," Estrella said.

"I'll be fine. The wind has changed in our favor, and it's easier for one wolf to sneak around than two. Have a little faith." She play-growled at me while her ears ticked forward in agreement. I ruffed a chuckle in reply before returning to the matter of the moment. "When I get back, Tilhack, you and

Jinta take Folar to my den. See if you can talk some sense into him. Estrella, I want you in your place, if you're willing."

"Would I be anywhere else?"

Only if death could catch you, I thought with a nuzzle for her.

～⌣⌣⌢

I had so many escape routes planned, I felt like I knew the forest by heart. Twenty-four trees, three logs, seventeen bushes, by the time I found a border marker left by Rajor, I was starting to count birds too. A part of me wished my mockingbird was one of them. I stood on my side of the border, Estrella ever solid beside me. If only I felt the same.

"Just tell me I'm crazy," I said. "Tell me so I know it's really me that decided to do this."

"You're crazy, Luna," Estrella said without emotion. "That's why this will work."

"Have a little faith?"

"See? You do learn."

A lie I can live with, assuming I actually live.

I had to swallow a few pinecones before I could go through with it. After all, I didn't have to. The right howls could get what I wanted, but not with the same impact. No, I needed to be sure all of the pack heard me, which left me only one way to proceed.

Another pinecone, and my paws moved. A few steps at a time, each one a violation of my sentence. They came with a thunder in my chest that pulsed through my body, for each one had a high chance of being my last.

I almost wanted a scout to see me. I wanted an excuse to abandon my plan. Wolfor never gave me one, because we never saw anyone, prey or wolf, the farther we crept into Rajor's territory. For a moment, I returned to the pup I once was. Every sound demanded my attention and drew an extra beat from my heart. A soft crack, or a shadow, or that leaf over there, any of them could bring my end. As an adult, I knew better. It just didn't help.

At last, my ears picked up a conversation. First, voices I never knew well but had heard before, then younger ones, then an older one I knew almost as well as I knew Toltan and Martol. Lonate was teaching the pups again. *Like he'd do anything else.*

I followed the sound to where the pack had always been. A steep hillside I once called home, that still bore the same den where I was born. Every tree and bush remained exactly the same as the day Toltan drove me off. From on top of the hillside, one could watch the whole pack, as Toltan did on many occasions.

Despite the low number, the pack looked well. Not a dozen wolves, pups included, but all looked strong from what I could see. Many of them were

152

asleep in the afternoon sun breaking through the trees, while the two pups bounced around an old bone. I found Rajor watching them from a distance, oddly quiet and sullen in a shadow.

But where is Lonate? I had heard his voice, so where did he go? Based on previous experience, Lonate would be the ideal place to start, if I could find him.

A short growl from the side startled me and Estrella into cowering. Fear of attack kept us there as Lonate emerged from cover. His tail and hackles were up, but he was otherwise silent. He stared at Estrella a moment with softer ears, then renewed his glare at me.

"I thought you said the humans took her," he said.

Estrella replied before I could. "They did. I managed to escape and make my way home."

"I'm glad to see you well. But you shouldn't be here, either of you. You know what it means for a lone wolf to return. Rajor won't be as kind as Toltan."

Maybe he wasn't so ideal after all. Too late now.

"I don't have a choice, Lonate," I said. "I have to speak to Rajor about…"

That dropped his fur. "You what? Are you nuts? The moment he sees you he'll—"

"LUNA!"

I knew that voice. The pack jolted, then froze as Rajor tore from his spot up the side of the hill toward me. Lonate's ears went flat, yet for some reason, mine never did. Not until I forced myself to go low, even appear submissive. Estrella tried to get between us, but I pushed my way in front of her. I had to give her a growl of my own to force her to back down. Rajor had to deal with me, or this wouldn't work at all.

Rajor's lips were curled back in a snarl as every hair stood on end. His sprint announced my doom with every step. I held my posture, praying it would work, or I'd live long enough to save myself if it didn't.

Rajor came, and I shook for fear of the pain I may be allowing to come my way. Thankfully, it never did. Rajor stopped cold right in front of me in full display. I didn't dare move now.

Rajor's snarl faded, but he was still growling when he spoke. "What are you doing here? You know the law as well as I. You know the price."

Well, here it goes. May Wolf or guide and protect me. Not necessarily in that order.

"Nothing compared to the price if I don't come. Rajor, I bring a warning."

"You dare? I don't care how many times you best me. This is still *my* territory. *My*—"

"That's not what I mean!" I allowed myself to rise, but slowly, with no hint of threat or challenge. "The humans are back, Rajor. Our packs are the only ones left. If we do nothing, none of us will live to see summer."

Rajor's growl stopped, though his glare didn't. "And what? You want to come back? Be protected?"

"No. I want you to join me in one great display. A united pack to drive the humans off once and for all."

Rajor's ears went straight. He looked more appalled than anything else. *This can't be good.*

"I don't believe this," he said. "You risk your neck to suggest that *I* follow *you* in an attack against the humans? Has solitude damaged you that much?"

I turned my ears back with a sigh. I had a hard time fighting past my pride to give a response that wasn't an insult.

When Estrella stepped forward again, this time, I let her be. It gave me a chance to regain my composure.

"Listen to him, Rajor. We can't live like this."

Rajor snorted at her, indignant as usual. "You seem to be fine. Luna said you and the others were dead."

"The others *are* dead. I escaped the humans before they could do the same to me. But I had help. If we're to survive, we have to—"

"No!" Rajor's growl returned, as did his raised tail. "My pack remains because it is the strongest. The humans won't dare risk coming after us."

Just what I didn't need. The foolish side of Rajor's pride. I countered with frustration escaping my control.

"Rajor. We can't wait to be the prey. We have to be the wolves we were born to be. We have to drive the humans off as we would a rival pack, or we risk losing everything."

Rajor instantly changed. His growl ceased, his ears fell, he even stepped back while his ears repeatedly turned back, as if constantly saying "no." His tail never tucked, but I could still smell the fear on him. It was almost the same fear I found on Martol and Toltan when the thunder first rang out in the forest.

"I've lost too much already, Luna," Rajor said. "I won't risk more on a fool's assault that will only kill those I have left. They are my pack. I must protect them."

I tried to be as gentle as I could. "This will protect them, Rajor. You have to—"

"No!"

I couldn't believe it when Rajor started trembling. From nose to tail, he shook like he might fall at any moment. He could hardly breathe as he stared at the pups below. When he came back to me, his glare was born more of fear than anger. *What happened to you, brother?*

"Get out," Rajor said. "Get out of here while I'm feeling merciful. Don't come back unless you want to die."

"Rajor," I said, "don't be—"

"Go, Luna! I will not ask again."

I didn't wait long to push Estrella away. We had our answer. Nothing we said would change it.

We didn't say a word on the way to the den either. I wouldn't have had anything to offer had we tried. I couldn't get the image out of my mind. Rajor, my proud brother, paralyzed by fear. Were he not already dead, Toltan would have laughed to death had someone told him. If only I could find such humor in the situation.

"Luna pack still strong and proud, Luna pack will lift the cloud."

About time he showed up. Haven't had a strong perk in my ears for a while.

"Thanks," I said as the bird wove around trees well over our heads. "I don't suppose you could offer any help."

"Luna, Luna, need no help, Luna, Luna, ain't no whelp."

He left chattering away from a playful growl from me and Estrella. Darn bird hadn't lost his touch.

We returned to the den where the others were waiting. Folar was still favoring his leg, but he didn't whimper anymore when Jinta licked it. I hoped it was only pain now, for he'd be no good to us hurt. Assuming he'd hunt with us, or rather me, at all.

Tilhack saw us first. He met us near my caching tree, a soft wag in his tail, the only thing about him that wasn't quite wolf.

"Well, you're both alive, so it can't have gone that bad."

I growled while flopping in front of the den near Jinta. "Might as well have. Rajor wouldn't listen. Pride, arrogance, fear, I don't know why. All I know is he won't help us."

Estrella laid beside me and offered a soft rub. "We'll find a way."

"You sure about that?" Tilhack said as he found a spot to settle in himself. "I mean, where does this leave us?"

"The same place," I said. "If Rajor won't help himself by helping us, fine. We'll do this ourselves."

"Luna. Five wolves against the humans? It's insane. If they were wolves, they'd never take us seriously. I don't want to think about what the humans would do."

"Five wolves?" I let myself hope while looking over at Jinta. "Then Folar has changed his mind?"

Jinta ruffed a chuckle while Folar laid his head on his paws, trying to fake sleep. His body relaxed, suggesting he might have found it anyway.

"I didn't give him a choice," Jinta said. "As you said, this has to stop. If my big brother is going to scare off the humans, then I owe it to him to be there, even if he did turn me down before. Folar won't let me go alone, which means he's forced to join us, no matter how much he hates it."

"Hates me, you mean."

Jinta's ears flashed back. She couldn't stop a whine either. "You have to admit, you stung him good as a pup. You of all wolves understand the nature of those scars."

I ticked my ears forward through a wince of my own. *Do I ever.* It's what made our parting so hard. At the time, I couldn't stomach the thought of driving away my only chance of companionship. Yet I had enough sense to know I had to. Toltan just made it easier by relighting my rage. Unfortunately, that same rage made me far harsher than I needed to be, and led to me turning away my mother not long after. The sight of the void behind her eyes still plagued my nightmares sometimes. As did Carlin's and Toltan's bodies, Folar, and many other wounds not yet healed.

"Stung me too," I said. "I had to make a choice. I knew he wouldn't last long with me. He had to go *somewhere*. He wouldn't accept it, so I had to force the choice on him."

Jinta ticked her ears forward, but otherwise didn't react. "I know that. I think somewhere he does too, but for all his pride, he's never really moved past that night. First, he lost his family, then his hero rejected him. It's hard to think clearly through that."

And unlike me, he didn't have anyone to keep him in line when the pain hit. "I know. I can only hope someday he'll understand. Maybe even forgive me."

"Don't count on it," Folar said from his paws. *Guess he wasn't asleep after all.*

I still flicked an ear back at him. He was young. There was plenty of time for him to change his mind.

After so much reflecting, and staring death in the face, my chest felt hollow. Somewhere, my mind thought to look to my cache, then back at Tilhack without a word. He ruffed amusement with a forward tick of his ears. There were still scraps there. I returned his ruff before heading over to settle my stomach. I wasn't really hungry. I just needed something other than emotion in my chest right now.

Estrella followed, close enough to feel, far enough not to crowd.

"Are you sure we can do this?" she said. "Five wolves is hardly the united pack you were looking for."

I dug into the tree and picked out a hunk of meat still left over from our latest kill. "Martol started ours with little more."

"Half of whom, including my parents, are now dead, without ever facing a single human."

My ears perked at first in surprise, followed by a turn of my head in confusion. *Her parents are dead?* Estrella cringed in pain, which kept me from asking the question.

She must have seen it in my ears anyway. "Jinta told me while you were checking our trail. Solas died in a hunt, a lot like Martol did, as I understand it. Carfen... her heart died with him. She barely lived long enough to give birth to the pups the pack now has."

So that's who they were mourning. When Jinta had come looking to join me, the howl of mourning may well have been for another lost pup, but more likely, they were mourning Carfen. The idea that the proud pair of Solas and Carfen were now dead turned my stomach inside out. As did the heavy question of what would become of the pack without them to provide new blood. *Of course, if we're all dead, it won't matter much, will it?*

Estrella had paused to cringe in her own sorrow. "My point is, as strong as the pack was, they've lost members against far weaker foes. Martol told us about hunts in which she lost members, and she never faced humans either."

"She could have," I said, conviction returning to settle my insides. "I have no doubt of that. Just like I have no doubt in them. Even Folar, for all his hate, I'm certain of. Five wolves, one wolf, it doesn't matter. The humans will tuck their tails soon enough."

I chewed into my snack while Estrella laughed beside me. "Never thought you'd be the one telling me to have a little faith."

"Like you said, I do learn."

A quick shadow announced the mockingbird before I saw him land in the branches above us. "Learn, learn, gather more, another comes to help the score."

Another comes? What is that bird talking about now?

When he said nothing more, I looked around, searching for the meaning. It wasn't long before I saw another wolf trotting our way. Took me less time to realize it was Lonate... alone... far, far away from the current litter. *The world must be ending.*

As he got closer, Lonate slowed, with his ears flat against his head and his tail tucked under him. He was acting like an omega begging for scraps. I couldn't form a word because I'd never seen Lonate act like that, not even around Toltan. The same thoughts kept my ears soft, which allowed Lonate to approach and cower before me.

"Luna," he said. "I'm sorry for violating your territory. There was no other way."

I had to shake my head before I could think again. *Is this the same wolf?* "Lonate, what are you doing here?"

"I'm here to join you on your hunt."

"What? Why now? What about Rajor's pups?"

Lonate spat as if hacking a bad meal. "*Solas'* pups. They'll be fine without me. I have to do this. I *need* to do this."

I could only stare and remember all the days Lonate spent standing guard after the thunder first echoed in the forest. That same wolf stood before me. He carried a wound none could see, but it bled just as much. I couldn't understand why as a pup. Now I had a chance to learn, and unlike Estrella's tale, I felt like this story was one I *needed* to learn. That said, for Lonate's sake, one change was needed.

"Estrella," I said. "why don't you take some scraps to the others? I'm sure Folar could use it."

Estrela tilted her head, confused, and probably a little hurt. "Luna? What are you—"

"Estrella. Please?"

I asked with my eyes only. I couldn't say it, perhaps because even the question might betray the moment. Thankfully, Estrella appeared to understand anyway. Despite a backward tick of her ears, she gathered a few scraps, then with the bird chirping and fluttering over her, left me and Lonate alone.

Once we were, I felt my insides grow roots. I didn't want to do this, but I had to know. I needed to understand what the humans stirred in him. It was the only way I could be sure he could handle the task ahead and, perhaps, help him get past scars of his own.

"Lonate, why do you need to do this? There's something you're not telling me."

Lonate cringed, then shook as if he were cold. It reminded me a lot of Toltan after I'd beaten Rajor last fall. The memory drove a tree through my heart, but it also kept me mindful of how much pain Lonate must be in.

"I have scars of my own, Luna," Lonate said. "Why can't you leave it at that?"

If only I could. "Because these scars could threaten my pack. I remember when the humans first came here. You said something about a past you left behind. I need to know what it is so I can help you face it."

"Face it, or answer for it?"

"I'm not here to judge you, Lonate. I want to help you, but I need to understand the wound before I can heal it. You can't face the humans until we do."

Lonate cringed so hard, his eyes closed. When they opened, they asked me, begged me not to let their owner speak. I stood silent. No posture, little emotion, only a pair of ears turned forward to catch every word. The same ears I'd used as a pup to learn everything I now knew. Lonate needed this as much as I did. Estrella had shared as much pain as she could, and the change had been immediate. Lonate was keeping all of his inside. He had to let go before it consumed him. I hoped I was helping him do so without doing harm in the process.

Lonate cringed again, then his eyes filled with tears. I was surprised he didn't sob when he spoke again.

"I killed them," Lonate stared at me as if I were responsible. "I killed my pack. First, my younger siblings disappeared, despite my best efforts to keep them safe. They were too curious. They snuck out, and I never saw them again, not until that last day. My brother and I found them, trapped, scared to death. We tried to free them, then they came. Humans. They killed my brother with their thunder sticks, and I ran. I ran to the only place I thought was safe. The humans followed me. I knew they were there, but I kept going. I led them to our den. The others... they..."

The sobs came as Lonate looked as if he couldn't breathe right. I felt the sting within, but I didn't move, or say anything, for more was coming. Even though I knew the rest, Lonate needed to say it for himself.

"I didn't stay to fight," Lonate said. "The humans came, and I kept running. I was so scared, I couldn't face them. All I could hear was that terrible thunder, and the whimpers of the injured before they were killed. My fault, my wrong, and I didn't shed a drop of blood for it. My father alone survived. He blamed me for their deaths, and so do I. He banished me for what I did. He told me I deserved a death worse than theirs for not protecting the pack when I had the chance. So you see, Luna? I didn't do anything then. I can't ignore the chance to do something now. It's my only chance to make things right."

He continued to sob, and I remained still as I felt the weight of a thousand trees on my back. What do you say to that? I knew it was coming. Partway through, I recognized the tale, yet I still wasn't prepared for it. Was it the story, or was it the legacy of that stubborn old wolf standing before me that did it? I couldn't tell, nor could I find a better thing to say in response.

"Driving the humans off won't change the past, Lonate. Nothing will."

Lonate glared at me not in anger, but conviction. "No, but it might give me something I can be proud of. Something my father could be proud of if he knew. The pup that led humans to his den grew up to be one of the few wolves who defended another pack from the same fate? That has to count for something."

"I'm sure it would."

I had my answer. More than that, I knew what to say now. We'd need to talk about what happened to his younger siblings, among other things, but that was a conversation for another time. The here and now was all about getting Lonate to reconnect with the blood that ran through his veins. I stood tall, trying to act the strong alpha I felt he needed.

"Lonate, if your father knew what you've done since that day, I know he'd be proud. I suspect he'd even forgive you."

His sobs and tears stopped all at once. I could tell from Lonate's glare that a growl wasn't far behind. "You don't know that."

I didn't back down, but I did offer a tap of my nose on Lonate's. If only he knew. "Yeah, I do, but enough of that. Come on. You should see where I've been living the last few years, and if you're going to hunt with us, you'd do well to learn the pack." I turned to lead the way back, but stopped when I realized Lonate hadn't moved. I found him stock-still, with his ears straight up. "Well? You coming?"

Lonate's ears twitched back, but he came to my side, at a trot no less. I nipped at his muzzle to get him to relax, which he returned while his tail floated behind him. We traded a panted laugh, then Lonate turned his ears forward with a snort.

"I'm with you, Luna," he said. "No matter what happens, I'll do better this time."

"I never doubted it," I said. "And Lonate, only you and I need to know your reasons. The others can settle for your desire to help. Make up whatever excuse you want for the tears. Your past only concerns me, and I've already forgotten it."

Lonate cringed again, but the softness of everything else suggested this one was pain. "Thank you, Luna. That means a lot."

Least I can do for Carlin's son.

~~~

Chapter 14

MY INSIDES WERE TIGHTER THAN A CRAMP after a long chase, but it couldn't be helped. We had to risk being close to the humans' meeting area during the day. I needed to be sure of their number, and to see if I could find any other weakness we could exploit. That meant watching them when they were most active, and at close range. Unfortunately, I found more reasons for my stomach to turn inside out.

The fourth pet wolf must have recovered from that night with Carlin. He was bounding around with the rest of them, playing with the humans like newborn pups. Simple games over lengths of vine, or a stick, or one game I couldn't believe or understand. A human would throw a perfectly round pebble the size of two paws, a pet wolf would chase after it, he would carry it back to the human, the human would throw it again, and thus the cycle went on. It had no point, no reason, yet both human and... pet found this fun. That's when they weren't begging for simple pats or rubs that seemed to bring them some amount of pleasure. I would have felt sorry for what they'd become if I wasn't so busy trying not to be sick.

At least they were too busy to notice me and Tilhack hugging tree and shadow to remain hidden. It had allowed us to get a good look at their pack over the last few days.

It seemed they'd brought another human pup besides the one Estrella and I killed. With the two dead, their numbers were back down to six humans, and only four pet wolves. *Guess the dogs they used to bring before the wolves died.* Their meeting area hadn't changed either. The same bombardment of strange sights and smells, humans sleeping in their odd dens, and of course at night, they continued to gather around a fire that never spread. No spider webbing for the pets though. Instead, the humans seemed to attach some kind of vine or thick spider thread to the vine around their necks. This kept them from leaving a tree whenever the humans went to sleep in their dens. On things went in the humans' meeting area, unaware of the two wolves stalking them day by day.

On this day, a low ruff from me told Tilhack we were done. After a third day in a row of seeing the same things, I was confident I had all I needed to know. Tilhack ticked his ears forward, and we slinked our way back to our den.

Folar made a point not to look at me when I arrived. *I suppose it's better than the growls he's been giving me.* Even so, it seemed he still couldn't let go of the hate. I turned my ears back at him, even as I thought about *my* distaste for Rajor.

It was Rajor's fault after all. It was his lie that got me banished, and his lie that caused me so much pain. Didn't I have the right to still hate him? I thought so, yet I looked at Folar, and couldn't help wondering. In my own way, I had wounded him as much as Rajor had wounded me. Folar still hated me for it, even though I was nothing like that anymore. I'd even tried to apologize, but he refused to hear me. It had me asking a lot of questions about my own feelings for Rajor. If he were to come to me, ears back and tail tucked, offering an honest apology, would I be any different? Then came the moment where Folar's hatred had almost cost him his life. Again, I had to ask myself: would my anger obstruct me any less? I tried to tell myself that I'd never let it get that far, but the lie had a hard time surviving.

"About time you got back," Estrella said.

No question how she makes me feel. A breath of contentment, and a quick flick of my tail, made it clear just how glad I was to see my mate again. She stood over a hunk of fresh meat almost as big as she was, looking more than a little proud of herself.

She wasn't alone, but that just made it better. Lonate and Jinta were both dragging huge pieces of meat, far more than the pack would ever finish. I had told them to be sure we were well fed. It would appear they tried a little too hard.

I turned my ears back with a quick pant of laughter, then shared a whine and a rub with my mate. Jinta offered the same to hers, though it took a little more prodding to get him to admit he still loved her, despite the choice she'd forced on him.

I tried to ignore it while accepting my share of the kill from Estrella. Lonate settled in to share his meat with Tilhack, while Folar and Jinta ate in silence. Another improvement over the last few days. Everyone had grown tired of their arguing. Even the bird had sung about endless anger, which only seemed to spur them on more. After that, he'd stopped commenting on it. *I could only be so lucky.* The only reminder was how much the two of them ignored the rest of us unless we involved them.

A part of me knew why, and it triggered another thorn in my belly. They'd set out to start their own pack after all. I couldn't expect them to merge with mine beyond the coming hunt. No matter how hard I wished otherwise, they were still their own pack. The moment this hunt was over, they would set out to establish that pack, which meant their instincts made it hard for them to be "one" with mine. *As it should be*, I thought, as much as I wanted to think otherwise.

"Learn anything?" Estrella said through her meal.

I turned my ears back while swallowing the first of mine. "Nothing new. Same numbers, thunder sticks, dens, unnatural behavior, still can't remember which pet wolf held which name beside the female Marron. I think we're ready."

"Ready for what is the question."

"We could still call it off, you know," Tilhack said. I gave him a gentle glare more as a test than true reprimand. "Someone needed to say it, Luna. We still have a choice."

The point was valid, which silenced any hint of anger. Yes, we did have a choice. One I still rejected, but Toltan used to say how important it was to consider all options whenever possible. Because of that, my glare softened, just not my position.

"Yes, we do," I said. "But I'm not changing mine. I'm still going to do this."

Tilhack snorted with a forward ear tick. "Then all I need to know is if you have a plan yet."

"What's there to plan? We treat this as if we're driving off another pack of wolves that poses a threat to us. We go in, we show them our fangs, if we have to, we add a few inspiring bites to get them moving."

Tilhack seemed to choke on his last bite. He ruffed his throat clear before turning toward me, ears up and challenging. "That will only get us killed. You don't know humans like I do. They scare easily, but are the most dangerous when in panic. More so than any creature you've ever seen."

I ignored his challenge once I realized it wasn't me Tilhack was challenging, but the plan itself. Even then, it was to make the point, not to disrespect. However, it kept me from laughing at his description of humans, especially compared to the tales I'd heard of Martol and the mountain lion.

"I've faced humans before," I said. "They have no claws or fangs."

"They have thunder sticks, Luna," Lonate said.

"Hasn't stopped me yet."

Estrella now glared her own resolve. "No, Luna, he's right. You've faced *individuals*, never a pack. We can't go in as we would wolves. They're too clever and too dangerous."

I growled in frustration. I'd thought they were committed. Now it sounded like they'd rather tuck their tails and run. I couldn't allow that, not with what was at stake. Even if we got away clean, Rajor's pack wouldn't. There's also the near certainty the humans would come after us sooner or later anyway.

Then what? Would we run again? I had done enough of that already. I refused to do it anymore.

"So what do you suggest?" I asked. "You seem to know so much. What would you have us do?"

Estrella's ears fell first. "We can't ignore their power. Their pets, wolf or not, are plenty fierce. Their thunder sticks can kill us, or worse, weaken us until we faint. We can't forget it. If it weren't for Tilhack, I never would have navigated their magic alive."

"Yet here he lays without a shred of wisdom to offer when we need it most."

Estrella snarled at me with every hair standing on end. Her sudden reprimand surprised me more than scared me, but I still flinched onto my side, my ears back in apology.

"I thought you'd grown out of that," she said.

She stared at me for some time. Long enough for me to wonder if she was going to bite me to further make her point. I would have let her too, because she was right. I'd left my sarcastic days behind me a long time ago, or at least I thought I had. I lowered my head and ears further to accept the just reprimand she had for me. She eventually dropped her snarl, though her glare remained.

Lonate broke the silence with a sigh. "We can't ignore their power."

Tilhack quickly added, "But we can't ignore their weakness either. Luna's right about one thing: they have no power of their own. Without thunder sticks and stone fangs, they're nothing to us. If we're going to scare them properly, we have to deny them those things."

I rolled back onto my paws, then flinched again at Estrella. Even though she hadn't moved a hair, I didn't want to test her temper again.

"How do you suggest we do that?" I asked slowly, eyes flashing between her and Tilhack.

"Catch them sleeping," Tilhack said. "The longer into it the better. Once they're in it, humans tend to sleep through anything. They'll be separate from their pets too. We have to get them in such a panic they can't find their thunder sticks. Their pets shouldn't be a problem for us from there. Especially if they're stuck to that tree."

"I thought you just said they're the most dangerous panicked animals out there."

"Because they seem able to think more when terrified. A scared deer has only one thought: run. A scared bird has only one thought: fly. Humans will think any number of things. We catch them when sleeping, they won't be able to think at all, and they'll be further away from their thunder sticks when they are."

"You sure it will work?" Estrella asked, finally forgetting me to stare at Tilhack.

"As much as any plan will," Tilhack said. "It's our best chance."

"And if they use their thunder sticks?" Lonate asked.

"Then we defend ourselves. One bite that breaks the skin should send any individual running. If that happens, the pets need to be a secondary focus. Otherwise, they'll delay us enough to let the humans get their thunder sticks. If that happens, we're dead."

Estrella snorted as if rejecting the idea, though she turned back to me with only concern in her ears. "You still sure about this?"

I drew myself up with all the pride I'd ever felt, then I let it soften into a teasing nip on her cheek. "Have a little faith."

Estrella ruffed a chuckle, then gave me a gentle nip of her own. Tilhack just flicked an ear before cleaning the scraps of his meal.

As the sun set behind the mountains, I suggested the pack get what rest they could. Display or fight, we'd need to be at our best. Unfortunately, they fared better than I did. Jinta and Folar were out cold almost immediately. Tilhack wasn't far behind, though Lonate stood vigil until I threatened to pin him until he fell asleep. Once he put his head down, he too found sleep.

I never did. I laid beside Estrella, even closed my eyes for a while, but I never slept. The last of the sunset faded, and I remained aware. Night came, complete with an almost full moon. Still I couldn't sleep.

After a while, I stood as carefully as I could and stalked my way to the river. *Maybe some water in my belly will remind it how full it is.* Instead, the thought made me think how full my mind was. The most I managed was to find a comfortable place on the bank to lie and pray.

"Would you like an ear?"

Estrella. *Guess I didn't sneak carefully enough.*

I flicked an ear forward, and she lay down next to me. For a while, I stared at the moonlight reflecting off the river water, and at my hackles, my "silver sheen," glowing in the same light. I listened to crickets and an owl or two. All the while, Estrella only looked and waited, ears ever attentive. She still knew how to wait me out. Not that I was resisting, really. I just couldn't figure out what to say.

I finally looked up at the stars and said, "You know, I remember when I was named. I was looking up in the night sky, just staring at the moon. My parents saw me and instantly knew that my name was Luna. Martol said something about me developing a silver sheen to reflect the light of Wolfor's home, which made it all the more fitting. Rajor always made some mocking comment about it. Now their little pup is the only thing that stands between the pack and their deaths. Now he is a full-grown wolf who is mature and strong, at least I hope he is. Yet, I am asking myself: is this a good idea? Even if it is, how much will it cost? Tilhack's right. We could leave. Find a new place to live where humans never tread. Am I wrong to force this confrontation? I can't be sure, and I can't stop asking."

Estrella ruffed a chuckle, then looked upward herself. "You know what I remember? I remember when you were willing to kill me before you let me live in your 'lonely world.' Now I'm about to go into battle by your side. You know what this means, don't you?"

That you're not going to answer my question? "Not really. It seems like nothing around me is the same. Nothing is safe or familiar anymore."

"It isn't the world that's changed, Luna. It's you. You are very different now. It's a change for the better, and no matter what anyone else says, *I* say that you are an honorable wolf. A wolf who knows the answer even if he won't let himself admit it."

Not exactly what I was looking for.

Or was it? We lay in silence for some time. Half a day? Just a moment? I couldn't tell, for time seemed to stand still. Long enough for my thoughts to drift through the years. All the things I'd seen and done came one by one. The day I was named, my first kill, my banishment, Folar, Estrella...

Carlin.

Somewhere along the way, I settled on the wise old wolf I had grown to admire. He'd offered a lot of himself during the short time I knew him, and I suddenly wished I could go back and listen again. Maybe this time, I'd ask questions, learn a few life lessons then that could help me now. Instead, all I had was that one conversation during the winter. I remembered Carlin's words, then my words, then out of the blue, I started laughing. *If only he knew.*

Estrella tilted her head at me, looking like I'd grown wings. "Luna? What are you laughing at?"

"A memory," I said. "Remember Carlin? While you and my parents were playing 'kill the wolf moose,' he and I did some talking. He said I had a lot of potential, I just had to let myself see it."

"This is funny to you?"

"What's funny is my response. I got sarcastic with him, as usual. I said, 'Potential? Potential to lead wolves to insanity, maybe.' Now here I am, on the eve of battle against a lethal enemy, with five insane wolves joining me in the fight."

Estrella looked toward the den where the others slept. "Looks like you were both right. You do drive wolves to insanity, but you also have potential you don't see. You've done great things already. Who knows what else you'll accomplish."

"'Even a lone wolf can do good things,'" I said. Estrella tilted her head again. "Something else Carlin told me. I brushed it off then. Now I wish I'd spent more time trying to understand it."

Estrella's ears turned soft, almost as if she were laughing. "You don't have to understand it. You just have to believe it."

"That I can do 'great things?'"

"Not *great* things. *Good* things. Anyone can be great. Even Rajor, in his own way, has done great things. The difference between you and him is that you do *good* things. *Noble* things. Things that make others see how great they can be. Things that make their lives better than they were. That's what Carlin meant. Even as a lone wolf, you've done a lot of good things... for all of us."

Good things. I could almost feel the words rolling around in my ears. The idea that I had the ability to do something special, "noble" as Estrella put it, filled me with a lightness I'd never felt before. Yet as I looked up at the moon, I realized, it wasn't because of me. It was because of them. The orphaned pup I led to a pack. The stubborn female I allowed into my life. The old wolf that... that gave so much of himself. Even as I tried to push them away, there was a mark left behind that somehow made them better. In an odd way, it made the scars I carried seem worthwhile. Though some hurt more than others, mostly because a few of those marks weren't there when I needed them most.

"I... I guess," I said at last. "I still wish he were here. I could use his wisdom right about now."

"He's still with you, Luna," Estrella said. "Just as you left a mark on him, he left a mark on you. I think you got more from him than you realize."

But is it enough?

I sighed. I feared so much, it hurt. All I could think about was how many of my pack I might lose this time. Losing my parents had almost broken me. As my gaze fell on Estrella, my heart melted at the thought of losing her. To say nothing of Jinta, Folar, Lonate, even Tilhack, whom I barely knew. What would I do if I lost any of them?

Estrella had avoided the question before, but now more than ever, I needed to hear her answer. If nothing else than to make the fear seem worth it. I stared at her, hoping she understood how much I needed to know.

"Estrella... do you think we can we do it? Drive the humans off for good?"

She didn't hesitate. "I do. With all my heart, I believe we'll see the humans running scared before us."

Now it was my turn to look toward the den. After that, I looked past it to the humans just beyond. Could we do it? Possibly, but how many of my new pack would I lose?

I didn't let my mind think about it anymore. I couldn't afford to worry about things I could not control. Carlin had told me to stay close to Wolfor's fur. So far, he hadn't led me wrong yet. I had no reason to doubt him now.

After more thinking and remembering, I turned back to Estrella. "You realize neither of us is going to sleep tonight."

"Not a wink," Estrella agreed with a ruffed chuckle.

Chapter 15

THE SUN PEEKED OVER THE MOUNTAINS, casting a soft glow over leaves and grass still wet with dew. As the foliage dried, a sweet scent filled the air that seeped into my muscles, bringing a level of calm I hadn't expected. While the aroma would not be enough to keep us hidden from the humans' pets, the personal benefit was more than welcome. It was as if the forest itself were rising up to stand with us. Or maybe I'd remembered how to lie to myself. I couldn't tell which.

One thing I didn't need to lie about was the state of my pack. Even Folar moved beside me in unison, smooth as clean fur, crisp as fresh ice, silent as dea... as pups hiding from a predator. Except this time, we weren't the prey. Hopefully no one would be.

I hadn't swallowed that lie either.

Our pack approached the humans' dens carefully, ears ever searching for trouble. Compared to all the times before, the humans were being oddly quiet. I could see two pets held to the tree by more of the human vines attached to their necks, then found another pet being led inside a den. The pet not only gave no resistance, a soft wag in his tail suggested he liked the whole idea.

I stopped the advance to rethink things, and to get some disturbing images out of my head. Despite our plan, I'd expected to have easy understanding of where each member of the human pack was. Instead I was missing one pet entirely, and I had no idea where all the humans were. The silence of the dens suggested they were asleep, but I couldn't tell how far in they were. *I let the pack sleep too long.*

"Luna?" Estrella whispered. "What's wrong?"

"We don't have as much information as I expected," I said. "I can't find all of their pack, and I didn't think about them sleeping in their dens. Our plan may not work as well."

Tilhack squeaked while holding in a chuckle. "How well do you think after you just woke up? I think now is the best time to get our point across. They'll be so droopy, they'll come out of their dens to find our fangs dripping into their eyes. They'll be so panicked, they won't be able to realize how small a pack we are. Should be quite entertaining."

I ticked my ears forward in approval. *That it would.* "What about the missing members?"

"Humans aren't like most animals. They often don't have members watching for danger. I don't see or hear any sign of one, so at worst, there might be one sentry that has his guard down. If we see one, we go for him first, scaring the others in the process just as we've planned. Trust me, Luna. We'll be fine."

I hope so. I wasn't convinced, but his argument was enough for me to risk proceeding.

I tossed my head forward, and we continued, moving as one unified pack. Each step brought a thunder within my chest, but years of hunting kept my legs from becoming knots of anxiety. Confidence kept my movements fluid, while wisdom kept my eyes dancing between each den, as well as the now dozing pet wolves.

My pack approached the meeting area without changing pace. The humans could see us now if they looked, and our scents would be on the wind, assuming any pets were awake to catch them. I could only imagine what the humans were doing, for I couldn't see any of them. All I knew was my pack was able to walk right up to the humans' dens without a sound from either pack. I glanced between my members asking for ideas. When none offered any, I went with my first hunting lesson.

With quiet ruffs, I had Jinta and Folar prepare to engage the pets. I then had Lonate and Estrella stand to the sides of where I'd seen the humans enter this particular den. I went to the opposite side of the den, with Tilhack standing just behind. They weren't rabbits, but I was sure they'd scare just the same.

When Estrella and Lonate were ready, I shattered the silence by digging at the humans' den. The sides of the den felt more like super thin fur or deer hide as I dug at it. My paws squeaked with each stroke, while my claws often caught on it much like they would on tree bark. Yet despite several strokes, I never broke through. After a short burst of digging, I stopped, too confused to continue.

I jumped back when the side of the den fell away with an odd buzzing sound. My surprise was replaced by a glare Tilhack echoed when we saw two humans sitting inside. Neither one had more than a thin layer of their strange hides, and their bottom paws were completely bare. Both of us growled, daring them to make a move. The humans were like stones that stank of fear. One of them soon stank of urine too.

A bark from behind sent everything ablaze. The pet wolves had found us. The other dens opened all at once, cries and barks from the humans erupting from everywhere. One of the humans in front of me grabbed a

170

thunder stick. He aimed it forward, except I wasn't there anymore. By the time the human leveled it, my paws were on his chest. I kept going, planting my jaws on the human's neck before he could make a sound. A blur, crack, and gargle beside me announced Tilhack had taken care of the other human.

CRAACKCRAACK CSHOOSHOO shooshoo shoo

Whimpers followed. My heart stopped, but only for a moment. I couldn't let myself think. I could only act now, to save what I could.

Tilhack and I burst from the den, right into the fray. Estrella had a human on his back, trying desperately to keep her fangs away from him. Lonate vanished behind a den, right in front of another thunder stick as it went off. The blast rang in my ears, but I knew it was too late to harm the pup sitter.

The human shifted his stick toward me, only to drop it so he could try and fend off a pair of rasping mockingbirds, both pecking at his eyes. *About time he did something useful with his beak.* I was already advancing toward him. By the time he chased the birds off, I was in the air. His eyes doubled in size right before my jaws hit his neck. He died the moment we hit the ground.

I had yet to see any sign of Jinta or Folar since the beginning of the fight. I heard whimpers and barks, some human, but I couldn't tell who was making which, or what any of them meant. That is, except for a pair of snarls I had no trouble identifying. I found two of the pet wolves charging toward me, intent on ripping me and Tilhack apart.

One rolled on the ground with Tilhack, both trading snaps. The female, Marron, tried to do the same with me. Turned out her snarl didn't fit her fangs, for she didn't place her attack well. Her first bite would have caught scruff at best, assuming it got past my nose. I sent my fangs straight into her, forcing her to recoil to avoid a return bite. Even then, I managed an impressive cut on her muzzle.

She and I snarled death at each other, dancing around one another as we traded glancing blows that meant nothing. My strikes drew blood more than hers, but we never quite got into a full tussle. Marron couldn't find a way to get in to me, and I didn't dare forget my surroundings, lest a human catch me off guard.

"I'm sorry this happened," Marron said. "I wanted to see you *after* we had our hunt. Would have been so much sweeter."

Sheesh. Rajor, Folar, now Marron? Are there any wolves out here that don't *hate me?*

"Your hunt ends here," I said aloud. "You'll not threaten my pack ever again."

"Too late for that, whelp. Even now, your pack feels the sting of our power. Your black alpha will die first, then his two pups, then all who remain. They'll pay for what you did to the human I loved."

Pups? My pack had no pups. And why such an exact number? No wolf would assume I had such a small litter. Not unless they'd seen...

My heart stopped solid this time. *Two pups? Black alpha?*

"Rajor."

Only then did I realize a pet wolf was still missing. That meant a human or two was likely with him, which meant someone was hunting Rajor even now. *He'll never survive. He doesn't know humans like I do. They'll kill him before he has the chance to defend himself.*

I was so appalled, I missed Marron's advance. My mockingbird, however, didn't. He descended from the skies, fluttering and rasping in her face. One peck nearly caught her eye, forcing her to slow so she could snap at him. Unlike me, she missed entirely. Then Lonate came from nowhere to tackle her from the side, his snarl loud enough to snap me out of my trance. I noticed Tilhack behind him, bloodied but still breathing, while the pet he'd been fighting lay to the side. The pet was covered in blood, with his head at an angle that made it clear he wouldn't be a threat anymore. Between two dens, I also saw Folar locked in combat with the remaining pet. Both their coats were marred in wounds, though thank Wolfor, Folar's previous wound hadn't reopened yet.

A blast of thunder rattled me again. While I didn't see who was hit, if anyone, I thought of how Rajor wouldn't fair as well. At best, he'd scare the humans a little before they killed him. The pack would likely follow. *Would there be a Lonate this time, or would they all die?*

Panic set in like I had felt only once before. The first time, I had been running from a father who'd just banished me. Now, I tore through the human dens, mostly forgetting the ongoing battle. Someone called after me, but thunder drowned it out. I never really heard either. I refused to let the pack suffer, no matter what the cost. No matter their crime.

I ran faster than I ever had. I blew through the forest, totally ignoring Rajor's scent marker. I couldn't let it happen. If anyone was going to kill Rajor, it would be me or old age, and I had already refused the chance. I went for the den area. The top of the hillside rushed toward me in a blur. There I saw the pet wolf Harso and a crouching human, thunder stick in his paws.

I pushed my legs for everything they had left. Harso turned to see what the noise was, but he didn't have time to recognize the threat. I blew past him, reaching for the human's neck and shoulder.

CRAACK CSHOO cshoo shoo

My fangs had hit him just as the stick went off. The thunder rang in my ears, too loudly to know if I heard whines or just imagined it. I knew my bites never found skin, or at least, I never found blood. I tore through some kind of thick pelt, but it was more fluff than flesh, and it never bled. The human fell to the ground, grunting more surprise than pain, while his thunder stick clattered out of his reach in the dirt.

I recoiled for a better bite at his neck, but felt someone else bite on my shoulder before I could try. I'd forgotten Harso. I yelped in pain, then it became a snarl as I turned to face the pet wolf. Blood stained my leg, pain warned of damage, but the snarl of the other wolf wouldn't let me heed it.

Harso recoiled, then charged. My sprint and injury allowed Harso to push me onto my back, but after so many fights with Rajor and others, I was not about to die that easily. I bit the side of Harso's neck before he could get to mine. The strikes slowed him enough for me to get back on my paws and meet him fang-to-fang.

Our jaws locked with each other in a stalemate. We would push each other to the ground, but neither could do any real damage to the other. Both muzzles, heads, and legs still bled as our fangs dripped with the blood of the other. Dust from our fight covered us like a fog. My shoulder screamed, but I ignored it. I would not lose to a pet. *Toltan would never forgive me for it.*

He pushed me to the ground again. When Harso tried for a final bite, my good paw came up and snapped his jaw shut. As he shook his head, I rolled onto my paws and lunged. Harso defended his neck, except I wasn't going there. My fangs hit right where I wanted: dead center of the left eye. Harso yelped and retreated as my fang punctured the eyeball. He pawed at his eye, still whimpering, giving me the chance I'd planned for. I knocked Harso over onto his side, and with him still whining in pain, I landed a lethal bite on his throat. He wasn't whining much longer after that.

I turned to face the human, then froze when I saw him standing there, still as a stone, with his thunder stick pointed right at me. My wounds were too serious too ignore any longer. I knew I'd never get to him in time. The human had a perfect chance, leaving me only to snarl, furious that I'd lose my life to this whelp with little fur and no fangs.

The human pushed the thunder stick into his shoulder. The end remained pointed at me, and I waited for it.

CRECRAACK CRESHOO shoo sho

There was some kind of flash near the middle of the thunder stick. The human immediately dropped it, yelping pain as he held one paw in the other. I was too busy trying to understand why I wasn't dead to react. Surely he hadn't missed. Had Wolfor somehow protected me from the blast? Had something gone wrong? Was I dead and just didn't know it?

Before I could find an answer, a streak of black fur flew in from the side. *Rajor.* He leapt into the human's chest and planted him in the ground. My brother tore the human apart before he could finish a yelp.

Rajor stood over the human, growling with each heavy breath. It was only then I noticed his left ear was bleeding. Upon closer inspection, I realized a nick was missing where his ear pocket should be. Too clean for any bite wound or hunting injury. That's when the last few minutes returned to my mind. The human had missed a kill by that much. Then I remembered the battle I left. *Estrella? My pack!*

I turned to run, then yelped as my shoulder made it clear it had nothing left to give. I fell onto my side, which only made it hurt worse. With one shoulder ruined, and another leg full of bite marks, it became a battle in and of itself just to find my footing. It didn't matter. I had to find a way. I couldn't stay there, not when they might need me.

A sharp voice knocked me down from behind. "Hey, cut it out. You'll only make it worse."

I looked back to snarl, only to have it lodge in my throat. I couldn't hide my fear when I saw Rajor standing there, alone. Now *he* had all the right. I'd been warned twice, yet here I was, a lone wolf, violating the territory of my former pack, too injured to run or defend myself. I managed a convincing glare, but I couldn't stop myself from shaking. Half from fear, half from anger. *To think, after everything, this is how it ends.*

Rajor's ears pulled back, not without a cringe, yet his lips never curled. "Don't. You have nothing to—"

"Don't you dare, Rajor!"

Both he and I turned straight eared toward the voice. I knew it better than Rajor long before I saw its owner. Estrella appeared like a spirit screaming our way, except she was very real, very alive, and very, *very* angry.

Estrella planted herself between me and Rajor, every hair on end, her fangs dripping with fresh blood, as did her fur from her wounds. It wasn't until a moment later that I noticed Lonate had come only a few steps behind her. He looked less injured than her, but no less fierce. *Why am I not surprised?*

"Don't you dare touch him, Rajor," Estrella snarled. "I don't care what the law says. He just saved your neck. You *owe* him."

Rajor's pack gathered on the hillside behind him. Even the pups were there, if at a safe distance. Rajor glanced back at them all, then stared at me, as best he could through Estrella, for a long time. Long enough for me to feel the blood run from my wounds.

Rajor's ears fell for a moment. When they rose, he addressed Estrella first. "Please, let me talk to him."

My ears perked straight. *A respectful request? From Rajor? What next? Estrella gets pessimistic?*

"What could you possibly have to say to him?" Estrella said.

What indeed? I couldn't leave without knowing. At the very least, I had to make sure this was really my brother who was saying these things.

"Let him speak, Estrella," I said.

When Estrella glared at me, I returned it with a forward ear tick. She sighed, pulled back her ears, then stepped behind me.

"I'm watching you, Rajor," she said.

She licked my shoulder while Rajor took deep breaths first. Even then, he kept swallowing as if he had a pinecone in his throat. At times, I wondered if he was going to faint, while others, I expected him to start snarling. Not once did I see the Rajor I'd grown up with.

"Luna," he said. "Luna, I have to know something."

This should be interesting. "What could I tell you?"

"Why did you never kill me?"

That got everyone's attention. Even Estrella stopped mid-lick to stare at him. I tilted my head, not quite sure I heard right.

"What?" I said. "What do you mean?"

"You've had the chance. As pups, you had the chance before you knew the law. As adults, you had more chances. Last fall, you had the chance, and all the right, to kill me. You never did. Why?"

Like you care about my reasoning. I couldn't get past the old bully I knew as a pup. I rose despite great pain and tried to look as proud as I could.

"You wouldn't understand," I said. "It's a concept beyond you."

"Luna!" Rajor said. He was almost whimpering. "Please! I need to know."

I almost left him to wonder. I almost left to exact the only revenge I could. Folar stopped me. Or rather, his near-miss stopped me. So much rage after all that time, and he'd had every right, as I did now. Except Folar's rage had almost cost him his life. *What would mine cost?* My life I could handle, but Tilhack? Lonate? Estrella? How many of them would pay for my rage? Did I have *that* right?

Then there was Rajor himself. Jinta said he wasn't the same wolf, and more and more, I agreed. Ever since the winter, he'd yet to try for even the smallest of insults or slights toward me. Now he stood there, so desperate for an answer, he was shaking like a leaf in the wind. Nothing like the brother I knew, just as I was nothing like the pup that drove Folar away. Yet despite my best efforts to prove that, Folar had refused to forgive me. Just as I didn't want to forgive Rajor. To say nothing of Toltan, whom I never forgave until I saw the pain he carried.

Finally, there was Marron. Her rage had ruined her ability to fight. Only our surroundings had kept me from tossing her aside and ending her. She wanted revenge, even after so much time had passed. Here I had a chance to exact some of my own. Were we so different in that desire?

I looked at my brother, trying to see the bully. I wanted to see the evil thing that had cursed me, gotten me banished for a crime I didn't commit. I tried hard. I used every lie. Instead, I saw the blood from Rajor's ear. How close he'd come. How close Folar had come. How much it had cost Marron. I couldn't let that happen again.

Not to myself, or Rajor, or anyone.

"You're my brother," I said at last. "Despite all you've done, you've never changed that. We share the same blood, as does much of this pack. I could no more kill you than I could kill my own pups. It was all I had left when I was banished." I rubbed against Estrella. "Turns out, that's all I ever needed."

Rajor had a hard time finding words at first. He still appeared to be in pain after he'd found enough to work with. "Then... then you... you came for me? You fought to... to save me?"

"You, them, my blood, my pack, they're worth dying for. They always have been."

Rajor stood frozen and silent. His pack looked amongst themselves, unsure what to do. I watched them all, praying my death might yet be avoided.

"Come on," Estrella said. "The others are wounded, but alive. Even the birds made it out in one piece. They'll perk up a lot when they see you."

"What of the humans?" I asked.

"Dead," Lonate said. "We had to kill them all. They insisted on fighting instead of running."

My ears slowly turned back. *Foolish creatures. What a waste.* "No one said they were the smartest of beings. Well, at least it's over. Time we went home with the rest of the pack."

Estrella stood beside me as I limped away. Lonate followed, keeping a close eye on Rajor's pack. To keep them away or to say a final goodbye, I couldn't tell which.

We didn't get but a few steps when Rajor called after us.

"Luna! You're going the wrong way. Your home is here. You belong to *this* pack."

I almost forgot I was injured. *Come again?* Estrella and I both stared at Rajor, unsure what to think. This wasn't a boast or tease. He meant it. By Wolfor, he actually meant it. I couldn't believe it. I wasn't sure I did.

Rajor used the silence to turn to the pack. He dropped his head for a moment before he spoke, loud enough to hear, but withdrawn like no one had ever heard from him before.

"I was wrong. As a pup, I lied. I swore that Luna killed our brother Calon in an attempt to ensure he retained lead of the litter. The truth is... *I'm* the one who wanted the lead. Luna did nothing to ensure Calon died. In fact...

in fact, Luna tried to *save* our brother. It was Calon who killed himself trying to get at Luna."

Rajor looked at me while I was still trying to believe I was hearing this. "I did see it, Luna, all of it. No one noticed me slip away to follow you that day. I thought for sure you'd give me what I needed to beat you. I got more than I hoped for. I used your silence to remove you as a threat. I see now how wrong I was. For so many reasons, I was wrong. I see only one punishment for my crime. I will take your place as a lone wolf. You will take mine, as alpha of this pack. They all knew you as a pup. They'll follow you, and Estrella. I only pray... I only hope someday you might... you could find it in your heart to..."

He couldn't say it. I couldn't believe he was thinking it. I still didn't believe it was *my brother* saying these things. As far as anyone could tell, the pack may not have either. Few were moving save for ears and eyes. The pups tried to get answers from their sitters, only getting commands to remain where they stood.

Rajor tried again, but he couldn't ask. I knew the question, but he couldn't say it. Finally, Rajor dropped his head and started walking. Tears were there, but not quite flowing, nor was he really crying. Still, I saw a different wolf than the one I grew up with. I saw a broken, defeated wolf. A wolf wounded just like Carlin, and Lonate, and Toltan. Perhaps as wounded as I had once been.

I tried to imagine Rajor out on his own. He'd survive, his pride wouldn't allow anything less. Living, however... I couldn't allow it. I'd lived that life, however briefly. To call it life would be an insult. Like Rajor said, I hadn't been able to kill him before. How could I do it now?

"Hold right there, Rajor," I said. Rajor looked at me, his ears flat, the one still bleeding. I limped close to him, with Estrella refusing to leave my side. "Where do you think you're going?"

"To unclaimed territory," Rajor said. "I will live my life as a lone wolf."

"Why?"

"As punishment for what I did to you. It's what I deserve."

I cringed, my wounds making me go tighter still. *There's that word again.* I'd heard it too often in my life, more so because it was always someone else using it. Yet not once did it ever feel right.

Or, maybe they'd been *too* right. Martol deserved better than I gave her that night. Carlin deserved more respect. Toltan deserved a chance to explain himself. Estrella... well, she deserved a lot more than I had given her. Now here Rajor stood, saying he deserved punishment, but I looked at his ear, at the blood still dripping from his head, and at the wound within him. I saw a wolf far removed from the bully pup I grew up with. This wolf deserved something, but my pain wasn't it.

"You're wrong again," I said. "You don't deserve that life any more than I do."

Rajor's ears went straight in shock, but it was Lonate who spoke his mind. "Luna? How can you say that after all he's done? Surely he deserves something."

There's that word again. "He's already had it. He knows the pain of losing pack mates. He knows the sting of a thunder stick. He knows the shame of a lie. A life alone will bring no justice." I stared at Lonate a moment, to make sure he alone understood the hidden message. "He deserves a chance to make right the wrongs he committed. So, Rajor, you will remain. This pack will remain your home as much as mine. It's up to you to decide your place within it, but I will not have my brother living alone. We've fought with each other too long. It's time we acted like the brothers we were born to be."

Rajor stared. He cringed, he cried, and he knew better.

"Thank you, Luna," he fought to say. "I swear to you, things will be different."

I panted a laugh. I couldn't leave that there. I just couldn't. "Well, I'd say you're off to a great start."

"Why's that?" Rajor asked.

"You left Wolfor out of your swear this time."

A panted laugh shattered the tension among the two packs... among *the* pack.

～～～

I paced outside the den with a growl not far from my mind. It had been hours, what was wrong? Was there something wrong? I wanted to go in, but I knew I would be run out in an instant, either by Estrella or by my sister Golte. *Some consideration.* Toltan always said late bloomers were the death of males. Now I know why. Having pups this late in the spring is bad enough. It taking this long for them to emerge was going to kill me.

Someone approached, but I didn't care to note who. I only cared about the hole in the side of the hill.

"Luna," Rajor's voice. "Give it a rest, will you? You're making me wish I'd joined Jinta."

Jinta. Not-so-little Folar hadn't let go of his desire to start their own pack. *Or maybe he still hasn't forgiven me.* Not that I could blame him, really. The humans had wounded him, again, this time a solid hit in the leg. He was impossible while his leg healed enough to be usable again. He barely spoke to me, and when he did, it often came with a growl or raised hackles, sometimes both. Given his scars, and the fact that he never directly challenged me, I let it go. To my surprise, not even Rajor disagreed with the decision. Once Folar had recovered, he and Jinta left for unclaimed territory,

178

taking one of the older members with them. Days later, their howls echoed among the trees, announcing the birth of their first litter.

I could only be so lucky. I still didn't have one. At this rate, I never would. I feared I wouldn't have a mate either. *Wouldn't that be a bite in the tail? I reclaim my life, my pack, gain a brother, only to lose my mate? Just dismal enough to feel possible.*

Rajor growled, flopped his head on his paws, and sighed again. "You keep that up, you'll dig a new den."

Less work for Tilhack and whatever female he can charm into—

A yip from the hole froze me. My ears turned to be sure and found only silence. Had I heard wrong? Had I heard right and I didn't want to know? When Golte came out of the den, my heart stopped while I waited to hear.

She glanced at Rajor, then back to me with an amused ear flick. "One loss, four gained in perfect health, and the mother wants to see you."

I was inside the den so fast I don't remember how I got there. I only knew that it was Estrella I found first, alive, alert, and laughing at me. She bent down to lick the closest of four tiny pups still damp from birth. All were sipping at their mother's milk with the same soft whimpers I had been imagining all day. I didn't see the fifth pup, but in truth, I didn't want to see it. The pain of the loss couldn't gain ground over the joy of the four healthy pups I saw. Not to mention the adult they were drinking from.

"About time you got here," Estrella said.

I gave a playful growl. Estrella laughed and rubbed her nose on the ground behind her. I took my place there and nuzzled my mate. I leaned in slow, making sure I had permission, and tapped the nose of a pup with my own. The tiny wolf gave a soft whine at the new touch, then reached up to repeat it. The other pups seemed to sense something new, as each one crawled their way toward me.

I tapped my nose to each and every one, getting the same soft whine in reply every time. It sent a thorn to my heart, for I remembered the same sensation from someone no longer there. It couldn't stop me from thinking how they would remember the touch with the same fondness I still did. Nor did it keep me from absorbing their scent into my soul and blood. I now understood why Carlin instantly recognized his pups. *If only you could have seen Lonate, Wise One. You would have been so proud.* The thought seemed to trigger a warmth I didn't bother to question.

"They're beautiful," I said. "I'm not sure I deserve them."

"Of course you do," Estrella said. "You're mature, and strong, and honorable, and you've suffered enough. I think this is Wolfor's way of saying it's time you had some real joy in your life."

I panted a chuckle at the thought. *Maybe it is.* Even if it wasn't, I no longer cared. These were *my* pups, born from *my* mate, destined to join *my* pack. The joy of those thoughts prevented any others from forming.

That is until, from outside, chirping could be heard. "Luna wolf has new tails! Luna wolf has new tails!"

Then the pack spoke as one, "Will you shut up?!"

Estrella and I nearly laughed ourselves to death within the den.

"He hasn't lost his touch," Estrella said.

No, he hasn't. "It wouldn't be my pack without him." I leaned in, careful not to worry Estrella too much, and nuzzled the pups again. "May the blessings of Wolfor protect them."

Estrella began the howl of birth. I was too happy to join in, allowing me to hear the pack echo the call. I laughed again when I noticed Rajor's voice rang the loudest among them.

Some things never change.

The End

———

Don't worry.
The wolves will return… sort of, in *Blood of an Alpha*.
Coming soon.

———

About the Author

FOREST WELLS is an author with a deep passion for all things wild canine, as well as pro football, hockey, and e-sports. Forest has authored a short story, as well as several poems, in the 2015-2017 editions of the "Wolf Warriors" anthologies, in addition to another short story in the March/April 2019 issue of Kyanite Publishing's collection of dragon stories.

Forest continues to work on his future stories, including a military sci-fi and a fantasy. He currently lives in his home town of Thermal, California.

Printed in the USA
CPSIA information can be obtained
at www.ICGtesting.com
LVHW092152111223
766262LV00025B/121